A FAR-FROM-ORDINARY CHRISTMAS

"'Vulgar'—my family motto. Though in Latin it means 'ordinary,' so maybe you'd better come up with a less toothless insult," said Giles. "Sorry. You're both going to have to try harder if you want me to crumble and weep. Princess, would you care to give it a go?"

"No, I do not think that would be wise."

"And do you always do what's wise?"

"I have not in the past, no. But since I find myself unexpectedly in York and ostracized from my favorite sister's wedding, it is probably past time I begin."

The lashes around Giles's vivid blue eyes were dark, much darker than the copper of his hair or the gilded stubble just beginning to edge his jaw. "Or you could wait," he said, "until after the new year. Allow yourself an unwise Christmas."

It was difficult to look directly at such blue eyes, like staring into the noontime sky. "I shall have that either way, since I am now a part of a quest for treasure."

Season
for # Desire

Theresa
Romain

ZEBRA BOOKS
KENSINGTON PUBLISHING CORP.
http://www.kensingtonbooks.com

First Printing: October 2014
ISBN-13: 978-1-4201-3245-8
ISBN-10: 1-4201-3245-8

First Electronic Edition: October 2014
eISBN-13: 978-1-4201-3246-5
eISBN-10: 1-4201-3246-6

10 9 8 7 6 5 4 3 2 1

Printed in the United States of America

ACKNOWLEDGMENTS

After four Holiday Pleasures romances (yay!), I have more people to acknowledge than ever. For supporting me with kind words and infinite patience while I wrote, deepest gratitude to my husband, family, and friends. Many thanks to Amanda for sharp-eyed and sharp-witted critiquing, to my brother for guidance on characters' medical issues, and to Kelly for her expertise on telescopes. And to my dear daughter, who made a nightly tradition of busting into my office and climbing into my lap while I was working on this book: no, *you're* the silliest.

I owe a great debt of thanks to the wonderful people who transform my words into books: my awesome agent, Paige Wheeler; my insightful editor, Alicia Condon; and the talented art, marketing, production, and publicity teams at Kensington Publishing Corp. And for keeping me grounded and laughing at the same time, I'm so grateful for the writers and bloggers who share their good humor and good sense with me online.

And of course, wholehearted thanks to my wonderful readers. I'm so glad you've found my stories and have joined me for another Season.

Chapter One

Wherein the Adventure Begins, Much Against the Will of Certain Participants

December 11, 1820

Sunset fell early over the wintry moorlands of northern England, and prudent men abandoned the road to the criminal, the desperate, and the mail coaches.

Giles Rutherford wouldn't exactly call his father prudent, but neither was the elder Rutherford criminal or desperate—for now. And though hale and fit for a man in his middle fifties, Richard enjoyed traveling through darkness no more than Giles, especially when travel came paired with steady rain. In the weeks before Christmas, their native Philadelphia froze under a snow blanket, but this frigid rainfall went to the bone more quickly.

For once, then, Richard marked the end of their day's travel with little protest. He was willing enough to be persuaded to pull up the carriage outside the Goat and Gauntlet, a post-house tucked within the ancient stone walls of York.

Once settled in a private parlor, Giles let the fire's warmth lick at his sodden boots as his father ordered a generous dinner from a servant. The room to which they had been escorted was low-ceilinged and slope-floored like many old buildings in this country. Lamps on the table and mantel cast pools of warm light in the dim room. A simple table and chairs were drawn up near the fireplace, a wide structure of smoke-blackened bricks. Within, the coal fire glowered at its own inadequacy.

Ah, there was the problem: The parlor window's wooden sash had warped in its frame, allowing the December chill to leak in. Before Giles could decide whether his aching hands were up to the task of setting the window to rights, the servant entered the parlor again with a stoneware jug. And . . . a man in a filthy red coat.

Giles lifted his brows. "That is not what you ordered for dinner, is it, Father?"

Richard ignored him, standing to accept the jug—coffee, how Giles hoped it held coffee—while also accepting an introduction from the man in red. "You are a servant to the Earl of Alleyneham? My, my, this is an honor." He sounded cheerful, as always.

"Are we meant to bow or to curtsy?" Giles took the urn from his father's hands, nodding a dismissal to the servant who had brought it. *Oh, blessed warmth.* The stoneware was hot enough to make his hands prickle as though quilled; every little bone and joint tensed, then eased into relief. Giles could almost have groaned as he poured out the first cup.

He seated himself with cup in hand, then realized he had missed the first part of the exhausted-looking servant's story.

"At first, Lady Audrina was thought to be visiting a friend," the man was saying. A footman, probably, because of his scarlet livery—now splashed and dirtied by long hours on horseback and muddy roads. "But when the hours for calling passed and she did not return home, the earl suspected an elopement."

"That suspicion seems premature. Why shouldn't he think she went shopping with her maid? Or calling on another friend?" Giles could almost *feel* his father's look of reprimand as Richard drew out a chair for himself. "What? Those seem more likely possibilities than that she eloped with some rakehell."

The footman's expression did not change, except that he blinked rather more quickly. "If you will pardon my frankness, sir, Lady Audrina is the sort of young lady far more likely to dash off to Scotland than to pay a call in Mayfair."

"She sounds exhausting." Giles took a sip of coffee. It was strong and scorched, bitter on his tongue and beautifully warm.

"The earl cannot permit his youngest daughter to elope," continued the footman. "His lordship and Lady Irving, with whom he said you were acquainted, are traveling here with greatest possible speed."

"Lady Irving," Giles said. "Perfect. Wonderful. This is your doing, Father, isn't it? So certain were you that she'd want to sell her jewels that you told her all the details of our planned path through England."

Richard seemed not to hear, which was a certain

indication that Giles was correct. "I had not thought Lady Irving was much of a traveler," he said to the servant. "I hope she's been well since we met her in London several weeks ago."

"Her ladyship is quite well, sir, I'm sure. She is willing to render assistance to Lord Alleyneham and was quite sure such amiable gentlemen as yourselves would be, too."

"I'm not the slightest bit amiable." Flexing his fingers, Giles grimaced. His hands were always more painful after a day of travel.

Fidgeting, the footman tried to straighten his wig atop his short-cropped hair. The headpiece had gone sad and flat, but white hair powder still clung to it. How had it survived the ride? The servant must have tucked it inside his coat, only to slap it atop his head before requesting entrance to the Rutherfords' private parlor.

These English and their priorities. Image was everything, wasn't it? Though Giles was half English by birth, he would never understand them.

Once his head had been properly covered, the servant continued as though Giles had never attested to his own lack of amiability. "Should the fugitives' arrival precede that of their pursuers, sir, his lordship requests that you arrest them."

"Arrest them?" Graying and ever elegant, Richard sat up straighter in his solid wooden chair. Giles had inherited his mother's raw-boned ruddiness—but though he little resembled his father, he knew well the animating expression that crossed the elder Rutherford's features. *This sounds like an adventure!*

"'Arrest,' Father, is one way the English say 'stop.'"

You *do* mean 'stop,' don't you, ah . . . man in the wig? And not anything more dramatic than that?"

"Yes, sir. I mean that you are requested to stop them, sir. If you would."

"Stopping a carriage could be very dramatic," Richard mused. "A few obstacles across the road, perhaps, to halt it. And then—rip the door open and carry the young lady to safety? What do you say, Giles?"

"I say that this has nothing to do with us whatsoever. One wild goose chase at a time is enough."

"Where is your chivalry, son?"

"I left it on the gangplank in Philadelphia." He'd had to. It was hardly chivalrous to leave five younger siblings on the verge of adulthood—especially Rachel, whose mind remained in childhood as years advanced. But Richard held the funds from which his younger children drew stipends, and for all Giles knew, this quest in England would beggar them.

In most families, sons formulated harebrained schemes and fathers tried to talk sense into them. For Giles and his father, the situation was entirely the reverse. Not that Giles had ever been able to talk his father out of any scheme the elder Rutherford set his mind to.

Which was why, after two months traipsing about every corner of England where Giles's late mother might have been thought to hide either jewels or clues, the Rutherfords now found themselves in the parlor of the Goat and Gauntlet with not even a whisper of a hunch.

Instead, they had found a dirty footman asking for help for some spoiled English princess.

Giles's wrists ached; he realized he was clenching

his fists, resting them like stones on the table. Time ticked raggedly, unpredictably, when he felt these aches. And it was harder to dismiss the quest, the reason they had crossed an ocean. The reason he'd bidden good-bye to so many loved ones who needed him.

Lifting his hands to shake out their tension, he frowned at the servant. "How do you know the happy couple hasn't already traveled beyond this inn? If you'd passed them on the road, you'd have seen them."

The footman swayed on his feet.

"Sit if you like," Giles added. "Here, by the fire. You must be cold." A sidelong glance at his father: *There, see? I'm not a complete monster.*

"Thank you, sir, but I couldn't seat myself. It would not be proper." The servant shook his head, setting the wig askew again. "I do believe the carriage broke down at some point, as its tracks left the road. I could not trace them once they left it."

"Why not? A carriage is large. As it rolled, it would have crushed grass and moved pebbles and—"

Richard cleared his throat.

"Well, perhaps such signs wouldn't be visible in the rain," Giles granted. The roads in this country were ancient and deeply rutted. Any moisture turned them into a sloppy stew, and rain and sleet had traded control of the sky for the past three days. Assuming frequent changes of horses, this was probably as quickly as a pair of eloping Londoners could reach York on their way to Scotland.

"They might choose not to stop at this inn, though," Giles added. "They could even be on a different road."

"They're not." Richard shrugged off the possibility of events proceeding other than as he wished. "This is the swiftest road from London. And if they don't choose to stop, we will *make* them stop. We'll stop every carriage if we need to. It will be an—"

"Adventure." Giles spoke the word along with his father, his mouth a wry twist.

Giles wanted to throttle whoever had coined the word *adventure*. Everything was an adventure to Richard Rutherford, from days on sleet-sludgy roads to his grandiose plan to establish a London jewelry firm to rival Rundell and Bridge.

"Perfect," Giles murmured again. "Wonderful. A plan without flaw. Do tell me, man in the wig, why is the earl set against his daughter marrying? Don't earls want their daughters married, as a rule?"

For the first time, the footman looked something besides tired; a stricken expression crossed his face. "That is a question best asked of his lordship, sir."

Maybe it was the man's sudden apprehension. Or maybe the fact that, for a wage that was likely no more than a pittance, he'd been willing to chase across England with nothing but the frailest of hopes, the smallest chance of success. To this footman, apparently fleeing was preferable to staying behind, and begging help from strangers was preferable to failure.

Giles didn't seek out adventures—but he was not, as a rule, a monster. And this man had ridden for his life as though pursued by a fiend indeed. "We shall help you," Giles decided. Not for the sake of the heedless eloping aristocrat, but for the tired servant.

"Of course we shall," Richard echoed. There had never been a question in his mind, Giles knew; to be asked for a favor was to do all in one's power to grant it.

Giles hefted the stoneware urn of coffee. "Take off your wig, man, and sit and have some coffee until your master arrives. I'll keep watch on the road."

As the youngest of the Earl of Alleyneham's five daughters, Lady Audrina Bradleigh had often dreamed of running away to Scotland.

This was *not* that dream.

A dream would never include the company of David Llewelyn, whose angular face wore an impatient expression as he peered down at her. "Finally coming around. Good. I thought you would sleep all the way to the border."

Nor would a dream include a pounding head, the jouncing of carriage wheels over ruts, or the sickish, bitter aftertaste of laudanum.

Swallowing a groan, Audrina shoved herself to a seated position. Slowly, slowly, making sure her head didn't fall off and her stomach didn't reverse course. Through slitted eyes, she took in her surroundings. Rain sluiced down the coach windows and thudded on the roof; the carriage lamps were lit against the fall of night.

There was light enough for Audrina to recognize the deep green of the velvet squabs on which she reclined. "Llewellyn, you rotter," she said through dry lips. "If you must kidnap a woman, use your own carriage instead of filching your mother's."

His mouth curled with humor, though he retreated to the opposite seat. "This is no kidnapping, my dear Audrina. It is the adventure you always wanted."

This had to be a dream. But the flask he extended to her contained water that spotted her hands and gown as she fumbled open its lid. Water that soothed her throat enough to ask, "The border, you said. You are making for Gretna Green?"

"Coldstream Bridge, actually. It's far closer. Unless you will marry me in England."

She capped the flask and tossed it back to him, not wanting his fingers to brush hers a second time. "Not in England. Not anywhere."

"What call have you to protest? We've already consummated our union, after all."

"Spare me such romantic twaddle. I know you have consummated with others before and since."

"True." His brows drew together, sharply dark in the flickering lamplight. "But I don't mind marrying you. We amused one another, did we not?"

"That depends on what one means by *amusement.*" If he meant the physical crisis—he'd enjoyed himself, certainly, but she had never achieved the same level of delight.

Another jolt; her teeth snapped together, setting up a drumbeat in her temples. The rain must be turning the roads to a stew of ruts. "Ugh. As soon as my wits are clear I shall throw myself out into the elements."

An empty threat. She was not even certain she could feel her fingers and toes.

"The laudanum is fogging your wits, I expect." Llewellyn looked as bland and unconcerned as though pronouncing upon the weather.

Had she really ever thought him attractive? Dashing? She had indeed; his dark elegance and risk-mad recklessness had once seemed a male version of her own hopes and wishes. But that had been months ago, foolish months ago. He wanted her dowry to cover debts, he had admitted in a careless moment. She had dropped him.

It seemed he felt entitled to the money all the same.

Audrina shut her eyes, letting her heavy head fall back against the squabs. "I expect you are right. I'm not in the habit of taking laudanum. How did you do it?"

"Get you to take it, you mean? Easy as anything, my dear. A small bribe to your lady's maid, and she was willing to add a vial to your evening tea."

"Do not," she groaned, "call me your dear anything. And please cease to call me by my Christian name. I insist you stop at the next inn." From which she would scribble a note about having her maid sacked.

"Of course! That'll give people the chance to see us together."

"*No.* You shall enter first, and I will . . ." Her vision was blurring; she squeezed her eyes shut, but could not imagine the next step to take. She had no chaperone and no money. Not even a change of clothing, unless the treacherous Sally had deigned to pack a few items. No one would ever believe she was a lady of quality carried off against her will.

"Don't worry, Audrina. I will take care of you." Llewellyn's voice seemed to echo, as though he called from a long distance away.

"I won't accept anything from you."

His laugh clanged from the coach walls. "You already did; you drank from that flask. Didn't even think to ask what was in it, did you?"

Water? Tinged with something else . . . still so bitter in her mouth.

"You rotter," she said again, weakly. Then the world went gray.

When color and sight returned, a new face was looking down at hers. This one was like a statue: still as if carved, all strong spans and hollows, with short-cropped hair that glinted copper in the light of the . . .

Not of the carriage, but a lantern hanging from a hook on a rough plaster wall. "Where's the carriage? Where am I?" Her head felt so heavy, but instinct returned before sense. She did not know this man who gripped her arms tightly. Quicker than thought, she kicked out, and he cursed at her.

With a strange accent. "You are American?" Good God, where *was* she?

"And you are not." He released her arms—not all at once, but slowly, letting her sag until her back found purchase against the solid wall. Then he lifted his hands at once, splaying them broad and empty. "But you *are* the wayward daughter of the Earl of Alleyneham. Correct?"

"I . . . suppose so, yes. What has become of . . . ?"

"That fellow with you?" The large man rubbed at his chin. "He'll be all right. You're at the Goat and Gauntlet, a post-house in York."

"York." Her knees went watery, and she slid, the plaster of the wall scraping against her wrecked hair and gown. Gaze darting around, she noted the small span of the room. An antechamber to keep out the cold, its floor muddy from many boots. Doors flanked her. Outside one, rain fell in drops fat and hard as marbles; through the other, voices spilled in lilting northern accents. "York. Good God. How much time has passed?"

"You must be hungry," the man said in a voice of stone. "I'll show you where to wash up; then you can join us in the private parlor for a meal."

"You and—"

"My father." He laughed, but the sound held as little humor as his previous sentence had held comfort. "And your father, and some harpy of a countess, and a poor footman who looks as though he's been frightened to a shadow."

Her father was here? This was too much to take in; Audrina shook her head. "Who are you?"

"Giles Rutherford." A dangerous smile crouched on his strong features. "And, princess, this is the end of your adventure."

Chapter Two

Wherein the Earl Disposes of His Daughter

If the earl's daughter was the pinnacle of English womanhood, Giles thought, then high society had declined in the generation since Richard Rutherford carried off his aristocratic bride. The young lady for whom an earl, a countess, a footman, and two innocent Rutherfords had been inconvenienced was haggard and confused.

Lady Audrina's bedraggled appearance was understandable, since she had been on the road for several days. But her confused manner when she roused from her stupor? Ridiculous. She seemed truly not to understand where she was or what the consequences of her actions might be. Drunk, probably.

And Giles had the charge of her while everyone else began dinner.

He slouched against the white-plastered wall next

to the door of the washroom, where the lady was supposedly setting herself to rights.

He wished *he* were drunk. Then he wouldn't care that he couldn't feel his frozen toes.

Lord Alleyneham's carriage had arrived not long before that of the fugitives, and the earl had insisted on being present while his tipsy daughter and her precious suitor were wrested from one another. Under his lordship's watchful eye, Giles had assisted the eloping gentleman forcefully from the carriage, then hauled him up the servants' stairs and locked him in a bedchamber. The earl distributed coins to the inn's servants to ensure they would remain deaf to any knocking or shouts issuing from that room.

"That will do for now, Rutherford." The earl did not so much speak as proclaim. "I shall decide what is to be done with him next."

Lord Alleyneham's mouth was a wide slash; his graying brows hooding deep-set eyes. An ebony-headed walking stick was clutched in one fist, less for support than—from what Giles had observed—hitting people in the ankles. A great lion of a man, the impression he gave was one of bulk, of a size so great that it could not be gainsaid. And Giles was hardly a small man; usually he was the one looming over people. To be on the receiving end of folded arms and a glower was both unusual and unwelcome.

But through his mother, Giles was the grandson of a marquess. Not that such a fact had any bearing on his life, ordinarily, but when faced with a haughty earl it helped him square his shoulders. "When you decide what's to be done with your unwanted guest, I assume you'll let me know if I can help," Giles had replied smoothly, letting the hard American consonants twang in his voice. "It's been an absolute pleasure so far, getting pulled into your family affairs."

The earl lifted his chin. "They may yet be yours, young man. I know why you and your father are here in England, and I can help you."

He knew? He couldn't possibly know the real reason. No, everyone thought the Rutherfords were simply in England to visit the late Lady Beatrix's relatives—and purchase jewelry, of course. Richard's plan for a London shop was known. But his plans for financing it?

"Impossible," Giles said. No one knew *that* except Giles and Richard. And no one believed in it except Richard.

"It is not impossible at all. Indeed I *can* help you— if you help me."

"*If* I help you? I've already helped you." Giles motioned toward the locked door, on which the would-be groom—Llewellyn, was that his name?— was now pounding. "There's your help, right in there, imprisoned by the sweat of my brow and the goodness of my heart. As I see matters, it ought to be my turn to be on the receiving end of help."

"That depends on what happens to my daughter."

"No, it doesn't. I've already helped you with your daughter by—might I remind you—walling up some-one who seemed perfectly ready to marry her. For my part in thwarting young love to suit your whim, you owe me whatever assistance you can provide."

"Impertinence!" The earl spat upon the floor.

In the narrow corridor, the men glared at one another. A competition of scornful eyebrow versus scornful eyebrow, clenched jaw versus clenched jaw, narrowed eyes and pinched features and squared shoulders. Giles had the advantage of height, but Lord Alleyneham brandished his walking stick in a most threatening manner.

Had Giles happened upon the pair of them posturing beneath the feeble light of a wall sconce, he would have turned away snorting with laughter. But within the moment, time stilled and teetered. If the earl knew—if he had a single clue that might help the Rutherfords—

"To what sort of help do you refer, my lord? Do you have information?" With some difficulty, Giles twisted his features into a conciliatory expression.

Stubbornly, the earl failed to be delighted at Giles's fit of manners. His hard mouth crimped, and he said only, "See to it that my daughter is sober before you and she join me in my parlor."

And off he stumped, leaning on his cane, in the direction of the private parlor. *Giles's* parlor; the one he and his father had hired no more than two hours ago with the hope of calm and respite.

And dinner. Giles's stomach pinched at the thought of boiled meat and heavy bread. English food might be predictable, but hunger could sauce and spice a simple meal into a feast.

All this had been no more than fifteen minutes ago. The earl had left his daughter's suitor locked up and had handed the care of his drunken offspring to a virtual stranger. How did he know Giles was trustworthy? For that matter, how did Giles know the earl was?

Unease made the back of his neck prickle. Maybe he shouldn't have interfered, adventure or no.

And surely the young woman had been in the washroom long enough. By now she had probably either escaped or swooned.

He hammered on the door. "Hullo in there. Did you faint again?"

"Calm yourself, sir." The voice answered at once, muffled by the wooden barrier. Then the door sprang open, grazing Giles's still-outstretched fist. "I did not faint."

The woman who exited the washroom was not, to say the least, what Giles was expecting.

To assist her drooping figure from the carriage into the Goat and Gauntlet, he had cradled her elbow, half supporting her. She was a sturdy woman, no small weight with all her muscles and curves, with a great pile of inky hair most untidily tumbled and mussed.

When given a bit of privacy, he had assumed she would tidy her dark hair, and indeed she had restrained its tangled curls. She had washed her hands and face; she had set her rumpled deep-red gown to rights. But the change in her was far greater than the removal of a few creases and smudges. Because as she strode past, she looked him up and down—quickly, a flick of chilly heat—then gave a little shrug. As though she saw every darning in his wool stockings. "Shall we proceed to the dining parlor, sir, or do you require a moment to compose yourself?"

Had she been this tall before? As she passed, the crown of her head was at the level of his eyes. And what sort of room was this that she could enter dizzy and souse-witted and emerge with arrogance and poise? He peered within the mysterious depths, but saw nothing more transformative than a pitcher and ewer and a folding privacy screen.

"How kind of you to ask, dear lady. But I'm fine." With feigned carelessness, he leaned against the wall. Letting his wet coat pick up the grain of the whitewashed plaster; letting his leather boots squelch and squish on the wide-planked wooden floor. He would wait her out. "Isn't there something you've forgotten?"

"A great deal, probably. Is there something in particular to which you refer?"

That damnable calm. She might as well have informed Giles that his help was unwanted. Not needed. Certainly not appreciated. Which was no more than he'd been hearing for months. Years, really; all the years since Lady Beatrix first fell ill.

His smile had a sharp edge. "Only the fact that people who wait patiently for young women outside of unfamiliar rooms are usually thanked."

"Are they? I cannot imagine why. Such behavior seems rather predatory to me."

Giles shoved himself free of the wall. "You seem to have recovered your spirit with a vengeance, princess."

"Lady Audrina Bradleigh," she said, her accent crisp as a toast point. "And you are Mr. Rutherford, if I recall correctly."

"You remembered my name. Good job."

Rude, but he was unsettled. Being ordered about by people he'd never met; being confronted with a wilted flower who had turned into a treacherous poppy.

And being offered the possibility of progress— real progress—in their quest for Lady Beatrix Rutherford's jewels. When she debuted in society, the marquess's daughter had been given an elaborate diamond parure. Earrings, a necklace, and who knew what else? The set of jewels had become the stuff of legend. And perhaps that was all they were, for no one had seen the gems in thirty-five years. When young Lady Beatrix's relatives suspected—rightly—that she was planning an elopement, they had searched her belongings, stripping her chambers and person of anything of value.

They hadn't found her diamonds, though. Richard was sure his canny bride had hidden them before she'd eloped with him to America, and he was equally sure he could now find them again. But he and Giles had traveled northward through the marquessate's properties, and . . . nothing.

Of course, they might have had more success if they'd been able to search in the open. Since Lady Beatrix had married her American lover without family permission, relations with the English branch of the family had been icy. The suspicious aristocrats granted Giles and Richard houseroom, but as far as the Newcombes were concerned, Lady Beatrix's jewels had been stolen by servants decades before. Filched, broken up, pawned, never recovered. Searching for them was unseemly and nonsensical.

In this, if nothing else, Giles was inclined to agree with his starchy relatives.

"What has happened to . . . the person who traveled with me?" The lady's low voice interrupted Giles's thoughts.

"He's enjoying a bit of privacy in a locked bedchamber. Well, *enjoying* might not be quite the right word, but he's there for the present."

A deep breath made her shoulders rise, then fall. "Good. That's good. So. We are in York, and you are the end of my adventure. Have I mastered the situation?"

"Nearly, yes. Your father is also here. And mine. And a countess."

"My mother?" Her brows knit.

"No, this one calls herself Lady Irving."

"Good God."

"That was my reaction too, yes."

"Have you met the countess before today?" At his *yes*, she brushed past him. "Then let us join the party, since its members are such old friends."

"Don't be too sure about that, your majesty."

She halted as though leashed by his words.

A thin smile played over Giles's mouth. "You and I, for example, are nothing but acquaintances. Now that I have been inconvenienced to serve in your and your father's schemes, we shall soon go our separate ways." He paused. "Also, you're heading the wrong way. The private parlor is the other direction."

He shouldn't have goaded her. He really shouldn't. Because even though he was tired and cold and hungry, she was all those things, too.

Turning back toward him, she stared, all shadowed eyes and set jaw in the candlelit corridor.

Words of apology were among the most difficult to pronounce, but he made a start. "Look, I didn't mean—"

"I think," she said in that lead-crystal voice, "that you are under a misapprehension about me, Mr. Rutherford. Perhaps several."

Her haughtiness closed off his apology before it got properly under way. "Doubtless, princess. I'm probably full of misapprehensions and mistakes. But I'm also the man who knows where the parlor is, where your father is keen to speak with you."

That lost look crossed her features again: wild, confused, terrified.

Yes, princess; actions have consequences. He didn't say this—admirable restraint!—but only stretched out a hand to indicate the correct direction.

She did not follow. "First, I am not a princess, but the daughter of a peer of the realm. You ought correctly to call me 'my lady.' Second, I am neither stupid nor intoxicated. I was shaking off the effects of being drugged. And third—which you might work out for yourself, given the second fact—I did not arrive here of my own accord." As she spoke, a steadying hand rested against the plaster wall. The flow of words seemed to sap her strength, though her voice never trembled.

"Fine," Giles said. "I understand. My mistake. Three mistakes." Many more mistakes than that, actually. He cleared his throat. "I'm . . . sorry."

Her head jerked, an awkward nod. "I'm sorry that either of us is in this situation."

"So—you didn't really elope with that sharp-faced fellow?" This was all he could think of to say.

"He is rather sharp-faced, isn't he? No, I did not elope with him. I never intended to have anything to do with him again." And she began to spin a frayed tale about laudanum and her maid—she had her *own maid*, of course she did—and waking up in the carriage, and being drugged again, and . . .

Finally Giles put up his hands. "Stop. Stop. I don't need to hear all that. You can tell your father, preferably while I'm sitting before a fire eating dinner and letting my boots dry out."

"But you believe me, do you not?" There was an unmistakable resemblance to the earl in the defiant way she lifted her chin.

Giles dodged the question. "Your father was certain you eloped."

"Was he? And is your father correct about everything you get up to?" One of her dark brows lifted, and there was something carnal, suddenly, in the way the words sang through the air, lush and low.

"No," he admitted.

"Then we need not consider the parental view of the matter, need we?" In the considering tilt of her head, there was judgment.

Now, how had Giles come to be judged? Lady Audrina was the one almost a country away from where she was meant to be.

Ah—no, Giles was split by an ocean from his home, wasn't he? And his dreams were as wild and distant as any laudanum-bespelled vision.

The lady stood beneath a sconce, and when he stepped closer, he saw strain tightening her features. Eyes of deep green, squinting wariness; a strong nose and cheekbones under shadowed skin; a full mouth, pursed as she held his gaze. Every clean line of her face held pride, but something else, too. Shame, he thought it was. She must be feeling confused. Betrayed. Even a little afraid.

All in all, it was a dreadful expression, as pained as it was painful. The force of it made Giles step back again. "I do believe you," he said. "And I'm sorry."

This time, it was not so much an apology as a statement of human feeling. Richard, Giles thought wryly, would have been gratified to hear his eldest employ such politeness.

Again, he extended a hand—just to guide her, not to touch her at all—and together they made their way to the Rutherfords' parlor. Which was now a minor holding of the Earldom of Alleyneham.

"There they are," barked an unfortunately familiar female voice as soon as Giles pushed open the door. "Satisfied that you've starved us long enough, Rutherford? May we have the dinner brought in now?"

Lady Irving. Giles had met her once in London, during the Rutherfords' brief venture into the settled bits of England. Richard had, at the time, been sure that he had only to ask and wave about his dollars, and the English would turn over their fusty old jewels to be reset anew.

Just as she had been in London, Lady Irving was dressed in silk brighter than any color in nature, her turban and gown clashing hues of red and orange. Though about the same age as Richard, her expression had none of the elder Rutherford's patient good humor. She was sharp: aquiline nose, angled eyebrows, hard jaw, set mouth. And her voice was the sharpest of all.

Giles ignored her barking as he would that of a misbehaving dog. "Father, you waited for us? I thought you'd have dined already."

Richard paused as a platter of roast meat was laid on the table, then drew back chairs for Giles and the troublesome daughter of Lord Alleyneham. "I thought it only polite since you were doing a favor for the earl and his companion."

"We require brandy," Lady Irving informed a servant, then fixed bright brown eyes on Richard. "You've got it all wrong, man. I'm already doing a favor for the earl, so your son cannot be doing a favor for me."

"Surely that's not so." Richard smiled. "One good deed doesn't preclude another."

"You forget to account for haughtiness, Father." Giles served out a plate of meat and vegetables, then placed it before Lady Audrina at his left. "Hungry?" The lady shook her head violently, as though he'd handed her a plate of smashed toads. After a pause, Giles took the food for himself. "Perhaps I forgot to account for haughtiness, too."

There were far too many nobles in this room, rarefying the air by putting up their noses. And the servants! Giles was unused to the presence of servants everywhere, slipping about the edges of the room, ever present yet ignored. Upon the arrival of his master, the tired footman had been required to hoist himself from his chair. Leaning against the wall by the brick hearth, he had fallen into a doze despite the argument that seemed to be ongoing between Lady Audrina's father and—

Well, everyone.

"As I was saying," the earl boomed above the din of his own cutlery, "I shall escort Llewellyn back to London myself. He must be seen to return to town without my daughter, so society will not connect their disappearances."

"Could I not travel to London with you instead, Papa?" Lady Audrina asked. "I tell you, Llewellyn took me from home against my will. Surely if I returned with you—"

"Your will does not enter into the matter." Lord Alleyneham smacked the table with the flat of his knife. "Were this situation to become known, it would not matter whether you intended to flee London or not. Your departure and your guilt are the same."

His daughter opened her mouth, and the earl held up a beefy hand. "No. No discussion. I cannot have you endangering our family's prospects with the scandal of your presence. I do not want you seen in London." He turned to Richard. "Rutherford, I need your assurance that Audrina will be permitted to travel with you until after the wedding. Naturally, Lady Irving will remain with the party to impart the respectability Lady Audrina requires."

Giles set down his fork. "Wedding? Whose wedding?"

"My third daughter's wedding to the Duke of Walpole on the first day of the new year."

"What does that wedding have to do with us?" asked Giles.

"Third? How many daughters have you?" This from Richard, who always took an interest in personal irrelevancies.

"Five. This one is the youngest." Without looking at the lady in question, the earl gnawed at a bit of roast, then drained a glass of the brandy Lady Irving had ordered. "I have no sons, so the disposal of my daughters in marriage is of highest importance for the reputation of our family. A union with the Walpole dukedom will be the finest matrimonial alliance London has seen in years, and I cannot allow the scandal of an elopement or an abduction to endanger it. Especially since my two eldest have allied themselves disappointingly, and the fourth seems disinclined to be a part of proper society."

This was all sensibly put, were the earl talking of the behavior of business partners. But his words were as cold as the winter rain. Didn't his children deserve more care? Richard's schemes always had family betterment at their heart, even if the end result was quite the opposite. Giles could not help but notice that Daughter Number Five sat stiff as a statue, not touching a bite of food. Not looking as though she was eager to be *disposed of.* Not looking, for the moment, as though she dared feel anything at all.

But Giles remembered the bleed of painful emotion that had overcome her in the corridor. "How uncooperative of your progeny," Giles said coolly to the earl. "It is obvious that dependent females ought to set aside individual will and do as you bid them."

Someone kicked him under the table. Honestly, it could have been any of them. "If Llewellyn's interference is unwanted," he added more loudly, "then why don't we simply tie him up and leave him in a cellar until after the wedding?"

An arpeggio of gasps, from the earl's drink-deepened rumble through Richard's baritone and Lady Irving's contralto. "I did, of course, intend that we should feed him," Giles said.

"You mistake the matter, young man," barked the latter. "He must be returned to London at once. You must see that if he arrives in the earl's company, it will be quite clear that he never eloped."

"He could have eloped with the earl."

The earl's complexion turned a deeper red. "You are vulgar, sir."

"Do you think so? I'm not even trying. Must be the gift of my American blood." Giles turned his attention to his dinner, adding, "As long as we're making observations about behavior, I don't think much of your manner of asking for a favor, my lord."

"You don't have to like it. It is, however, in your best interest to obey."

Giles felt a pang of sympathy for the earl's offspring.

"And if you do, giving me your word as gentlemen—assuming such a thing matters to Americans," Lord Alleyneham continued, "that you will remain with Lady Audrina and Lady Irving until the ducal wedding goes forward, I will tell you where to find a puzzle box."

Across the table, Richard's dark eyes snagged Giles's. "A . . . puzzle box, you say?" He had to clear his throat before the words resounded clearly.

"One belonging to your late wife." Could the earl be thought human enough to experience joy, the expression on his face might have read as gleeful. "I told you I had learned of your business in England. You, Mr. Rutherford, are on a treasure hunt—and with the right guidance, you shall find what you desire in time for Christmas."

Chapter Three

Wherein the Candle Burns Low

This unpretentious York public house was much like a London dining room in one regard: While they dined, people talked around Audrina and about her, but never to her. It was not at all difficult to slide back her chair and slip from the parlor unnoticed.

In the corridor, she wrested a dripping candle from its sconce. Clamor rolled up from the public room below; speech, laughter, the thump of tankards and platters. Near yet unseen, just like the people in the parlor. Unaware of her being aware of them.

As she held the acrid-smelling tallow candle, its flame flickered in the stir of her breath. She shivered, her limbs as chilled as they were weary.

Your departure and your guilt are the same . . . I do not want you seen in London.

This, from her own father. He would rather spend the journey back to London with the man who had stolen his daughter from home than with the daughter who dared to be imperfect.

Though she had rinsed her mouth, the remnants of laudanum made her stomach heave—as did finding herself in York with no warning, tied to a scoundrel, her only potential ally a hulking, impatient American stranger.

The young Mr. Rutherford *had* said he believed her, though. Which meant he had to be better than no ally at all. And though his demeanor had been brusque, his hands were kind. Careful, not presumptuous. Far more respectful than his words.

But it was Llewellyn with whom she needed words now.

Knowing that Llewellyn was *enjoying a bit of privacy*, as Rutherford had put it, Audrina had no trouble locating him. The story above the parlor was lower and plainer than the rooms on the ground or first floor, with small bedchambers on either side of the corridor. From one of these, thuds echoed against the door. The corridor, Audrina noticed as she affixed her candle into another sconce, was devoid of servants. Her father must have paid them off. He thought of everything.

Everything except noticing with whom she had spent her time months ago. A bit of parental intervention could have stopped all this nonsense with Llewellyn before it started. Flirting, daring, exploring the pleasure of her own power, she had sped along a reckless path, thinking someone would stop her soon. Any time. That someone would notice and care what she was doing.

But no one did. And now she was truly lost, terribly far from where she had intended to be. She had never been good at stopping herself, not with the shadow of her family's disapproval always to flee.

With thwarted anger giving her new strength, she pounded the door with her fist. The thumping within stopped. "Who's there?"

"It's Lady Audrina. For God's sake, Llewellyn, stop that racket or I shall have you tied up and thrown in the cellar." Another bright moment generated by Mr. Rutherford. Really, it sounded like quite a good idea to Audrina.

"Audrina. Finally. Let me out!"

"Not likely. Since you dragged me in a cold carriage all the way from London, I think you can stand a bit of solitude in a nice warm bedchamber." Lowering her voice, she spoke into the seam between door and frame. "You shall remain here overnight. In the morning, my father intends to transport you back to London with him. You shall travel with him peacefully and we shall never see each other again."

"Oh, is that how he wants to play it?" The arse sounded amused. Audrina could imagine his expression: mouth a wicked, smug curve; thick, hawkish brows arched. He fancied himself quite the rake.

She no longer fancied him at all. "This is not a game. There is no question of play on my father's part."

"Play is what it's all about, dear Audrina."

"I will not respond to you unless you salute me appropriately."

He released a sigh heavy enough to send a chill down her back. "Fine. My lady. It's all a matter of money. Either you marry me, or I shall get your dowry some other way."

"No, you are mistaken. Marriage is the only way to get my dowry, and I shall not marry you." She tugged at the bodice of her gown, slumping against the door. Perspiration made her neck and breasts itch, yet her extremities were still clammy. She wanted a hot bath. In her own home. In London.

She wanted it to be a week ago. Or three weeks from now in a bright new year, with her elder sister Charissa safely married to the Duke of Walpole. With the family fortunes safe for a while longer.

"How pedantic you've grown, dear lady. You used to be an entertaining sort. But if you want to be exact, then yes, I should have said I would be content with the equivalent of your dowry." His voice sounded close, too close, like a murmur in her ear, and she jerked away from the wooden barrier that suddenly seemed not nearly solid enough. "If you won't marry me, your father shall instead be required to pay me to keep silent about our romantic journey to York. An investment, shall we say, to avoid the scandal of the fastidious Walpole canceling the ducal wedding." These last words were spoken with a sneer.

Her father could not pay, Audrina knew. The earldom's farm rents had declined year over year since the disastrous winter of 1816. A few months ago, a ship carrying tea and silks had been lost, dragging the earl's investment to the ocean floor with it. Though their dowries were safe in the Funds, protected by their parents' marriage settlements, the Bradleigh sisters had seen the family's income plummet in the past year. Yet another reason why an alliance with a solvent dukedom was vital.

"And if he cannot pay?" Audrina hated her voice for catching on the words.

"Earls can always come up with necessary funds. If he needs a bit of encouragement, dear girl, I have

a pair of your garters in my possession. Your maid
has assured me they are quite distinctive. Bespoke,
aren't they? There will be no question that they
belong to you."

Damn. Damn. Damn. Her maid ought to be tied up
and thrown in the cellar alongside Llewellyn, since
they got along so famously.

Really, that was not a bad idea. "Then keeping you
tied in the cellar until the new year seems like an excellent plan. Mr. Rutherford thinks you should be fed,
but I am not at all sure that would be necessary."

"Tut, tut, my pigeon. I am not a fool. You should
have known I'd take precautions to ensure my own
safety." He chuckled. "When I said your garters were
in my possession, that was not strictly true. They are
with an accomplice of mine, and if I am not safely
returned to London by the last day of the year, one
of your garters shall be sent to Walpole. He will then
have a day to reconsider his marriage to the sister
of . . . such a woman."

A woman who had done nothing more—and in
fact, far less—than Llewellyn himself had done. Who
was being blamed *by her own father* for Llewellyn's
disrespect of her. As though his crime reflected her
worth, not the rotten state of Llewellyn's heart.

No, it wasn't her worth her father was concerned
about. It was his own.

When she next spoke, she managed a scornful
tone. "I must still be fog-headed, because I do not understand how you will benefit if my sister's wedding
does not take place."

"To whom did Walpole almost become engaged
last season?" The soft words wound about Audrina
like a snake. "You remember, don't you, my lady? My

sister almost entrapped him, until yours began flinging herself at him. He could not resist her coin. But coin won't be enough to hold him if scandal touches your family, and my dear sister will make sure she's at hand to console him."

True; very true. The Duke of Walpole was a serious sort, conservative and traditional. He had almost drifted into a betrothal with the colorless Miss Llewellyn, until the laughing, chattering Charissa turned his head in another direction. Should their betrothal be severed—should there be a scandal—

Hands fluttering behind her, Audrina caught the wall by the door. Coaxed herself back; gently, not making a sound, not jarring her exhausted frame. If she did, she might shatter.

Llewellyn did not require the full attention of his audience to perform a soliloquy. "So you see, I shall have your dowry or a . . . let us call it a settlement. Or I shall be brother to a duchess. I do not care whether you're ruined or not. You are a means to an end, my dear."

It did not befit an earl's daughter to slide to the floor and wrap her arms around folded-up legs, nor to hide her face in the cradle of her weary limbs. But there was no one here to see her, and for the moment, she didn't give a damn how an earl's daughter ought to behave.

Especially when Llewellyn realized she wasn't going to reply and began hammering on the door again.

A quiet voice slid below the thumping. "I'm sorely tempted to tie him up, no matter what the illustrious Lady Irving recommends."

Audrina's head snapped up. Giles Rutherford was

crouched on the floor at her side, his large frame neatly folded like a stack of lumber.

"What are you doing here?"

His teeth flashed bright in the warm light of the candle overhead. "I noticed that you have a habit of not being in your expected location, then instead turning up in the company of London's most fascinating gentleman." He tilted his head toward the door. "What's going on? Are you trying to talk him into sense?"

Against his tanned, ruddy skin, his eyes were light and clear. *He said he believed me*, Audrina told herself. And so by way of reply, she simply said, "Yes."

"How's that working?"

"Not terribly well."

"He has a fool's ingenuity, doesn't he?"

"If he is indeed ingenious"—and after learning that he had thought ahead to snatch a pair of her garters, she had to grant that he was—"we should not consider him a fool."

Rutherford rocked back on his heels. "If he weren't a fool, he wouldn't treat a woman as he has you."

"How chivalrous of you." She allowed her tight grip about her folded legs to loosen a bit, her head to sink back against the support of the wall.

"Was it? Sorry, princess. I won't let such an uncharacteristic remark pass my lips again. What I meant to say was—if he weren't a fool, he wouldn't sap his strength hammering at this door." Raising his voice, he beat his square fist on the door—just once, then grimaced and shook out his hand. "Stop that racket, you thief," he called. "We all know you're in there, and no one will let you out."

When he turned in his crouch back to Audrina, she

said, "Should I call you 'peasant,' Mr. Rutherford? If you are to exaggerate my status by calling me a princess, I ought to return the favor."

One of his brows lifted. "Draftsman might be more accurate, in that case. Or tradesman, if you've an objection to a man who uses his hands."

"That depends on the man," Audrina replied.

His mouth twitched. It was rather a nice mouth, mobile and sharply cut, with a small scar slicing one side of the upper lip in a pale line. After this hellish day, she was glad that he felt human enough to smile and that she felt human enough to enjoy the sight.

Unfolding to his great square height, he leaned over and extended a hand. "Hop up, your ladyship. We might as well talk a little farther away from your would-be bridegroom."

She allowed his hand to close upon hers. It was a solid hand, broad and strong, its fingers and palm rough and warm. A shiver ran through her body; the warmth of his touch reminded her again how cold she was, and how long she had been that way.

Once he drew her to her feet, her eyes were at the level of his mouth. She was accustomed to looking down on half the men in London; it was rather a nice change to have someone watching over her. The flickering candlelight traced his cheekbones, and she noticed: "You have freckles?"

The mouth with the tiny scar curved into a half smile. "Is that so odd for a big redheaded lout?"

Llewellyn was hammering at the door louder than ever. How could he not be tired by now? She felt she could lie down and sleep on the wooden floor. "You're not a lout."

"Princess, you'll make me blush. And no one wants

to see a redhead blush." Releasing her hand, he
turned back toward the stairs.

"My candle," she blurted. "I can't leave it."

Rutherford waited at the top of the stairs as she
popped the tallow taper free from its holder again. It
felt safer to have something to cling to, even if it was
only a cheap stick of hardened fat.

When they reached the turning of the stairs,
Llewellyn's din faded and the light and noise began
to leak up from below. Holding her candle in one
hand, Audrina worked a nail into its soft surface. "I
had to leave the dining parlor," she said. "My father
did not require my opinion for his plans. And after
that creature"—a tip of her head to the upper story
and Llewellyn—"fed me laudanum, I could not bear
the idea of any food."

"I wondered if it was something like that." He
reached into a pocket of his dark-blue woolen coat
and pulled forth a cloth napkin, extending it to her.

With a cautious hand, she flipped open the folds.
"Bread. You brought me a slice of bread?"

"It's not very good, unfortunately. Pretty dry. It
might be from yesterday's baking."

She found a wall holder for her candle, then broke
off a bit of the bread. It was hard, as he'd said; so hard
that it scratched the inside of her mouth and she
wound up sucking at it like a boiled sweet. The oaty
crumbs began to dissolve, slowly, and as she swallowed, her protesting stomach began to quiet a bit.
"Thank you."

It was difficult to look at a man when he had seen
one at one's weakest and worst. Instead, she peered
over the handrail of the stairs but could see nothing
but more stairs, winding up and down. "I learned

how to make bread," she recalled. "I sneaked into the kitchens and asked the cook to teach me."

"Why?"

The stairs seemed to stretch out long, then collapse. Tired; she was so tired. Shaking her head to clear her vision, she turned back to Rutherford. "Because I wanted to know how it was made. Wouldn't you? It starts with all these flat dry ingredients and ends in something so light. Well—sometimes it does." She popped another stale morsel into her mouth. "That was a long time ago. My father found out, told me it was unsuitable for one of his family to be in the kitchen, and threatened to dismiss any servant who allowed me in there again."

"I can imagine." Rutherford was quite good at keeping a bland expression on his face, even as his light eyes were full of mischief. "Wanting to know how something is made, then taking steps to pursue that knowledge, seems a most unsuitable and hazardous attitude for a young Englishwoman. The sort of behavior that should be squelched at once."

"Yes, well, it is the only way a young Englishwoman can learn something besides the directory of the peerage and a bit of worthless embroidery." Her companion's smile held a sympathy she did not want, and she picked at her bread just as she had at the candle. "What was decided after I left the dining parlor? Everything was, I assume—but in what way?"

"You know your father's methods well, I see. Yes, it's settled that we'll all leave tomorrow. Llewellyn and your father shall return to London in Llewellyn's carriage—"

"His mother's."

"What? Are you joking?" Rutherford cleared his

throat. "Fortunate fellow, to have a parent willing to aid him in an abduction. She'll have her carriage back in a few days, for your father intends to begin the journey south at first light. Lady Irving's carriage shall bear her, you, and my father and I to Castle Parr, a few hours' ride from here."

"The home of the Viscount of Dudley? Why should we go there?"

"Listen to you, as good as a book of reference. You weren't exaggerating when you said you knew the peerage."

She crumbled a bit of crust between her fingers. "All elegant young women memorize the peerage of England, so as not to neglect an opportunity of making themselves agreeable to gentlemen of quality." *Elegant.* Ha. She felt, and probably looked, as though she had been stored in a dirty closet. This red gown had been her favorite, but the cotton was creased beyond repair.

And now it would remind her of Llewellyn. She wouldn't wear it again.

But she had nothing else to wear, did she? She had no possessions with her at all. Wadding the napkin around the stale bread, she asked, "What of servants to accompany us? A maid?"

"Lady Irving will allow her maid to serve you both. I think she's brought along a bunch of baggage for you so you can be more comfortable. Your father's footman will also come with us. They'll ride in my father's carriage, since Lady Irving was convinced hers would be more comfortable to the tender backsides of the nobility. No offense meant."

"I am far too tired to take offense. Probably." She

handed him back the napkin-wrapped bread. "You still have not told me why we are to go there."

"True enough. The answer, my lady, is that we are chasing a wild goose because my father believes it lays golden eggs."

"I am also far too tired for metaphors."

"A pity. That was a good one, I thought. Somewhere in Castle Parr, says your father, is a puzzle box that belonged to my late mother. He had the information from Lady Irving, whose marvelous network of servants and informants seems to know everything in England. And somehow, says *my* father, that puzzle box contains a fortune."

Audrina unspooled this information. "Then we had better find it."

"There's more to the matter than that." Rutherford's mouth drew flat and grim. "If you want to return to London in time for your sister's wedding, your father insists that you be betrothed. Otherwise he won't allow you in the church."

Oh, for God's sake. She caught herself on the handrail before she could sag to the floor. "He is the second person to try to marry me off against my inclination today."

Rutherford looked not upstairs toward Llewellyn, but away—in the direction of the parlor, maybe, or just of the *anywhere else* he surely wished to be. Worry tightened his strong features. "Sorry to be the bearer of . . . news. I'm not sure what adjective to put to it."

"I'm far too tired for adjectives."

When he looked back at her, his expression was smooth again. "Of course. Let me show you to your chamber. Or would you rather return to the parlor?"

Her stomach pitched. "No. Not the parlor."

"Not much point, really," Rutherford agreed. "Your father and Lady Irving are arguing about which of them is more indebted to the other. My father, meanwhile, is ignoring them both as he finishes his dinner. Since he has six children, he's used to ignoring a din."

He retrieved her candle—not much more than a stub now—and led her to a door that, she was glad to note, was not within earshot of Llewellyn's cacophony. He handed her a key.

"You're safe for tonight. Lock yourself in. Lady Irving's maid will probably check on you soon." Rutherford fell into shadow as Audrina took the candle and opened the door. "Sleep well, princess. Fruitless quests require an early start in the morning."

Chapter Four

Wherein Illness Is Narrowly Averted

Another day, another unwanted carriage ride. As Audrina was conscious and clean for this one, she supposed she ought to consider herself fortunate.

She had not quite managed to feel that way yet.

Lady Irving's carriage was glossy and comfortable, as though splatters and stains dared not inconvenience the countess. From her seat on the squabs of striped velvet—orange and red, of course; no peaceful colors for her ladyship—Audrina watched the ancient walls of York relax their grip and slide behind the carriage. The farmland around the city faded into unbroken moor as they drove north.

"How long is the journey to Castle Parr?" she asked. Not as though the answer mattered. Until someone let her out, she was trapped in this gilded box.

"No more than three hours, with these fine horses

to pull such a comfortable carriage." With a gracious smile despite his ill appearance, Richard Rutherford inclined his head to Lady Irving.

The countess and Audrina had the forward-facing seat; the two Americans had stuffed themselves onto the back-facing bench across from them. No more than five minutes after the horses clopped away from the Goat and Gauntlet, Richard Rutherford had begun to sway and turn pale, all the while protesting that he felt quite well.

Now Giles Rutherford gave his father a nudge in the side, which caused the elder man to shudder and heave. "Father, you look terrible. You know you become ill if you face backward in a carriage. Do go sit on the other seat."

"Son, where is your chivalry?" Richard croaked. Audrina had not known a suntanned man could turn such a sickly color. Like that shade called *drab* that had been all the crack a season ago: green and brown together.

"Father, would it be chivalrous to get sick all over the inside of Lady Irving's carriage?"

"I should say not," said the countess, wearing an expression of some alarm beneath her violet turban. "Audrina. Quickly, girl. Trade places with that Rutherford before he shows us what he had for breakfast."

Richard closed his eyes. "Nothing, my lady. It's safer that way if I know I'm to ride in a carriage."

"Well, good heavens, man, how do you expect to get through the day like that?" Lady Irving sounded even more annoyed. "You've got to eat if you want to keep up your strength for dragging people around England to look at treasure boxes."

"Puzzle boxes." A faint smile, though a dew of perspiration had broken out across his forehead.

"Mr. Rutherford, you look very ill. Do trade places with me, please. I never get ill when I travel." Audrina thought she heard Giles Rutherford snort. "As long as no one has given me laudanum, that is."

The carriage hit a bump, and not even the well-oiled springs could keep its frame from bouncing. Rutherford swallowed heavily, then nodded, his eyes still shut. "Thank you, my lady. I—very well."

Gingerly, he rose from the seat into the crouch permitted by the low ceiling of the carriage, and Audrina echoed his movement. Another bump on the road made them sway, and Audrina steadied herself with a quick reflex: one hand pressed flat on the ceiling, one catching—

Giles Rutherford's hand, which had shot out to hold hers. *Oh.* "Steady, princess." His fingers were as rough and sturdy as the rest of him; she had not imagined the unfamiliar strength of his grip last night.

"I am perfectly steady," she replied, shaking free her hand—though a tipping sensation that was not unpleasant slid through her belly.

"Excuse me, Lady Audrina," said Richard. "If I might just move a bit . . ." Sway, sway, and the shuffle of bodies within the moving carriage made Audrina feel like a die being shaken by a gamester. Richard's booted foot knocked against hers, and unsteadied, they both fell onto the opposite seat with more force than grace.

In Audrina's case, she landed squarely in Giles Rutherford's lap.

Arms and legs a-windmill, she struggled to right herself. "I beg your pardon, sir." He was solid beneath her thighs, all buckskin and clean soap and scratchy wool.

"Please don't," he said as she slid to the seat at his side. "It's an honor for me to have a royal backside in my lap."

"You are vulgar," said Lady Irving, whose own lap Richard Rutherford had missed by a scant few inches.

"Always, or only just now?" Though he regarded Lady Irving with a curious gaze, he managed to shove Audrina upright next to him with one broad hand, warm on her upper arm.

"I have not yet decided. Probably the former."

"Good to know," Giles said. "I'll have it embroidered on my handkerchiefs. 'Vulgar'—my family motto. Though in Latin it means 'ordinary,' so maybe you'd better come up with a less toothless insult."

"Son," moaned Richard from his slump on the forward-facing seat. The elder man's color was returning to normal, though he had again closed his eyes. "Please."

"That's not very insulting either," said Giles. "Sorry. You're both going to have to try harder if you want me to crumble and weep. Princess, would you care to give it a go?"

"No, I do not think that would be wise."

"And do you always do what's wise?"

"I have not in the past, no. But since I find myself unexpectedly in York and ostracized from my favorite sister's wedding, it is probably past time I begin."

The lashes around Giles's vivid blue eyes were dark, much darker than the copper of his hair or the gilded stubble just beginning to edge his jaw. "Or you could wait," he said, "until after the new year. Allow yourself an unwise Christmas."

It was difficult to look directly at such blue eyes, like staring into the noontime sky. "I shall have that either way, since I am now a part of a quest for treasure." She smoothed her lavender skirts; an insipid shade she had never cared for. A final defiance from her traitorous lady's maid, who had packed a trunk of Audrina's belongings for Lady Irving to bring on the journey. "Tell me, what is this puzzle box you seek? It must be important to draw you across an ocean."

"Yes," said Richard.

"No," said Giles.

Father and son looked at each other, Richard sitting up straight. "How can you say no, Giles? When you never expected we'd learn of any clue at all?"

"All right, maybe," granted Giles. "Maybe there's something to this. If there is a puzzle box, and *if* it belonged to my mother."

"There is, and it did," said Lady Irving. "I am never wrong about such matters." Both Rutherfords blinked at her, and the countess lifted her chin. "Honestly, Rutherford—a pair of Americans darting around England to buy up jewels? Highly suspicious behavior. You can't be so naïf as to expect that I wouldn't winkle out your secrets. Why, what if you were dangerous criminals?"

Audrina spoke over Giles's choked sound of protest. "Assuming Lady Irving's information is correct"—now she ignored the sound of protest from Lady Irving—"what do you know of the box, Mr. Rutherford?"

"I think it will be a *himitsu-bako*," said Richard.

"*Himitsu-bako*? What sort of a heathen name is that?" Lady Irving, of course.

"A Nipponese name." Richard's voice had regained

its steadiness. "These boxes were invented in Japan, and the finest are made there. They are constructed of interlocking panels that must be slid apart in a specific order; otherwise the box simply won't open."

Audrina was caught on the first part of this speech. "How would a box from Japan come to be in this part of York?"

As though to remind them of the remoteness of their location, the carriage slowed, all but mired in a muddy stretch of road. Out the window, Audrina saw nothing but brown and gray land under a cloudy bolt of colorless sky.

"My late wife's father was a marquess," said Richard, "but her mother was of Dutch extraction and brought a fortune from trade to the marriage. To the Dutch alone did the Japanese open a port, and my wife's grandfather carried home beautiful objects like *himitsu-bako* for his bride and his daughter. When Lady Beatrix came of age, her mother passed them along to her. That was shortly before our elopement."

"And you think the box contains a treasure?" Lady Irving sounded skeptical. "How large is this box?"

"We have no idea what it contains, but most likely it's not very large," said Giles. "I've never heard of one longer than my forearm. Some are much smaller." Stretching forth an arm, he invited the comparison. His coat-clad arm seemed to Audrina as sturdy as a great oak branch, stretching to be climbed. To be spanned with her hands, testing its size and strength.

Steady, princess: her own thoughts mocked her. There was no sense in allowing oneself to become attracted to a man simply because he had not treated one horribly.

And because he had laughing eyes, and broad

shoulders, and because he had no sense of propriety whatsoever.

Steady, princess.

She looked out the window again. The dullness of winter was a much safer sight than Giles Rutherford's blue eyes.

"Why did you agree to accompany us?"

Audrina thought Giles had addressed the question to her, but Lady Irving replied. "As though I was going to miss out on this sort of scandal? Not likely." She gave a snort.

As she looked from the window back into the dim, close confines of the carriage, the tipping sensation within Audrina's belly turned into a sickening plummet. "You would serve my mother so, Lady Irving? After your long friendship?"

"I wouldn't do anything to hurt your mother, girl—except amuse myself when she wears an idiotic fashion." With a triumphant smile, she patted her violet silk turban. "No, the only thing better than a scandal everyone knows about is a scandal no one knows about except oneself. You can trust me with your secrets. All I want is to know them."

"Have I become ill, too, or did that nearly make sense?" Giles said.

"I have not yet decided," Audrina replied. "But—thank you, Lady Irving."

"What about you, princess?" asked Giles. "What brought your royal backside into this carriage, and then so delightfully into my lap?"

Was he flirting with her, or trying to provoke a rage with his teasing? No smile softened those hard features, though his blue eyes crinkled at the corners. Sitting at his side, she could see the freckles on his cheekbones, flecked over lighter skin as if an artist had shaken a brush of golden paint.

She drew herself strict and upright, hands folded neatly in her lap. No flirting, no rage. "What was the alternative to traveling with your party, Mr. Rutherford?" Her consonants snapped with careful breeding. "Being left alone in York? That would never be permitted for a gently bred young lady. Returning to London with Llewellyn and my father? I cannot think whether I would have disliked that more, or they."

"So you honor us only by default."

"Be that as it may, you are still honored," she said sweetly. "Do try to remember that the next time you are tempted to speak of my backside."

"Vulgar," said Lady Irving—but Giles Rutherford smiled.

At last there was something to see besides Rutherfords, more Rutherfords, Lady Irving's turban, and the grayness of wintry moors. Through frozen fog, Castle Parr's wings of golden stone drifted into view. The central structure was tall and domed like a great crowned head. All in all, it gave the impression of an elegant lady stretching out her arms in an embrace of welcome.

When the travelers piled out of the carriage, the elderly Lord Dudley was just as welcoming. Audrina guessed that her father had described the callers as dear friends and holiday guests, and the viscount's eager reception betrayed his loneliness. Though he appeared frail, a small stooped man with a fringe of snowy hair, his eyes were brown and bright and merry.

Lord Dudley waved off his butler, guiding the

guests into the stately house himself with a shuffling
stride. "Travel is beyond us now," he said in a hoarse
but carrying voice. "M'lady and our daughter-in-law
and I rattle around in this great pile with scarcely a
bit of company. Glad to get Alleyneham's message
that you were nearby. I was a friend to his father in
our youth, and I remember the present earl as a
child. Quite a rotten boy, but then eldest sons so
often are, eh?"

Richard chuckled. "As you're my host, I shouldn't
disagree, but since my eldest son is at my side, I
cannot agree either."

"Is he?" Lord Dudley tilted up his face, studying
each member of the party in turn. "Lady Irving,
welcome. Ah, and you're Alleyneham's daughter. And
you"—his dark eyes fixed on Giles—"are the fair spit
of your mother."

"You knew her?"

"Everyone knew Lady Beatrix." The viscount waved
a gnarled hand as he began to lead his visitors
through the echoing entry hall. "Tall, she was, and full
of mischief. And I could never forget all that red hair.
Or her laugh. She had a marvelous laugh, didn't
she?"

"I don't remember her laughing much," Giles said.
"But then, she was ill for years."

"Heel!" A high, scratchy voice carried into the
entry hall, followed by a clatter and skitter and thump.
Within a few seconds, a motley bunch of canines came
into view at a subdued trot. Almost lost at the center
of the pack was a woman as elderly as Lord Dudley,
with a face like a carved apple and the straight bearing of a general. This must be the viscountess—though
she was dressed plainly, in an old-fashioned round

gown of dark-green stuff, and her long white hair fell unpinned down her back like a young girl's.

"About time you all got here," she called to her visitors in a voice like a rusty flute. "Dudley and Sophy and I have been waiting luncheon for at least a half hour."

"She sounds as cheerful as Lady Irving," murmured Giles Rutherford, a tickle of sound in Audrina's ear. "This should be interesting."

"Sophy is our daughter-in-law," explained Lord Dudley as hound after hound—good God, were there *eight* of them?—nosed his hands and wound tight circles around his legs. "A friend of your late wife's, I think, Mr. Rutherford? So said Lord Alleyneham's letter. Sophy spends most of her time in the library because the dogs aren't allowed in there." His laugh was a bark. "They'd chew the bindings."

"I don't want to go into the library. I don't have time to read with eight rascals to keep me busy." Her ladyship's words might have been wistful had her tone not been so brisk. "So. Who have we here? A Mr. Rutherford, I presume." Her eyes were as dark as her husband's, though drifting—first to the elder American, then his son. "And another Mr. Rutherford, eh? And let's see—you would be . . ."

"Lord Alleyneham's daughter," prompted the viscount. Audrina performed her curtsy.

"And Lady Irving," he added. Lady Dudley turned to the last member of their party. "I remember when you were Estella Oliver. I was as old during your London Season as you are now. You used to be quite a pretty girl. What happened to you?"

"Drink, gambling, and rakish men." Lady Irving rolled the *r*'s over her tongue like toffees. "All the delights of London were worth a few wrinkles and gray hairs. What's your excuse, Lady Dudley?"

"I'm too old to make excuses for the way I look." Lady Dudley folded her arms, allowing her back to fall into a stoop. "Dudley, I'm hungry." She sounded plaintive.

Richard Rutherford cleared his throat. "I am sure we're sorry for any delay on the road that caused inconvenience to your schedule."

"I'm not," said Lady Irving. "We were jostled enough as it was. No sense in killing ourselves or the horses to shave a few minutes."

Richard Rutherford shot her a look similar to the ones Audrina had seen him direct at his son: brows lifted, lids dropped; the tiniest shake of the head accompanying it. Rendered into words, it might read *Hush, now, and don't be rude.*

Amazingly, Lady Irving fell silent.

"Before we meet Sophy and go in to luncheon, my lady, I wonder if I might inquire"—Mr. Rutherford paused delicately—"does she have in her possession a puzzle box? Have you noticed such an item? It was a gift from Lady Beatrix, and . . . ."

Lady Dudley tilted her head, hair falling like spider silk over one shoulder. "You get right to the point, don't you, Rutherford?"

"Yes, Sophy has it." Lord Dudley steadied himself with a hand on the head of a long-legged hound. "It's a pretty thing of gold. She never could get it open, but I don't suppose that matters. If you shake it, it's clear that it's empty."

Chapter Five

Wherein a Brighter Turban Is Required

Silence dropped like a cloak over the entry hall.

But it wasn't Lady Irving's hall, or her quest—and therefore she need not be silent. "Empty, eh? That's a spoke in your wheel, Rutherford." Her voice echoed on the stone walls, bouncing to the ceiling dozens of feet above.

"It might seem empty to your daughter-in-law, my lady," said Richard. "But if we could examine it—if your daughter-in-law doesn't mind, that is—Giles might be able to open it. For, ah, posterity's sake."

"Sophy won't mind. She doesn't mind anything except being around the dogs." Lady Dudley reached into a pocket of her dark gown and pulled out a handful of tea biscuits. A canine ecstasy of panting ensued as she dropped a treat into each dog's mouth. "But what do you think you'll find?"

With a lift of his brows, Giles looked to his father. "That's a fair question. What *do* we think we'll find in an empty box?"

Richard clapped his son on the shoulder, his handsome features brightening. "One never knows, son. That's the adventure of it!"

Adventure, yes. For adventure, Estella had agreed to hare up to York with her oldest friend's husband; adventure, and the love of knowing things that no one else knew. A longtime widow, Estella had nieces and nephews and grand-nieces and grand-nephews aplenty, but most of her time was her own. This meant she was free to pursue her favorite pastime: collecting information. And as with any collection, the pleasure was in the getting and the keeping, not the sharing.

If she were to be frank with herself—which was not a habit in which she ordinarily indulged—she would rather spend the days before Christmas on strange, frozen roads than at the fringes of a family Christmas. In Castle Parr, they were all uprooted. All strangers.

In a way, this knit them.

"Adventure," she murmured. "It is."

Giles rolled his eyes. "That's my father's favorite word."

Crow's feet marked the corners of Richard's eyes, a pattern laid by years of sun and smiles. His grin showed overlapping incisors, a small imperfection that added to the impression of full-body delight. "It's a wonderful word. Everyone ought to have a favorite word."

"How about luncheon?" Lady Dudley took on a hopeful look.

"We've got to fetch Sophy first. And maybe the guests would like to freshen up. You won't starve in another half hour, will you?" Dudley winked at his wife, who snorted.

"Can't say. How many biscuits have I left in my pockets?" She shook back her long white hair, then turned to Richard Rutherford. "Dudley said your wife knew Sophy long ago. Did she ever mention whether my son Jack had—"

"I'd be glad," Estella interrupted loudly, "for the chance to tidy up before luncheon. Could we be shown to our rooms?"

Everyone stared at her as though she'd shouted curses. Fine. Let them stare, as long as Lady Dudley didn't finish her sentence. Lady Irving was known to say outrageous things. To be blunt, rude, or selfish. Sometimes, though, it served a selfless purpose.

Because it seemed Lady Dudley's wit was leaving her. Her speeches were odd, her manner was absent. Without the animation of her question, she looked lost.

"Of course, of course," Lord Dudley rushed to say. "Take all the time you need. Lady D, let's get the hounds to the stables."

The viscountess's face cleared, and she snapped her fingers. "Heel!" Silently except for the click of canine nails on marble, the pack of dogs left off nosing around Lord Dudley—or should that be herd, or flock? Estella had never been a literary sort, and the intricacies of naming groups of animals were beyond her.

Lady Dudley marched from the entry hall with more force and pique than she had entered. Well, let her. It wouldn't do her any good to discuss her son before a group such as this; the result would be either lies or pain.

Sometimes Estella regretted collecting information.

One of those times had been a decade before, when through a chain of servants' tittle-tattle, she learned that John Parr had died not in his home, but in Bedlam. After striking his head, the viscountcy's glib and charming heir had turned gruff and mercurial; this everyone knew. But his outbursts of violence? Those were meant to be a family secret.

Though there was no such thing as a family secret, really.

Estella wondered whether Lady Dudley had started taking in dogs as a way to protect herself from her son. Or maybe they had gathered over time, a collection of warm-hearted beasts to chase away the lonely cold.

"Well." She let her voice carry through a space that seemed far too silent. "Where did our footman and maid hide themselves? Their carriage ought to have arrived by now, and they might as well make themselves useful."

Talk of servants snapped the group back into action, and within a few minutes the quartet of travelers were shown to their bedchambers. Audrina and Estella had adjacent rooms, and the countess found hers to be as soft and dark and cluttery as a Christmas pudding. The room held a vanity and glass, a bed, a wardrobe, a writing-desk and chair, an armchair, a scatter of lamps, a wooden chest, and enough gewgaws to open a junk shop.

The Rutherfords were in chambers of their own at the plainer end of the corridor. There was no stickler for rank like an English butler, to whom no amount of fortune could compensate for the lack of a title.

Estella had felt that way once herself. Certainly she had encouraged her nieces to marry titles—but she would never have urged them to ignore their hearts. Not as she had done.

Standing before the generous fire, she coaxed her heavy silk turban from her head and laid it over a clutter of bottles on the vanity table. Beneath it, her hair was cropped short. In the past year or two, strands of gray had dimmed the former auburn. Now she simply looked faded. Old.

She had never really had the chance to be young.

Lord Irving had been much her senior, loose-mouthed and vulgar, but willing to buy her for a high price shortly after her debut. For the few years of her marriage, she'd endured his careless infidelities and spendthrift ways, his roughness with her in the marriage bed and his indifference outside of it. If an earl could act in such a way, then what the devil did rank guarantee a woman?

Nothing. Nothing at all. Thank God she'd got a generous income for life, so she need never rely on anyone but herself again.

Herself, and her maid. When Estella fell into the doldrums, she wore something bright to help pull herself out, and she obviously needed to don something brighter before luncheon. The castle had one of those modern bell-pull systems, and it was easy to ring for Lizzie. To sink into the armchair and slide off her slippers; to shut her eyes for a moment, allowing the maid to fuss about and ensure the safe transfer of the countess's belongings to the wardrobe.

"You'd better find me another turban to wear, Lizzie," Estella said as the maid bustled about. "Did you pack the aquamarine?"

"Yes, my lady. It's right here." Her eyes still closed,

Estella heard the soft thumping of hatboxes, the rustle of one silk headpiece exchanged for another. "Oh, ma'am—one of the paste gems is coming loose. Shall I mend it right now?"

"Yes, do."

Lizzie was unflappable and efficient—a skilled lady's maid, though Estella sometimes missed the voluble opinions of her French maid, Simone. It had been more difficult to fall into the doldrums around Simone because there was simply no silence. No opinion went unanswered, no clashing costume unchallenged.

"There, my lady. It's quite secure now," said Lizzie after a few minutes.

"Thank you, Lizzie," she said. "You may go. Please check on Lady Audrina before you return to your quarters."

"Yes, my lady. Right away."

Estella allowed herself a few more minutes to warm her feet before the fire, then slid back into her slippers and stood. Hips, knees, ankles popped as she did. Not a sign of age, surely; she was merely cold. No one in England was ever warm enough in December.

The aquamarine turban had been repaired; Lizzie did good work, not that Estella wanted her to become vain about it and demand a higher salary. This was Estella's favorite garment: the color of a summer sea, with plumes the shade of a vivid sunset and glass gemstones bright as the Crown Jewels. As she placed it atop her head, she smiled at her reflection, and a few years seemed to drop from the granite-faced woman in the glass.

* * *

When she and Audrina entered the dining room of Castle Parr, Estella noted that the Rutherfords and Dudleys had preceded them. Neither the Americans nor their host and hostess had changed clothing. They remained content to wear drab colors, fortunate souls.

The dining room smelled like lemons over mustiness, the telltale scent of a room cleaned often but used seldom. It stretched high, with windows nearly two stories tall and curtains heavy with embroidery, so heavy that they tugged and sagged against their corded ties. Lustrous paper-hangings in shades of tan and cream gave the space a pleasant lightness, but not even the two fireplaces could banish the feeling of cold one gained from looking out those windows to the frosty barrenness outside: skeletal trees and defeated brown grass, unadorned even by a blanket of snow.

Estella reminded herself that she was wearing the aquamarine turban.

"Quite a nice spread you've laid before us." She eyed the sideboard between the fireplaces; on it, an assortment of cold meats, cheeses, and dried fruits were arranged. "Are we to see the mythical Sophy sometime soon, or shall we eat without her?"

"Mythical? I do like the sound of that."

The voice from the doorway was crisp yet warm, like a ginger biscuit straight from the oven. The occupants of the dining room turned in its direction.

"Ah, Soph!" Lord Dudley's hoarse voice squeezed. "Finishing one of your notes, were you? Sophy looks through a telescope all night and transcribes her notes all day."

"I'd be mythical indeed, Papa, if I truly did as you say. Won't you introduce me to the guests?"

The mysterious Sophy proved to be nothing like the frail, flowery creature Lady Irving had imagined. A woman of about forty years, she was of average height and build but gave an impression of uncommon vigor. As Lord Dudley made the introductions, Sophy Parr removed her pince-nez and shoved the small spectacles in the pocket of her sensible black gown. The eyes thus revealed were gray and astute.

"Lady Irving, pleased to meet you." Sophy's handshake was as firm as her curtsy was abrupt. "I suppose her ladyship told you I don't like the dogs? It's her favorite thing to tell people about me, but it's not true. I like them fine from a distance. Any closer, though, and I start to sneeze."

"They are out in the stables for the afternoon, Sophy." Lord Dudley laughed, genial under his crown of white hair. "If you can manage a sneeze from that distance, I'll credit you with supernatural powers."

"A sad waste of supernatural powers," remarked Giles Rutherford, "if sneezing is the only manifestation."

Lady Dudley, standing at his side, declined to comment—though the expression on her face was worth a few choice sentences.

Overall, Sophy—for so she insisted they all call her—looked as though she didn't miss much, but didn't dwell on what did pass her by. After a marriage to the unfortunate Jack Parr, Estella supposed these qualities had stood her in good stead.

"Where is the footman who traveled with us?" asked Giles Rutherford.

Estella coughed. *Americans*. As though the Parrs

would be bothered to know the location of servants not of the household.

"He is resting in the servants' quarters." This from Audrina, seated demurely and seeming not to notice the looks of surprise on everyone's faces. "Lady Irving's maid, Lizzie, informed me. After several long days of travel, he felt unwell."

Giles frowned. "Sorry to hear it. He looked half-dead on his feet yesterday."

"Take him in as one of your strays," Estella said to Lady Dudley. "Feed him biscuits and teach him to heel."

"That sounds about right for training a footman." Lord Dudley gave a wheeze of laughter. "They don't all get biscuits, though. Maybe they should."

Lady Dudley's hair fell around her face. "Daughter of Alleyneham, you should keep an eye out for strays and send them my way."

"Call me Lady Audrina, please." The girl had spirit to go with her manners, Estella was glad to hear. She tossed off the correction with a smile, never pausing as she cut into a slice of beef.

"What sort of a name is that? I've never heard it before." Sophy sounded interested.

"It's my father's name, in a way." Audrina kept the smile on her face, though her hands went still. "He is called Adrian. I am the youngest of five sisters, and by the time I came along, he knew he would never have a son to take his name. I was given it instead."

"So you *are* Daughter of Alleyneham." Lady Dudley sounded triumphant.

The knife and fork resumed their motion. "That was never in question, I hope. But I also hope you will not blame me for that, any more than you might blame me for having dark hair or looking a certain way."

Estella snorted. "Oh, I don't think anyone's likely to blame you for the way you look, young lady." Audrina took after her paternal grandmother, if Estella recalled that lady aright, which meant the fortunate girl had escaped both her mother's weak chin and her father's harsh brow.

"Rather cold in here, isn't it?" Lord Dudley spoke into the midst of another conversation, cupping at his ear. "Fireplaces don't seem to be drawing correctly. Only let me know if you get chilled"—he winked—"and we can add a splash of something to the afternoon tea."

The conversation took few unexpected twists after that, as Richard Rutherford raced through his meal and cast approximately ten thousand sidelong glances at Sophy. Wondering about the puzzle box, maybe, though Estella felt all the difference between Sophy's fresh forty years and her own fifty-eight. Giles seemed preoccupied as well, too much so to let off another of the verbal cannon-shots with which he'd entertained her in the carriage. It was left to Audrina and Sophy and the Dudleys to chat, mostly about the home. And since no one bothered to call it *a great drafty pile in the middle of godforsaken moorland*, their observations were hardly worth listening to.

"May I offer you some cheese, Lady Irving?"

She blinked at being addressed, and realized Richard Rutherford was the one who had done so. He stood behind her chair, near the sideboard, and held a small knife with which others had carved sectors of Cheddar from a fat wedge.

Estella's stomach gave a gurgle of acceptance. She

had taken little food—her corsets were getting more and more difficult to lace—yet her appetite stubbornly refused to vanish. "I don't eat cheese, Rutherford. Cheese is vulgar." Her voice sounded more snappish than she intended, and not the good sort of snappish like a warm ginger biscuit.

Rutherford only lifted his dark brows, as though her observation was perfectly pleasant. "Do you think so? If you're hungry, you might try it all the same. Vulgarity can be delicious."

Her stomach gave a silent, surprised flip. "Are you flirting with me, Rutherford? At our ages?" *Because your age must be nearly mine; certainly you've long since passed forty years.*

His head tilted slightly. A handsome head, with steely-dark hair and a pleasantly weather-worn look. "I'm . . . offering you cheese."

Not an answer, but the tilt of his head provided all the finality his words had lacked. *What a ridiculous notion.*

"See to it that you don't," she replied. "Flirt. Or offer cheese. Either one."

Aquamarine, she reminded herself. She was wearing aquamarine.

And as a small silver lining, she had finally lost her appetite.

Chapter Six

Wherein the Recalcitrant Puzzle Box Is Encouraged to Reveal Its Secrets

"I might be able to open it," Giles granted.

Even before Sophy Parr heard of their interest in the puzzle box, Giles could tell she—like Richard—had a favorite obsession. The permanent mark of the pince-nez; the dedication to her astronomy notes. As the group finished their cold lunch, she pushed back her chair and said she must be returning to her work. But when Richard mentioned the item at which they wanted a look was a puzzle box—with a significant glance at Giles, who dutifully spoke his line about being able to open it—off Sophy darted to her chamber to retrieve the box in question.

The party of travelers met the inhabitants of Castle Parr in the drawing room. As it was early afternoon, pale sunlight grappled with the fog and won passage through the room's tall windows. The plaster ceiling was determined to remind them they were in a castle: flowered and trinketed and jeweled and painted in fanciful ways. The dark damask paper on the walls was the same sort favored in fine Philadelphia houses, though, and the furniture looked comfortable scattered around a great marble fireplace. The deep chairs and the heavy carpet bore scratches in their rich fabrics, as from canine claws and jaws.

Giles dragged a little tea table close to a window for the best light. Sophy sneezed several times as soon as she entered the room, cradling a cloth-covered object tightly.

"You had the dogs in here today, Mama," she said. "I suppose you fed them tea and biscuits?"

"Of course I did not. What sort of fool would give a dog tea?" Lady Dudley craned her neck. "Let's see the thing, Sophy."

Sophy laid the object on the table at the center of their group, tugging away the handkerchiefs in which she'd wrapped it. "I beg your pardon," she said, clutching them to her face as another fit of sneezes overtook her.

"Is that the famous puzzle box?" Lady Irving peered over it, her garish turban blocking all sight of the box. "All this fuss over a tiny little thing. What could it possibly hold, Rutherford?"

"I have no idea," said Richard. "That's the adventure." Giles mouthed these words along with his father. Audrina's mouth curled, a smile that felt like a secret shared between them.

To one who had never seen a puzzle box, the reality might be disappointing. Rather than a chest large enough to hold pirate treasure, it was small enough to rest within Giles's broad hands when he lifted it from the table.

Though the size was not unusual, the detail work was beyond any Giles had ever seen. The box was golden, with elaborate patterns incised into its surface: diamonds, pinwheels, crosses within crosses. Within each pattern, another and another, all beautifully tessellated and laid out in diagonal stripes. The eye never grew tired of looking at such riotous order, but only hungered for more, more, seeking out further and deeper art in the tiny lines carved so long ago.

For a moment, Giles cradled it, letting the anticipation of the moment suffuse him. What if this was a treasure, after all? What if his mother's final words had been literal rather than the laudanum dreams of a dying woman?

No, it was far too small a box to hold such possibility.

For one thing, it wasn't made of gold. It was much too light for that. Giles had had a fair amount of metallurgy drummed into his head, since Richard was sure he'd want to become a jeweler one day. Was there ever a father who didn't inflict his own thwarted dreams on his son?

Giles set the box down again on the tabletop, and the others leaned in to look, as though it might have changed during its minute in his hands. "Gilded wood of some kind," he said. "I haven't seen many *himitsubako*, but all the ones I've looked at closely have been made of wood."

A memory teased Giles, and he bent over the box and inhaled deeply.

"Does it have a scent?" Sophy asked. "I never noticed one—but then, I spend most of my time sneezing."

"No, it doesn't. I expected it to. When I made a

puzzle box for my mother years ago, she said she wanted it of rosewood because she liked the smell. But this one is—well, I don't know what it is."

"It's golden. Does anything else matter?" said Lady Irving.

"Getting it open does."

Before he could begin in earnest, each person had to take a turn hefting the box and testing its sealed lid. Even the person who had owned it for thirty-five years and could have been presumed to have given all this a try at her leisure.

"Sophy, how did you come to be friends with Lady Beatrix?" Audrina traced the whorls and incisions on the box lid. "You must be quite a bit younger than she was."

"I should say so," muttered Lady Irving. "Not close in age to Rutherford at all."

Sophy shot the countess an odd look, which was something Giles wanted to do about ninety percent of the time. "My elder sister was of an age with Lady Beatrix. Since I idolized my sister, I idolized her friends, too. I was a curious child, as you can imagine, and my sister was kind enough to tolerate my presence when her friends called." She pressed the bridge of her nose. "Some of them, that is. Some of her friends wouldn't allow a child to stay in the drawing room when they called, but Lady Beatrix always did. She said I reminded her of her own sister."

"That makes perfect sense." Richard, cheerful.

"That makes no sense at all. Are you talking about Lady Fontaine?" Giles had met his mother's younger sister during their first month in England, and a more shriveled, crabbed woman than Lady Fontaine was difficult to imagine. Arthritis had wrecked both sisters at an early age. If anything, it seemed to have wasted Lady Fontaine even more quickly than it had her older sister. Though it had spared her life for the time being, she was confined to a wheeled chair and had to be carried up the steps of her own home.

"She was young and healthy then." Sophy's voice held the wounded haughtiness of an expert whose opinion was questioned. "Perhaps your mother didn't always communicate with her own family so well as she did others. Considering she had no contact with her relatives from the time of her leaving England—"

"Let's have a look at that puzzle box," Giles cut in. "Maybe I can get it open. Even after this immense stretch of time during which Lady Beatrix's American and English families became utter strangers to one another."

He flexed his hands, trying to dismiss the thread of pain that raced from wrist to elbow. No one knew when or how the arthritis would progress, if at all.

Wordlessly, Sophy handed the box to him.

"Sorry," he muttered. "Thank you, Sophy, for keeping it safe for so long."

Her gaze fled as though she were embarrassed. "Think nothing of it. I was happy to be remembered by her."

Giles began to test the surface of the ancient gilded wood: a tug at an edge here, a tap at a corner there. Holding it up to one eye, he squinted over the surface to find the fine lines at which the patterned pieces were joined. The diagonal patterns led the eye astray; within the box, intricate straight edges and corners held its secrets.

"There's nothing in the box." Lady Dudley folded her arms.

"It could have papers inside," said Richard.

The viscount laid a quelling hand on his wife's forearm, which she shook off. "What papers? If they were important, Lady Beatrix would have kept them with her."

"She couldn't bring anything of value with her," Richard replied. "Her belongings were sifted and searched. The marquess and marchioness were hardly pleased that their daughter wanted to marry an apprentice jeweler from America—though I had good prospects. Beatrix and I had to make for the Scottish border, then the Atlantic."

Giles had heard this story at least ten thousand times before, to put a conservative figure to it. But with a new group of listeners, the hoary old tale seemed alive in a new way. He couldn't help but think of Audrina, dragged almost to the Scottish border against her will. But what an adventure—dear God, now *he* was using that word—if instead one eloped in the course of a love affair.

He caught Audrina's eye; she was looking a bit serious and pale. Setting the puzzle box down again, Giles stretched his arm across the small table and chucked her under the chin. "And your father thought your elder sisters married poorly, princess. Just imagine if an American tradesman turned up and threatened to take them halfway around the world."

She batted his hand away. "He would probably prefer that to our staying in England besmirching his good name."

"Would he really say 'besmirch'? Do people here talk like that?"

Audrina raised a brow. "Lady Irving, if you could accidentally step on Mr. Rutherford's foot?" Giles supposed he deserved the countess's hearty stomp on his boot, though she could have done it with a little less enthusiasm.

"All right, your foot's been flattened, young Rutherford," grumped Lady Irving. "Now get the damned thing open. We've all waited long enough. If I want to hear a tragic family story about illness and whatnot, I'll visit our fine feathered wastrel of a king and ask him about his mad father."

Giles stared at her just long enough for her to understand he wasn't obeying, then began testing the panels of the box again.

"There's nothing tragic about what I said," Richard protested. "These puzzle boxes are a nice tradition."

"It's plenty tragic," retorted Lady Irving. "When you speak of Lady Beatrix still as your wife, though she's been gone for three years."

"She's the only wife I've had. Why should I not call her that?"

"Someday, Rutherford," said Lady Irving, "I am going to get you to lose your temper."

"Why?"

Lady Irving made no reply, but the expression of her shoulders was eloquent.

Under the pressure of Giles's fingers, the ancient wood of the puzzle box gave a creak. He fumbled with the tiny panels, feeling large and clumsy. "I've got one side, I think—oh, no, I haven't."

Audrina crouched to peer at the box from tabletop level. Looking straight down at her, Giles could see the pale parting in her pinned-up hair. A fine line of naked skin, soap-scented and clean from a bath the night before.

So he assumed. Not that he knew for certain. But it

only made sense, cold and gritty as she'd been after her long days of travel, that she would want to sink her proud weariness into a great copper tub, and . . .

"Is there a problem?" Still crouching, Audrina looked up at him. Was that a knowing smile on her face? He had no idea what the expression on his own looked like, or whether it was possible for her to read *I was starting to imagine you undressing for a bath* across his features.

"Somewhere in the world, there certainly is. But if you're talking about the puzzle box, it's working exactly as it ought to." He laid his hands flat on the table; the right angle of palm to forearm made the tendons in his wrist scream, then sigh their relief. "The puzzle box I built required only six moves to open it. Even so, you could play with it quite a while and never hit on the right combination of which side to pull first, or which panel ought to slide in which direction. And this one is far more complicated."

"Then just break it," said Lady Irving. "We don't want to stand around this tea table for the rest of our lives. The box looks fragile. Here, just drop it on the floor."

"No!" Giles shot a hand out to prevent her from touching the box—as did Richard, Sophy, and the now-standing Audrina.

"Besides"—Giles drew the box back toward himself with careful hands—"sometimes a vial of acid was enclosed in a puzzle box with documents. If the box was jarred too heavily, the vial would break and destroy the contents."

Lady Irving shook her head, setting the sunset-bright plumes on her turban to wagging. "You really think that your mother gave Sophy a box of secret documents and acid when she was a child. *Really*. What would be the earthly point of that? 'Dear Sophy-girl, someday my son who doesn't exist yet will come along, and I want his hands to pain him. Please guard this box carefully for more than three decades, then present this acid to him with my compliments so he can shake it all over himself.'"

Giles blinked. "It's not going to be anything like that. If there's anything in there at all."

"All right," Lady Irving said into the silence. "So she wouldn't have been so formal."

"She left this behind before I existed," Giles bit off. "So the contents, if any, are not for me. Just—just give me a few more minutes to get it open."

"Hours," corrected Audrina.

"Fine. Hours. Maybe."

"Days? Weeks?"

Possibly, yes. For that matter, *never* was entirely possible. "Of course not that long," Giles lied.

"While you are working," said Lord Dudley in his hoarse voice, "shall we do a bit of festive decorating? The footmen have cut garland and holly. Rutherford, maybe you can climb about on the furniture to hang it. Lady D and I aren't so young anymore."

Richard appeared delighted. "I'd be glad to help, my lord. Where is the garland? That would be pleasant swagged across the chimneypiece." Already a few strides away from the tea table, he tossed back, "Son, if you get that box open, give a shout right away."

"*If* he *ever* gets it open." In a sweep of scarlet and ocean blue, Lady Irving joined the others across the room.

Sophy sneezed. "You will get it open eventually,

Mr. Rutherford. Though you might wish to keep a log of the attempts you have made."

A good point. "You are right," Giles muttered. "To track and record the movements I've tried. Best to be systematic."

Another sneeze. "I'd best return to the library before my head falls off," Sophy said in a stuffy voice. "If you find yourself on the verge of a miniature architectural triumph, do let me know."

By all rights, she should have been the one to work on and open the box. For so many years, it had been hers. But if she were to work endlessly upon a project, Giles suspected she would rather work on her own, something to do with her telescope and all the notes she took.

"Are we the only ones left to pursue this mystery to its end, then?" Audrina asked once Sophy had departed in a flurry of sniffles.

"Looks like it's just us, yes." Giles found a light tone difficult at the moment. The last time he and Audrina had been alone together, they'd been in the corridor away from family, away from Llewellyn. This felt even more alone, standing aside with others near, yet out of earshot. They could say anything, a hidden secret, and all would appear proper.

She was a brave creature, this English princess. She could not possibly want to be here, in York with near strangers, yet she managed to smile.

She was smiling now, a wry twist of red lips. "I hope you will not give me stale bread this time."

So she was thinking of it, too. A strange sort of intimacy to bind them. "Probably not necessary, since we've all just had luncheon. For my part, I hope you won't dart off to talk to a dangerous young man."

"That's not necessary either. You are the only young man here."

"Are you implying that I'm dangerous, or simply convenient?"

"I cannot think of a man who brought me bread as dangerous, nor a man who saw me in such distress as convenient."

"What about a man who saved you from a terrible situation?" he blurted, then forgot to breathe in again.

"It required several people to do that, Mr. Rutherford, including my father and Lady Irving. So I am not sure whether to consider any of you dangerous, but I am convinced none of you thought of me as convenient."

Across the tea table they faced each other, the golden box between them. She was as much a mystery as the contents, he now thought. He'd been inclined to regard her as gilded yet empty, but she had proved him wrong almost at once. What she was truly made of, though, he had no idea. She was too proud to give any hint, and he was too proud to ask.

Above the room's marble chimneypiece, a sprig of mistletoe was clutched by the hands of a sly-faced stone angel. What if Giles drew Audrina to the fireplace, to kiss her beneath the excuse of those waxy green leaves? Would she forget her cool façade, or the fact that she didn't want to be here?

Not that he had meant to spend so much time in England himself. If they both had their way, they wouldn't be anywhere near each other.

That was not a thought he liked at all, even though it was inevitable. By all rights, the Atlantic and a few blue-blooded centuries of haughtiness would separate them.

Besides that, there was the matter of his hands. A reminder he carried about with him, every moment, always, that there was no time for romance in his unwinding life. That he needed to be efficient and vigilant with the time he had.

Which meant, for now, that he needed to shake the numbness from his fingers and the ache from his wrists, then turn his attention back to the puzzle box. It was the only thing holding together their party of travelers. "Our stay in England has brought many inconveniences, princess. But you can hardly expect me to tell you if you're one of them, can you?" He looked up for a flicker, just long enough to see her dark brows draw together, then returned his gaze to the puzzle box. "Not even an American would be capable of such rudeness."

"Mr. Rutherford, I've no idea of what Americans are capable. They seem not to be capable of opening puzzle boxes, though."

Giles shot her a filthy look.

"A persuasive argument," she said. "Very articulate and well-reasoned. I'll get a paper and pen so we can begin to make note of your attempts."

Off she glided, soundless over the deep pile of the carpet. She moved with such grace, the confidence that whatever she did must be utterly right. Such confidence seemed too deep to pile up in one lifetime, instead collecting over the course of generations like coats of shining lacquer.

"Sleigh bells would be wonderful!" Richard's low voice rang from the end of the room, and Giles straightened up to regard his father. "Shall we hang them from the back of the door? Every time someone enters, he will be greeted with a pleasant jingle."

"Pleasant once, maybe." Lady Irving tossed aside a bit of garland. "After that, I shall stick a poker in my ear to be spared the din." Her hand drifted to her turban, and she granted, "Well, maybe not a poker. No sense in wreaking permanent damage."

Giles grinned. While Richard made it his life's work to be agreeable to everyone, Lady Irving seemed determined to be the opposite. "Perhaps someone stuck a poker in *my* ear, your ladyship," Giles called. "Because I'm sure I can't have heard you correctly. Did you really retract a threat?"

"As it was only a threat against myself, you needn't start frothing at the mouth with excitement, young man." With a sniff, she turned back to Richard. "Sleigh bells would be . . . not horrible."

Richard placed a hand over his heart, his tanned features falling into the familiar lines of a smile. "It shall be my slogan from this moment forward," he said. "'Richard Rutherford: His decorating decisions are not horrible.'"

"If you plan to set up shop in Ludgate Hill, Father, you'll need a more persuasive slogan than that."

Lady Irving snapped her fingers in Giles's direction. "Young Rutherford—yes, you, with that vulgar Irish hair of yours. If you want to chatter, you might as well make yourself useful by hanging up some more garland. But no fa-la-la-ing while you do it, or I'll see to it you break your neck."

By the time Audrina located an ancient bottle of ink and a few quills in the pigeonhole of a writing desk, the drawing room had rearranged itself. The tea table was abandoned, the puzzle box winking like a forgotten gift. Lord and Lady Dudley had eased themselves onto a velvet-covered settee that, like every other piece of furniture in the room, bore the claw marks of canine enthusiasm.

And Giles Rutherford stood atop a dark-upholstered side chair before the fireplace, hanging a bit of garland over the hands of a stone relief sculpture of an angel who already had a fistful of mistletoe to go with her smug smile.

"Move the garland to the left," said Lady Irving. "No, that's too far. Back to the right again."

"He mustn't cover up the mistletoe," said Richard.

"Go find yourself a sleigh bell to play with, Rutherford," barked Lady Irving. "I'll handle this."

"I'm going to fetch the dogs back from the stable," decided Lady Dudley, rising with some effort.

From his perch on the chair, Giles Rutherford grinned down at the clamor. A dimple carved itself into his right cheek, giving the hard lines of his face a soft place for the eyes to linger.

Since he wasn't looking anywhere near Audrina's corner of the room, there was no harm in letting her eyes linger. And wander. And . . . and wonder. How did one get him to smile like that? He would have to admire a person first, she supposed; something he would never feel for Audrina after seeing her at her most shaken and low.

When he stretched to loop the evergreen garland over the hand of the angel, his plain wool coat hitched up—revealing that, though his gray trousers were loose-fitting in the leg, they hugged the taut curve of his arse closely.

Proper English ladies would no more look at a man in that way than they would visit the kitchens to learn how bread was made. Yet men looked at women in that way all the time. Evaluating them. Deciding whether they were worthy of desire.

Was she?

Llewellyn wanted only the money Audrina represented; her father only cared whether she reflected well on him. Here in Yorkshire, she was alone and pallid in the color of half mourning. Her fists were full of stained quills and a black vial of ink. Her hands were dirty.

Maybe this was why every gluttonous gaze at Giles Rutherford came twinned with wariness. Because he had been self-possessed when she was drugged and sick and folded into a ball in a strange corridor. Because her father was helping him find a treasure he didn't even believe in, when Audrina would be satisfied simply to have her life returned to normal.

And, just a little, she resented him for not looking ridiculous atop that small wood-framed chair, his large boots almost covering the dark seat cushion. The drooping sprig of mistletoe fell from the angel's hand, jostled by garland, and Giles picked it up from the mantel with careful fingers and tucked it gently back into the angel's grasp.

She resented the mistletoe, too.

Chapter Seven

Wherein Paper Takes on a Complex New Shape

The next day brought snow to brighten a long morning spent in the drawing room. Clouds shook a fine frost over the ground, just as Audrina shook sand over page after page of ink-dark notes.

Page. After page. After page.

She and Giles had met after breakfast to work at the puzzle box again, while Lord and Lady Dudley shuffled from room to room accompanied by their pack of doting hounds, servants with arms full of garland, an eager-to-help-decorate-the-castle Richard Rutherford, and an eager-to-criticize Lady Irving.

Swiftly, she and Giles Rutherford had developed a process. They had assigned a number to each panel, and a list of notes unspooled in a neat line of cursive as different attempts were made:

P1 down, P2 left
P1 down, P2 right
P1 down, P3 left

. . . and so on. And on, for an hour and a half, as cups of tea cooled at their elbows. Pale light reflected off of clean new snow, slanting higher and higher through the tall drawing room windows as the morning drew on.

"You don't have to work on this with me." Teeth gritted, Rutherford tugged at P17. "This is my father's mission, not yours."

"Don't be arrogant, Mr. Rutherford. This is my father's mission, too. Do you not recall whose plots and schemes directed you here?"

P17 gave a squeak of distressed wood, and Rutherford released it at once. "He directed you here, too, for that matter."

"I did not mean to imply anything to the contrary." She smiled, all the more brightly when Giles Rutherford looked suspicious. "Come now, Mr. Rutherford. You must have seen enough of England by now to know that a proper English lady would never contradict a gentleman."

"And do I count as a gentleman?"

"That is for you to decide. But I am quite sure I count as a lady."

Usually. For now. With the help of Lady Irving's maid, she had pawed through her trunk until she found a gown to her liking: a thin, drifting muslin printed with sinuous vines, its bodice of deep green sarcenet that set off her eyes—should anyone care to look at them. For the first time since leaving London,

Audrina felt properly assembled, as though she had put on all of her armor. Even if no one wanted to fight her, she felt more protected.

"I'm quite sure you do, too," he replied. "Though I'm not sure what name I ought to apply to the sort of person who drags a lady to a city against her will."

Audrina turned to look out the window. In the distance, a bird flew and swooped like a tossed stone. "I should call that ordinary."

"Vulgar, then, as Lady Irving would have it."

"I would never contradict a gentleman," she said again.

"So you do think of me as a gentleman." He sounded pleased, his words tightly corralled by hard consonants.

"I do not think of you at—" She cut herself off before she could utter a lie. Or a contradiction. "Panel seventeen was next, was it not? Have you tried shifting it first of all?"

He didn't reply, and after a silent few seconds she was forced to look back at him. Hands lightly clasped atop the table, he had set aside the puzzle box and instead turned his scrutiny to Audrina.

Rather unnerving. "Panel seventeen?" she prodded, lending a cool lift to her brows.

"You're not as proper as you pretend to be, princess."

The curve of his mouth might as well have been a sickle, so much did those small words wound her. Fortunately, she had a deal of practice hiding her true feelings. "Everyone pretends. For example, you could not truly hold little hope about this quest for some forgotten treasure of your mother's, or you would never have agreed to leave your work and travel to England."

"My work is with my father." His lips pressed together

in a hard line, making the thin scar through his upper lip stand out paler against his skin. "I notice you don't protest anymore when I call you 'princess.' Why not?"

"A matter of the propriety you think I do not possess." Audrina brushed fine-grained blotting sand from her fingertips, noting that her right hand had become speckled with ink. She had learned a neat script, but the process of writing always left her a bit untidy. "I told you it was not an appropriate name to call me, yet you insist. I can only conclude that you are too foolish to remember, in which case it would be unkind of me to remind you of your incapability, or that you wish to give offense, in which case it is unkind of you, and I should not pay you any heed."

Gently, his thumb traced one gilded panel of the puzzle box. "Beautifully reasoned. Can't argue with a bit of that. Though there's one possibility you didn't account for."

"Oh?" She watched his thumb slide over the smooth wood. Low in her belly, a wary warmth trembled.

"I thought you ought to have a nickname."

"Oh?"

"You also didn't tell me you didn't like it. You only told me it wasn't appropriate."

"Oh." *Really, Audrina? One syllable? Come up with something more impressive than that.* Her mind blank, she pulled a sheet of paper toward herself, then folded over a vertical strip. Sliding her nail along the edge to weaken it, she tore off a thin strip. Then another.

The smooth actions helped order her thoughts. "No, it is not appropriate, but it might be all right. Why do you think you must nickname me? Is it to belittle me or to create a bond between us?"

"I'm not sure which is the right answer," he replied.

"To be honest, at first I expected you to be selfish and spoiled."

"Such compliments will give me the vapors." Smoothing her strips of paper, she began pleating them into a little spring. If her hands trembled a little, he would not notice.

"Only at first, when I thought you'd run off to Scotland and made your family worry." Pushing back his chair, he rose to stand before the window. "When you told me you'd been carried off against your will, I realized I'd wronged you. You must have been afraid, but you didn't break down. You were—well, like I imagine a princess would be."

"Oh," she said again. "You managed to turn that into something resembling a compliment. Well done, Mr. Rutherford." Under her crisp words, her heart stuttered; she was both dismayed and flattered at being seen so clearly.

"Now I feel as though I'm being condescended to." He turned, a silhouette against the window. "Won't you call me Giles, my lady? If for no other reason, it'll be more efficient when my father is around. No more having to specify which Mr. Rutherford is the object of your scorn."

Audrina set aside her pleated paper spring. "Your father seems like a nice, well-mannered man. I should never scorn him."

He laughed. "One little piece of a truce at a time, I guess." With a nod, he indicated her paper spring. "What's that you've made?"

"I like to make things," she said. "It was just paper before, and now it is different." She compressed it, then let it go, smiling as the folded paper popped out to its full length. "But it's useless. I should have left the paper alone." She scooped it up, ready to crush it in her fist.

"No!" Giles lunged for the table, catching himself on the edge. He cupped Audrina's hand in his as gently as he had plucked up the fallen sprig of mistletoe the day before. "Don't destroy it. It's interesting."

Surprised, she went still. He looked a little surprised himself. "That is—it might be good for something, even though we don't know what yet."

"You truly think a paper spring might be good for something?" She tipped it into his hand, drawing back her own to a safe distance.

"One never knows." He brought his hand close to his face, studying it. "I like that pleated shape. Almost like a bellows, don't you think? I would never have thought of making such a thing out of paper." His gaze roved the sweeping ceiling, the span of the room. "A bellows. I wonder whether one could be fitted to the fireplace to drive the warm air inward. If—" He shook his head. "Well. That's far outside of my ability to design. I'm a brick-and-board man. Or—a gold-and-stone man." He dropped the spring on the table before Audrina.

"Stone? Do you mean precious stones?"

"Jewelry. Yes. Remaking heavy old pieces into modern fashions. It's my father's dream to be a jeweler, you know." His words were clipped, his smile tight.

"I know." She took a sip of tea from the cup at her elbow. It was bitter and strong and cold, but it gave her a reason to pause before saying, "Giles."

He lifted his brows. "Well, now. That wasn't so difficult."

She ignored this reply. "What would you like to design?"

He repaid her by ignoring the question. "Do you want to hang garland? Look, Lady Dudley left a pile of it behind. I could only put so much of it onto one mantel."

"Giles," she said again. "What would you like to design?"

She wanted, very much wanted, to know the answer to her question. She had never wondered about a man's occupation before. The roles of the men she knew were no mystery, because theirs were the same as hers. All of them were part of a long line, and the weight of tradition and legacy rested on their shoulders.

Absent such a heritage, would one feel lighter? It seemed not. In one generation, a father could bow a son to his will.

In one generation, a father could bow a daughter. Almost.

"Once I hoped to design buildings." He stretched out a hand to her, drawing her to her feet. Just a quick clasp of hands; then he strode to a walnut sideboard on which now-dry evergreen garland had been heaped. "Philadelphia took a beating the last time our countries fought. I can't say I wanted to be a soldier since I had so many siblings to take care of, but I did want to help my city rebuild. I went to university to learn anything I could about mathematics. Geometry. I talked to people who draw up building plans as a profession. Architects."

"And what happened?"

"Nothing." Dry needles fell as he lifted a garland.

"The war killed Philadelphia's shipping industry. These last few years, everyone wants to ship through New York City. Safer, I guess. Money's leaving Philadelphia, and no one needs to build grand new homes or warehouses there."

She began a phrase of sympathy, but he spoke on. "They do need paper, though. So there's the paper mill to oversee. Paper milling was never my father's dream, but it supported his family. Now he's on a mission. A quest. Whatever you want to call it. And at the end of it, he'll have the life he ought to have had a generation ago." He dropped the garland. "So he hopes."

"For now, he has given you his dream?"

"So it seems. All that geometry allows me to design a marvelous brooch. That's . . . worthwhile. I suppose."

"Of course it is. The world needs beauty. And if you have a son one day, then maybe you could turn him into an architect," she said lightly.

He did not seem to want to look at her, so she picked up a garland of her own. The dry needles poked her hand; hissing, she dropped it to the pile. "These branches will shed themselves bare in a day. I don't think we can do anything with them."

"No, I suppose not." He had retreated behind a wall of folded arms and averted eyes. He had told her more than he intended, maybe.

Good. Let him feel naked for a change.

Not literally, of course. Only figuratively.

Right. So there was no reason to imagine those broad shoulders flexing as he tugged a shirt over his head, nor to wonder whether he was freckled anywhere besides his cheekbones.

None at all, except for the fact that—he was honest, and that was a quality more heady and attractive than she could possibly have imagined.

Also, his shoulders *did* look uncommonly fine. In his close-fitting coat of dark-blue wool, no padding made excuse for flaws of form.

He nudged a few fallen needles into a neat pile atop the sideboard, then stretched out a hand. "More puzzle box? What do you say?"

"All right." Quickly, she grabbed the needles again, letting them stab her into coherence. Then she trailed back across the room after him. "You really are fortunate," she said as she dropped into her chair. "To know that your father is pleased with you and that he trusts you. I cannot say either of those things."

Audrina had been raised with only one goal, one occupation: to marry well and make her family proud. The two were linked and inextricable. Without the former, she could never accomplish the latter.

I do not want you seen in London. Don't return unless you're betrothed.

On her own, she was not good enough. And so she had failed.

"Don't let yourself get too envious." Giles sat and sifted through her closely written notes, squinting. "My father is proud of me in the way a man might value a dependable employee. He knows I'll do what I say I will. I'll do what I'm asked even if I don't want to."

"For example, if someone asks you to stop a wayward carriage?"

"Something like that." Dropping the stack of notes, he flattened his hands atop the table and stared at them. "My mother was ill for years before her death. Pain, constant pain. My father traveled often for business, and I had five younger siblings at home. Who else was to take care of them?"

"So you became the man of the house."

"Nothing so respectable. In your language, I was the governess and the bootboy and the footman and—"

"The cook?"

"Thank God we had one of those. My family would have gone hungry relying on me. But I *was* the valet." His teeth closed on the hard *t*, lingering on the sound, and he rubbed at the thin scar on his lip. "I taught my younger brother to shave. Not well enough, though. When he practiced on my face, he left me this memento."

His light smile granted Audrina permission to laugh.

"I was glad to help, though." At last, he pulled the puzzle box toward himself, though he seemed reluctant to take up their task again. "Usually. I loved—love—my family."

"They need you." Audrina picked up the quill she'd been using, then set it down in a hurry when it rubbed ink on her fingers. "It must be nice to serve a purpose."

"They don't need me as much as they used to. Now they're almost grown, much as I hate to think of it. My youngest sister Sarah's going to be married next year, if she has a dowry. I'm just here in England to make sure my father doesn't spend a real fortune looking for a fake one."

"And then what?"

"And then"—he lifted the box, shaking it lightly—"I return to America to run a paper mill, or design jewelry. Or both."

"What about designing a building?"

"Not in Philadelphia. I'd have to move to New York City for that." The words were a flick of dismissal.

"Too far away from your family?"

"Almost a hundred miles."

Her brow knit. "But. . ." The distance from London to York was far more than that—to say nothing of the distance from America to England.

He could not possibly be unaware of this. So he must wish to design buildings less than he wanted to be near his siblings.

The thought brought her sister Charissa to Audrina's mind, along with a gray wash of guilt. The three years separating their ages had seemed a huge gulf when they were younger, but as the last two sisters at home, they had recently become confidantes. The threat of missing Charissa's long-desired wedding was a punishment. A judgment for testing the waters of scandal, trying to bait her family into caring about her.

Giles, for his part, had taken a nobler path, winding his relatives close to him with responsibility and care.

But Audrina knew, people couldn't be made to care. Not out of exasperation, not out of gratitude. Not for any reason except the tender tendencies of their hearts.

She rubbed her ink-stained fingers together. "That box is empty."

"Yes, I think so, too." He set it down, then pressed at his temples. "But remember, princess, I do what I say I will. And I told my father I'd get it open."

"And so off he went to decorate the house, leaving this precious possession in your care. He does trust you. You see? You are fortunate." Giles's father wanted to cross an ocean with him. Audrina's father didn't even want her to come to London.

He caught her eye and smiled, but it wasn't the sort of grin that brought out his dimple. It was more shadowed. Wary. If the usual smile resonated like crystal, this one rang a bit false. "Such praise from you, princess? I guess I really am fortunate."

"One day soon," she said crisply, "I am going to come upon you while you are asleep and—and ink a mustache on your face."

"Will you really? I'm even more fortunate, then."

"Why is that?"

"Because you'll be prowling about my bedchamber. With a pot of ink in hand and facial vandalism on your mind, true—but nonetheless, the situation you describe is intriguing."

Her face went hot.

"I should try to resist, of course, for the sake of my reputation. I've no great fortune or rank; nothing to lose but my good name. But you know how it is in England," he said conversationally. "The aristocracy must be allowed to do whatever they please. If you slipped into my bedchamber to seduce me, I'd put up a token resistance. But ultimately it would be disrespectful of me to decline any offer you might care to make."

"You are not as improper as you pretend to be," she said, playing upon his earlier words.

He leaned forward across the table, granting her a sapphire wink. "You mustn't say so aloud. If anyone knew what a genuinely kind and delightful person I was, I'd be deluged with admiration."

"Your secret is safe with me." She could breathe him in: the scent of evergreen soap, the spice of tea grown cold on his lips. "I promise not even to hint at it by excessive admiration."

He shot her the dimpled grin, then returned his blue gaze to the golden panels of the puzzle box.

All a joke; only a joke.

But his words were more seductive than he had intended, making her arms prickle, her fingers tingle. He teased her about seducing him, as though—as though it were ordinary for a woman to pursue a man. To want passion; to seek it; to chase after her own desires.

And then he left the subject in her hands to drop or pick up as she saw fit.

Every other man and manner of society had denied any of this. All of this. It seemed as far-off and mysterious as one of the bright, blobby stars she'd sometimes peered at through her father's telescope when she was a child.

Before he told her she must not touch his things and threatened to sack any servant who allowed her into his office.

The only power Audrina had at the moment was to follow, to obey. To stay away from her sister's wedding so as not to remind society of her undesirable existence—unless a betrothal rendered her, again, acceptable.

Yet Giles saw her differently. Giles, who had seen her weak and afraid: two things she pretended never to be. He must be made to forget that. If he would grant her power, she would take it.

But why must she wait for it to be granted?

Her thighs loosened, and she sank heavily against the slatted back of her chair. "I am not going to draw a mustache on you while you sleep tonight," she began.

His eyes flicked up to meet hers. "Oh, good. I'd look unfashionable." With a frown, he considered the puzzle box again.

"But," Audrina continued, "I do want to look through Sophy's telescope." She wanted to see something new, and she wanted to see it with someone who thought she might be good for something. Even if neither of them knew what yet.

"Excellent *non sequitur*. Might I suggest you talk to Sophy about that?"

"I will. Then would you look with me? At the stars?"

Tugging at another panel of the box, he said, "I never cared much about the stars. There is too much to learn and do on the surface of the earth."

She folded her arms.

After a moment, he caught on. "But I am wrong. Obviously. I'm twenty-seven years old, so I guess it's time I changed that."

Relief swamped her, followed by a thin, crisp edge of anticipation. "I am twenty-four. So I suppose I have three more years before I have to change the sort of person I am."

"Only your attitude toward telescopes," he said. "The sort of person you are, princess, you need never change at all."

Chapter Eight

Wherein Two Dozen Heads Are Made Festive

After twenty minutes of climbing around the great staircase of Castle Parr, winding evergreen branches around the stair rail and each baluster, Estella understood the look on Lord Dudley's face. *I'm exhausted,* said every line of his wrinkle-wreathed expression, *but I cannot admit it, because this was my idea.*

Estella accepted a length of juniper from her host's thin hand, then shoved the garland untidily around the last baluster. She rubbed her hands together; they smelled like a gin distillery.

Or a warm, resinous evergreen scent, if one preferred to think of things in that sentimental way.

"I think you've earned a rest, Dudley." As she straightened, a stitch in her side reminded her that she was no longer as flexible as she'd been in the eighteenth century.

"Oh, no." Lord Dudley's voice was a rusty file. "No, no. I'm quite all right, dear lady. I'm sure there's not enough greenery in the drawing room, and we haven't decorated the antique passage yet."

"There's a passage? Is it a secret passage?" Richard Rutherford sounded delighted even as he scrabbled on the landing for dropped needles and twigs.

"No, it's not a secret passage," barked Estella. "Good Lord, Rutherford. Let the servants pick that up. You were married to an aristocrat. You should know better."

"Know better than to make myself useful when I can?" Rutherford smiled, handing the gleaned decorations into the arms of the footman following them about. "No, I don't suppose I do."

Estella narrowed her eyes, which only made him smile more brightly. He had a troublesome habit of putting her in her place when she meant the opposite to happen.

A *very* troublesome habit. She was beginning to forget her place—and his.

When she turned back to Lord Dudley, her voice was all sugar. "Lord Dudley, at a house party hosted by my nephew-in-law, Lord Xavier, I learned a trick that serves wily gentlemen well."

"You serviced gentlemen at a house party?" Lady Dudley had wandered back up the stairs and into the edge of their conversation. "Are you short of funds?"

Estella wanted to snort with laughter and cover her face at the same time. She settled for a harsh "No" and turned back to the viscount. "The trick is that there's a type of brandy just the shade of brewed tea. You can have it served out any time of day and Sophy will never know the difference."

"I would know," said Lady Dudley.

"Know what, my dear?" The viscount's heavy white brows had lifted with innocence.

"That Lady Irving serviced men at a house party."

A strange heat suffused Estella's cheeks. *Embarrassed?* Surely not. Though she couldn't quite look at Rutherford as he spoke. "Let's get you settled with some . . . tea, Lord Dudley. And you, my lady—would you like the dogs brought in from the stables?"

"Yes, it's time." The viscountess tucked her long hair behind her ears, looking pleased. "Yes. Good. They can have biscuits when Dudley has tea."

Lord Dudley directed them to a chamber he called the "yellow parlor," which Estella approved as being bright enough to chase away despondency. It was almost the same shade as her yolk-yellow turban, though the turban had the undeniable advantage of being spangled with paste gems in fiery colors. Once tea was ordered—and brandy, to be served to the viscount in a teacup—Estella was satisfied that her host and hostess would ease themselves before the fire for a while.

"Rest here, and don't worry about anything," she said. "If you do, I'll find out and I'll be monstrously annoyed."

Lord Dudley laughed, closing his eyes as he sank back onto a long sofa. In repose, his face turned toward his wife, and a smile lingered on his worn features. Lady Dudley perched, eager, on the edge of a chair seat, awaiting the arrival of her dogs.

Tired, but together. Though they were in their twilight years, they sought means of keeping their lives bright.

When Estella exited the yellow parlor a few steps

behind Rutherford, she felt as though the sun were eclipsed.

"What are we left with, Lady Irving?" Rutherford's straight brows were furrowed as he nudged the remaining pile of trimmed branches with one black boot.

Estella blinked at him through watery eyes. What, indeed? A fortune and a solitary mansion? Put in that way, her life sounded like that of Lord and Lady Dudley, though she hadn't even an ailing spouse or a bluestocking daughter-in-law to keep her company. "I—" She could say no more before her throat closed.

Richard waved his hand at the pile of greenery. "Here. For use in the house. What do you fancy?"

Oh. Again, her cheeks went hot. As though her face thought that this was the year 1780 once more, that she was a maiden in her first Season hoping to catch the eye of an earl.

Idiotic face. Idiotic maiden, too, for that matter.

"No holly or ivy until Christmas Eve." Her voice came out more harshly than she intended. "That's bad luck."

"Is it really?" Rutherford tilted his head, appearing fascinated. "What do you think would happen if you hung it sooner?"

I would find myself so desperate for company that I'd take up with two Americans and my oldest friend's lost child.

I would find myself looking at a man—really looking—for the first time in decades.

I would want him to look back at me and like what he saw.

She gave her turban a steadying pat. "I don't know, but it's not done. It's a tradition. Do Americans understand traditions?"

"Of course. What may we use instead?" The

footman—Lord Alleyneham's servant, who had stated his name was Jory—had carried off the fallen leaves and tiny sprigs left after decorating the staircase. Rutherford crouched to sift through the remaining stock of evergreen.

Looking down on him, she saw silver and dark brown threading equally in his hair. At his temples, he had gone entirely gray, but seen from above he looked a bit younger. He still had a nice form, the build of a man who kept himself active. Good shoulders within that bottle-green coat.

"How old are you?" she asked.

Rutherford picked up a branch and held it to his nose, breathing deeply. "Fifty-five." He stood and extended the branch to Estella. "Rosemary. I like the scent. Is this acceptable, or is it bad luck, too? Will the roof fall in if we hang it?"

"Don't you want to ask how old I am?"

He grinned, refusing to be withered by her most withering tone. "Even in the wilds of America, that would be impolite."

"Well, I'm fifty-eight," she muttered. "And I can't answer for the state of the roof. But if it falls in, it won't be the rosemary's fault."

"All right. As long as we won't be blamed for any destruction." Rutherford scooped up the pile of cut branches. The armful was large enough to hide most of his face as needles and leaves and sprigs crushed, fragrant, against one another. "Do you know the passage Lord Dudley mentioned? The one you were quite sure wasn't a secret passage?"

"He gestured in this direction." Rapping on Rutherford's arm to indicate the way, she led him back down the stairs to the entry hall. Around its echoing width were scattered several doorways, two of which she knew led to the drawing and dining rooms. At the northeast corner, a pointed arch led to what she had presumed was the family wing. "Worth a look."

"I can't see, so you'll have to look for me." Rutherford's voice was muffled behind his burden.

Estella swept through the archway, and—stopped short. "Yes. Yes, I think we've found the antique passage."

A corridor of pale golden stone stretched several dozen yards before pausing at a stained-glass window and making a turn. Pointed arches lifted the passage's ceiling into vaults, and many-paned windows sliced the weighty walls. Between each window, framed in a recess by stone pillars, was a head.

A stone head on a plinth. And another, and another, all the way down the passage. In all, Estella guessed that there were two dozen stern-faced Romans and Greeks lopped off at the shoulders, the neck, or—in some unlucky cases—the chin. A gauntlet of blank eyes and stern jaws. An entire corridor set aside for being glared at.

It was so cold that the stone floor chilled Estella's feet through her slippers.

"My, my." Rutherford crouched to lay down the branches, then stepped to Estella's side. "Who do you suppose this fellow is to our right? He must have been someone significant to have his head carved in stone and kept around for a thousand years."

The stone bust stared with vacant eyes, its nostrils a haughty flare and its hair chipped and cracked.

"Maybe he was once," said Estella. "But what good does it do him now to be looked at? No one remembers him. No one knows who he is or what he did. He's no better off than if he'd winked out before someone chiseled his face in marble."

"You are a philosopher, my lady."

"Nonsense. Philosophers are men with long hair and tight trousers who beg money from their relatives." She sighed. "I'm just . . ."

No, it would be stupid to finish that sentence in any honest way. Rutherford would only give her one of his patient smiles, and she would start looking at his eyes and wondering whether they had a ring of blue or of gray about the dark center of the iris. Which was not the sort of information she usually cared to collect.

"I'm just ready for a brandy," she finished.

"Brandy sounds marvelous, but we have to earn it." With a sideways scoot of his boot, he shoved some of the branches before Estella. "Go on, your ladyship. Give these poor forgotten folk a laurel crown."

"We only have bay and juniper."

"Juniper should amuse them." Rutherford seated himself on the floor as easily as though it were a silk pillow. "They can distill gin from the berries and have a wild bacchanal tonight, when we're all asleep and they're left alone on their plinths."

"Nonsense." Yet it was difficult not to smile at all, and impossible not to fall into a crouch at Rutherford's side and begin twisting the spice-sharp branches into crowns.

"Yew," she murmured. The needles were short, the berries starting to shrivel but still red. "Rather poisonous."

"Well, then you mustn't eat it." Rutherford squinted, then gave a finishing twist to a wreath of bay leaves.

He seemed to radiate joy, but it was a cold light that reminded Estella of what she didn't feel. "Thank you," she grumbled. "For turning Lady Dudley away from the subject of my prostitution. *Alleged* prostitution."

"I assumed you didn't want to talk about your scandalous past." When she huffed, he shot her a wink.

"You have a dangerous sense of humor, Rutherford."

"Do you think so? I think it's more dangerous to have none." He sprang to his feet and plopped the crown onto the head of the Emperor of Chipped Hair.

Estella sank back onto her heels—oh, this cold made her ankles ache—and shoved a dangling bit of yew into the crown she'd fashioned. "Here. You can stick that on the head of one of the other gargoyles." Struggling to her feet, a hand pressed to a chilly wall, she added, "What the point is of decorating someone else's house, I can't imagine. We probably won't even be here at Christmas."

Each of Rutherford's footfalls was a dull echo. "The Dudleys like it. And it's not so easy for them to climb around this castle anymore. We're doing them a favor."

He tried the yew wreath on the head of Chipped Hair's neighbor, then laid it instead over the diadem of a grim-faced woman. The green transformed her expression from *I hate being a marble bust* to *I think this crown is ridiculous but I will wear it to please you.*

"I don't do favors unless I'll get a favor in return," said Estella.

"Why not?"

"Why should I?"

Rutherford shrugged. Estella had seen him make this gesture often enough to understand its meaning. *I disagree, but it wouldn't be polite of me to say so.* "We are getting some return. Lord and Lady Dudley are granting us houseroom, and Sophy has turned over the *himitsu-bako* to Giles. He'll figure out its secrets."

"Why are you so sure?"

"Because the last thing my wife told me before she died," he said, "was that I must go to England and find the puzzle box. She said it was her inheritance for her family."

"Oh." Estella's hand drifted to her turban, trailing over the bevels and mazarins of the false gems.

"I know, it sounds unlikely. Giles thinks so, too. Beatrix had been ill for so long, eased with laudanum and hardly talking sense, that it seemed like a fever dream. But she left England with nothing. What happened to her jewels? A diamond parure given to her, irrevocably, when she made her debut. We met when she had it valued by the jeweler with whom I apprenticed." His face fell into the soft expression of a pleasant memory, and he chucked the grim-faced woman under her stone chin. "Thousands of pounds' worth of gemstones, and it vanished."

"I'm surprised no one was imprisoned for theft. Or transported."

"Well—we were transported, in a way." He walked back to the pile of greenery and picked it up, then marched down the passage laying branches on each plinth. "We had to leave England after we married. Though it was a relief, Lady Irving, not to have a fortune weighing on us."

"Bosh. A fortune never weighs on a couple. Only poverty does that."

"A fortune shared, maybe. But if she married me with wealth and had to fit into the straitened life I could give her?" He distributed the last of the branches, then turned back to Estella with a shake of his head.

"If she sat in a silk gown before a chipped brick hearth, rocking in a handmade chair—she'd grow unhappy with me. Instead, though, we started with nothing but a small family mill and a willingness to work. We were even, if that makes sense."

Yes. But just as a pretty face and a biddable nature had caught Estella an earl forty years before, she had nothing but a fortune to recommend her now. "No. And I'm still in disbelief over your statement that a fortune wouldn't benefit a pair."

He shrugged. That *you're wrong but I'm not going to argue about it* gesture again. "It probably depends on the pair."

"And what if the inheritance was a fever dream after all? Because it's obvious the box is empty."

"Just because it's empty," said Rutherford, "doesn't mean there's no message inside."

"Your sister will not be joining us today?" The Duke of Walpole frowned. "She usually does, for the sake of propriety."

Charissa Bradleigh, third daughter of the Earl and Countess of Alleyneham, curtsied to her betrothed before retaking her seat in Alleyneham House's fashionable Egyptian parlor. She always met the duke here, at the front of the house, where the gentle noises of Mayfair traffic rang through the silk-draped windows. The hoofbeats and whickers of carriage horses, the industrious *ching* of their metal harness fittings; the call of a master to a footman. It was impossible in such a space not to recall one's proper place in society.

"Not today, Your Grace. Lady Audrina is"—Charissa

fumbled for the excuse her mother had given her—
"accompanying Lady Irving on a Christmas visit to
friends in York."

Don't ask any questions, Lady Alleyneham had said,
a worried expression on her gentle round face. *That's
all you'll need to know. Think happy thoughts, child! You'll
be a duchess soon.*

That was indeed a happy thought. Charissa smiled,
but Walpole didn't smile back.

"I never heard Lady Audrina mention friends in
York." Walpole swung his ivory-handled malacca cane,
a neat parabola of impatience.

The Duke of Walpole was of no more than middling height, but his face was as handsome and neatly
carved as a Roman bust. He was the perfect gentleman in dress and elegance. The black waves of his
hair would dare not fall over his brow; his cravat
would not dream of wilting from its intricate arrangement.

Charissa herself was of no more than middling
looks. Despite auburn hair, her gray eyes and colorless
cheeks inclined her complexion to the insipid. Her
teeth were good, though, and the habit of smiling a
great deal and talking even more had served her well.
A generous dowry made her more attractive, too: her
hair more gilded, her laugh more silvery.

"They are Lady Irving's friends." Charissa recovered a bit of her usual chatter. "You know how her
ladyship feels about Christmas, Your Grace. She
cannot bring herself to stay in London unless she has
family to stay with her. So this year, when she chose
to travel, she asked if she could bring one of us. Lady
Irving has always been fond of us."

"That is quite a compliment to you." The duke seated

himself facing Charissa; the arms of his chair were tipped by Sphinx faces. "I was not aware Lady Irving was fond of anyone."

"Oh—well, she is. Maybe because she never had daughters of her own. Or maybe because she was glad never to have daughters of her own? But that is why Mother said Audrina could go. I mean, I could not because of our marriage. Clearly."

"Clearly." The strict line of his mouth turned up at one corner. Charissa could hardly imagine it pressed to hers for a kiss, much less crying out with passion.

But it would, wouldn't it? And soon.

She wished it were sooner.

She looked down at her hands, neatly gloved from fingertip to the blond lace cuffs of her sleeve. She was every bit the proper bride on the surface, and her London family was equally appropriate for a ducal alliance. Just as long as her future husband did not inquire too deeply into her thoughts—or into the nature of Lady Audrina's departure.

"I do hope Lady Audrina will return in time for our wedding," the duke said. "It would be most irregular should the bride's sister fail to be present."

"But Lady Romula and Lady Theodosia—" Charissa bit her lip. "My elder sisters might not be in attendance. That is, my parents invited them, but we've heard nothing about whether they actually intend to come. If they are absent, I don't think it will be to give offense, but because they do not feel at ease."

The two oldest sisters, Lady Alleyneham had put about, had suffered from a lung ailment the previous year. In truth, they had caught smallpox. Though their health had returned after a long convalescence in Littlehampton, their pale complexions had been pocked and scarred. Too badly to catch a titled husband, their mother said—which was quite all right with them, as Romula had fallen in love with her physician and Theodosia with a country squire.

The two older sisters had resigned themselves to a quiet life in the country, one with which they professed themselves happy. They did not even express much enthusiasm for the fashion plates Charissa sent to them every season, or the bolts of satin and the plumes for new bonnet trimmings.

And then there was Petra, the fourth sister. Dreamy and solitary, she had been in Italy for a year since the urge to study art had seized her with sudden violence. No one expected her to return for the wedding. Such a notion had not even been considered.

"Your two elder sisters," the duke said as he seated himself facing Charissa, "have chosen a different sort of life. If they do not wish to return to the bosom of society, that is their right. But until Lady Audrina marries, she lives under your parents' roof and should abide by their wishes."

"She should," murmured Charissa. She never had, though. Charissa herself had always accepted her parents' wishes: to mix in society, to become a young lady of fashion, and to marry a duke.

"I am glad we are in accordance." His Grace smiled, a curve of his stern mouth that made his dark brows and eyes soften. "Lady Charissa, I have been considering a matter of great consequence. Since we are to be married in little more than a fortnight, I wonder—but no, perhaps it would be asking too much."

"No, please—Your Grace, ask me anything you wish. I am sure it will not be improper."

"I hope not." He folded his hands over the ebony head of his cane. "I was thinking that, since we are to be wed soon, you might call me Walpole instead of 'Your Grace.'" His head tilted. "If you mind, you must tell me at once."

His first name, she knew, was Roderick. Roderick Francis Matthew Elder, Duke of Walpole, Earl of Carbury, Baron Winterset.

So many names. Soon some of them would be hers.

"Mind? Oh, no—Walpole. Not at all. I should be very glad."

His smile matched hers, soft and bright, and her heart gave a quick, flustered flutter.

She *should* be very glad as the future Duchess of Walpole. And if only she knew where her sister and her father truly were, she would be very glad indeed.

Chapter Nine

Wherein Celestial Bodies
Are Not What They Seem

After an early evening supper and a cursory cup of tea—which the Dudleys, Lady Irving, and Richard seemed to enjoy far more than usual—Giles drew Audrina off in search of Sophy and her telescope. "You wanted me to look at the stars," he reminded Audrina. "Well, I'm not going to do that unless you do, too."

She raised a brow.

"No, sorry," he said. "I can't be intimidated by the movement of a few facial muscles. If you want me to sop up some unwanted knowledge, you have to come along and sop it up, too."

This was nothing but bravado. The idea of being alone with her in a darkened room, with stars gloating down at them, was startlingly attractive.

As was taking the chance to prove to her that he

had listened to, and remembered, every word of what she'd told him earlier.

Sophy was located in the library, as they expected. They found her seated in a ladder-back chair before an enormous secretary desk. A litter of scrawled notes, drawings of angles and radii and spheres, covered the surface of the wood. In the light of an Argand lamp perched precariously at one corner, the wood shone a burnished red. When Giles explained what they were after, Sophy's pince-nez caught a silvery reflection that made her eyes impossible to see.

"You want to use my telescope." Sophy's face turned from Giles to Audrina, then back. "Now? Tonight?"

"Tonight did seem a better choice than tomorrow morning, yes," said Giles. "I'm hardly expert, but I've been told it's easier to spot things through a telescope at nighttime."

Her mouth pulled up at one side. "You were told correctly. Have you also been told how to use a telescope?"

"What is there to know?" he replied. "Point one end up at the sky and look through the other. If everything looks smaller instead of bigger, turn it around."

"Do not turn my telescope around, Mr. Rutherford. I assure you, I have the right end *pointing up at the sky*, as you put it." Plucking off her pince-nez, she pressed at the bridge of her nose. "Are you any more familiar than he is, Lady Audrina? Really, I ought to adjust it for you. If the keys were to break—"

"We won't adjust it at all," Audrina assured her. "We will only look at whatever you have trained it on, then we shall leave it alone."

Sophy looked startled, the first time Giles had seen

that expression cross her capable features. "What would be the amusement in that? No, no, you must look at whatever you like." With a tilt of her head, she indicated the telescope on a Pembroke table at the far side of the room, in front of a window. "This telescope has quite a good lens and mirror. You can spot the rings of Saturn and tell apart the different colors of stars. Do you want any gridded paper for drawings or measurements?"

"Yes," said Audrina, just as Giles said, "Er—no."

Sophy handed Audrina several sheets of paper and a string-wrapped marking pencil. Then she paused, shuffling her notes into a neat pile. "Right. Well. This should be a good evening for watching the sky. The sky is clear, and the moon will not set until morning. It's waxing gibbous."

"Don't think I won't ask you to explain that," Giles said. "You're probably used to English gentlemen who pretend to know everything, but I have no idea what that means."

Shoving her papers into a drawer of the tall desk's hutch, Sophy explained that the moon was tending toward fullness. "No matter the phase of the moon, winter is the best time to look at stars because the sky is clear. I like to think that they freeze, waiting for humans to look at them." She ducked her head. "Just a fancy, of course. I know they do not change."

"And why should they not?" Giles asked. "What do we really know about the stars?"

With steady hands, Sophy transferred the Argand lamp from the desk to her abandoned wooden chair. "We know, Mr. Rutherford, that they are unimaginably far away." Tipping up the folding table on which she'd been working, she closed it away behind the doors of the desk. "Enjoy your time looking at the sky. Do try not to break the turn-keys while you are adjusting the altitude and azimuth."

Giles decided it would be wiser not to say, *Adjusting the* what? "We won't," he said.

Once Sophy had departed the library, Giles motioned toward the telescope. "After you, Lady Galileo."

Audrina smiled, then led him to the Pembroke table on which the telescope stood. Two of the table's dropped leaves were opened, making of it a fattened semicircle much like the shape of the moon.

The telescope itself was smaller than Giles had expected, considering it was the focus of Sophy's life. Two feet in length, with a diameter about that of Giles's fist, it perched on a graceful brass stand with ornamental curves and a sturdy trio of legs. The surface of the tube was brass, too, shining as though Sophy polished away every finger mark.

If Giles loved something as much as Sophy loved her telescope, he would treat it with similar care.

"So why are we here?" he asked as Audrina trailed her fingers up the tube, not quite touching its bright surface. "Do you want to look at something in particular?"

"No, I just want to *look*. Without worrying that anyone will chase me away or tell me this is an unsuitable interest for a woman of my breeding."

"I would never tell you anything like that, and Sophy certainly wouldn't either. Go on, you take the first look."

Audrina set down the papers and pencil; then stepping behind the telescope, she bent over its eyepiece. Several minutes followed in which she made nimble adjustments to a pair of skeletal brass keys below the telescope's tube, checked the view, adjusted, checked, *hmmmed.*

Giles didn't mind her preoccupation at all. Because while her posture was bent, the bodice of her dress dipped to an intriguing shadow. Such a curve of pale skin, like reflected moonlight, and then hidden secrets like the night sky itself.

He shook his head. Fanciful. He'd do much better to find himself a book about something useful. Like the peerage, upon whose whims his father hoped to build a new business. Or fashion plates to show him the sort of jewelry people were wearing these days.

With a shudder, he moved away toward the hearth. Every window in this sprawling castle seemed designed to leak in as much cold air as possible, and each was taller than a normal story of a house.

Though this room seemed warmer than the others in the stately home, maybe because the library was small. Or because it was insulated on all sides with massive bookshelves, with a heavy carpet underfoot. The draperies were pulled back, causing the room itself to feel like a telescope, all solid narrowness with a clear end, a beautiful view.

The sky, of course. The sky was what he meant. Not the woman in a gown the color of emeralds.

After a long interval of silence and staring—at the sky on her part, at her on Giles's—Audrina stood. Stretching and rolling her shoulders, she squinted toward the firelight. "Giles?"

He returned to her side at once. "Do you like what you see?" He could have bitten his tongue. Or not.

Audrina blinked, then looked down at the telescope. "I don't know what I saw. I don't know the names of any of the stars, or how far away the planets are. But I finally got to *see* something. Saturn's rings, and some stars that were almost red, and others I never knew were there at all." She grabbed his forearm. "Take a look, Giles. Look at the moon. Did you know the moon was so dark and rough?"

She yanked at his arm—which was fine with him, really, and it was also fine that she kept hold of it while he crouched before the eyepiece. Sky filled his sight, blue-black and spangled.

"What do you see?" Audrina's voice almost broke, as though she was swallowing her excitement. "Do you see the moon?"

"Not yet." Remembering the keys beneath the tube that Audrina had turned, he nudged each with his free hand. At his touch, the telescope edged up or down, left or right.

He was aware, as he skimmed objects far away in space, how close Audrina stood to him. So close that he smelled the traces of evergreen that still clung to her from the needles they'd crushed earlier.

The telescope found the moon, sudden and huge and glowing. He reared back in reflex, then pressed his eye to the eyepiece again and scanned it. What seemed silver from afar was dull and gray up close, a steely pockmarked half pie of scarred rock.

Something within him gave a lurch of painful feeling. "It's not the way I thought it would be." He straightened, tugging his arm from her grasp. "Go ahead, look some more if you want to."

His breath stirred a tiny wisp of dark hair at the nape of her neck. Her expression was all shadow—and then she smiled, a slip of movement in the moonlight. "I'm not as proper as I pretend to be, you said."

And before Giles could say *Yes* or *Right* or *I'd like to think so,* she caught his hand again and tugged him down to sit on the floor. "If we had blankets, this would be like an indoor picnic." Somehow she sounded as crisp and cultured as ever, each word a pearl.

"Just a second." Giles leapt to his feet and, striding to the fireplace, lit a branch of candles from a paper spill. He found a cast-off shawl by Sophy's abandoned chair and returned to Audrina. "Sunshine and a blanket. Have your picnic, princess."

Within a minute, she had arranged the woven shawl on the floor and placed the candles at a safe distance. The shawl, Giles discovered when he seated himself on it, was laid in the perfect location to look out at the sky without craning one's neck. And if one lay down on the floor and folded one's arms behind one's head—even better.

Audrina hesitated, then settled herself at his side. Giles estimated the distance between them at one forearm, one wrist, one hand.

He kept his hands to himself. The lady only wanted to look at the stars.

"It's Christmas in less than a fortnight," she said.

"Yes."

"I have never been away from my family on Christmas before."

Nor had he. Never since the births of his younger siblings had Giles been so long away from them.

Next year at this time, Sarah would be married. If Richard's plans for a London jewelry shop worked out, Christopher and Isaac would be running the Rutherford Paper Mill. Alfred seemed inclined to study law. And Rachel—Giles missed Rachel most of all. The closest to him in age, she had been born small and early following Lady Beatrix's bout of measles. With her sight and hearing limited, her speech delayed, Giles had thought to protect her. Coddle her.

And so, when she was four and he was six, she had thrashed him for telling her she *shouldn't* or *couldn't*. Giles never underestimated his sister again—though that didn't keep him from keeping a close eye on her. On all of them. They were just beginning to build their lives; they had hardly gotten used to the absence of their mother. How would they get along this Christmas without Giles? Their third parent?

How would he get along if they didn't need him anymore?

Giles didn't think of Richard as someone on whom he needed to rely. Maybe the younger Rutherford siblings were feeling the same way about Giles himself.

Now that was a thought that brought on that lurch again, a pain right below his breastbone.

"Maybe you won't be away from your family on Christmas," he finally replied. "As you said, there's plenty of time. Twelve days. By then, your father will have relented, and you'll be—"

"No," she cut him off. "No, he will not relent. Not with the family's reputation at stake."

At Giles's side, she shifted. The nearby branch of candles cast warm gilt on her face; the moonlight left her skirts and neatly half-booted feet silvery-cold. "Never mind that. It's all right. If I do not return to London, then I . . . then I will be somewhere else."

"Nicely reasoned," Giles said.

One of her feet kicked against his shin in what was surely not an accident.

"As it is almost Christmas," she said in a tone of frightening cheer, "shall we look for a special star in the sky?"

"What, as though we're Magi following it?" Giles shook his head, rocking it upon his folded-up forearms. "Sorry, princess. I wouldn't know a special star from an ordinary one."

"But would you follow a star? Or—a dream? If you were permitted to have one?" Her laugh was low and a little bitter.

Giles considered. "Following a star is no wilder than some of my father's other schemes. He's tried making paper not only from rags, but from wood pulp—what a disaster that was. And remember, we came to England solely because of a fortune that no one thinks exists anymore except for him. So if I'm willing to follow a whim that isn't even my own, why shouldn't I follow a star?"

"Because you don't believe in it." Her voice was low and soft. "You wouldn't follow a star on your own. You wouldn't be here on your own."

Her words sounded like a criticism, echoing within his hollowness. *There's nothing you want. Those dreams are all borrowed from someone else. You don't have any of your own.*

Maybe he didn't anymore. He'd let them go when his wrists grew painful; the first of many things that would inevitably slip from his grasp, just as illness had taken everything from his mother.

But it wasn't as though he'd done nothing with his life. He had made himself instead into the family's valet, bootboy, governess—and Richard's dutiful son, who could manage the accounts of a paper mill or design a new setting for an ancient jewel.

"If," he answered, "I am willing to come along so a person of conviction doesn't have to be alone, isn't that worth something?"

"I suppose, if you do so for the sake of providing company."

Not if you do it out of mistrust. This remained unsaid. Did she think it, though? It was such a grimy thought that he shied from it himself. "If I can't tell a special star from an ordinary one, maybe I'll treat them all like they're special. Or are we even talking about stars anymore?"

"We were never talking about stars," she sighed.

They lay on the woven surface, simply looking at the moon. Now that he had seen it through the telescope, to Giles it seemed closer, the shape of a grin tipped sideways. Hanging just out of reach, as though if he stretched out his hand he could capture the whole of it. Appearing so much smoother and brighter from a distance than it did when one looked at it closely.

Well. A lot of things were like that.

From the corner of his eye, he saw Audrina shiver. "Are you cold?" he asked.

"I am fine."

"Liar. Your sleeves are like little puffy flowers. They can't possibly be warm, especially when you're lying on a library floor."

He rolled to a seated position and began the tedious process of easing off his coat. The snug cut made it difficult to accomplish on his own, but he succeeded by working one sleeve down over the heel of his hand, then sitting on sleeve and hand alike to pin them in place as he eased out of the rest.

Throughout, Audrina watched him from her reclining position atop the shawl. The set of her mouth was grave—as though Giles was something to be looked at through a telescope, considered, then turned away from again.

"Here you go." He shook the coat out, ready to lay it over her like a blanket.

But somehow, in reaching over to cover her, he forgot to draw back again. Somehow his eyes caught hers, dark in the low golden firelight, and he forgot to do anything at all.

Poised on one elbow, his other arm spanning her body, he drank her with his eyes, with his breath, with a soft sigh of wanting.

After a few long seconds during which he couldn't quite seem to get himself to move, the solemn line of her mouth curved into a smile. And then she captured his face between her palms, pulling it to hers.

Chapter Ten

Wherein Moonlight Extracts the Truth

Before Giles could think better of it, he had brushed his lips over hers, and they sank together to the floor, his coat trapped between their bodies in a rough bundle.

Think better of it? What could be better than this?

Resting his weight on one elbow, he devoted his full attention to her mouth. A taste, rubbing his lips over hers until her tongue brushed against them, until her teeth nipped at him lightly. *Yes.*

A deeper kiss, then; one with mouth on mouth, opening for tongues to touch. She tasted of sugar and tea and—and who the hell cared, because he was kissing her, finally, finally. Hot as starlight, and her hair smelled so good, and that sound she made in the back of her throat—*mmm*, as if kissing him was delicious—

was enough to make him instantly hard. Oh, he could kiss her for days.

In a way, he had been. With every movement of his hands over the puzzle box, he'd wanted to trace the lines of her face and stroke his hands over her body. Every time she had made a note of a new attempt, then looked up at him with questioning brows, he'd wanted to shove aside the small table between them and wrap his arms around her. And the flecks of ink that spattered her hand as she wrote; he had envied the flecks of ink, for God's sake.

The hands that had cradled his face slid back to catch in his short hair, then down to grip at his shoulders. She tugged him until he was twisted, his torso atop her, his legs balancing at her side. Bracing himself with one boot against the legs of the Pembroke table—not hard enough to jostle it, for he owed this telescope a great deal of gratitude—he scooted closer, careful not to let his hard length brush against her body. Through his loose trousers, she could probably feel it. Would, if he pressed closer. And that would be so much more than a kiss, a quick burst of mutual passion.

Except: "This is already more than a kiss," he murmured. Her throat was smooth, and she shivered when he kissed her there, down, down, to her collarbone.

"Yes." She stroked the cords of his neck, making him quiver with pent-up tension. That damned coat; it had turned into a wall separating them.

She must have shared his eagerness to be rid of it. Skating her hands between them, she tugged the coat free and pushed it away. And then her hands slipped over him again, trailing down his back, then beneath the suspenders at his shoulders to claw him with delicious sensation.

That blessed coat, to have been removed from his body.

She arched upward, brushing her breasts against his chest. "You can . . ."

"I can . . . ?" He could no longer count on his ears to hear anything but what they wanted to. One elbow supported his weight, leaving one hand completely free to roam her curves. When he laid his palm over one of her breasts, a tender sigh slipped from her lips.

"Yes, whatever you like," she murmured. Her hand covered his, guiding it beneath the edge of her bodice. Slipping beneath stays, the tight lacing eased by their prone position, to find the satin curve of her breast, the firm nub of her nipple. He caught it, pinching lightly between two fingers, until it hardened yet further and she moaned. Then with his thumb, he rubbed just the tip, that sensitive tip that made her twist under him. To still her, he hitched one leg over her hips, catching her in a cage of his own limbs. An embrace. Again he kissed her, his thumb teasing at one nipple, then the other. Her hips began to rock, to push against his leg.

"Giles." His name was a gasp on her lips as she broke the kiss. "More." She worked her arms around his body, clutching tight first at his sides, then digging her nails into his buttocks. Unmistakable invitation. Instinct told him to cover her body with his, to push her down and grind his erection into her hip until her thighs parted.

Good plan, that. Shifting his weight, he raised himself up over her. The tiny bones in his wrists popped and burned, but he ignored them. He notched one thigh between her legs, her long skirts a new barrier between them—but that hardly mattered, because good God, this woman could kiss. More than kiss. Oh, a mouth such as Audrina's—one that uttered bitter truths, heated hopes, sharp desires—could fascinate a man forever.

Yes. He would kiss her for days, for all the days until Christmas, until the calendar turned from the old year to the new. And she would kiss him back. Rub against him, just like this. Make sweet moaning sounds as he sipped at her lips . . .

. . . but his wrists began to scream, blunting the pleasure of the moment. He tried sinking to his forearms, hoping the pain would fall silent. No, his arms had gone nerveless, biceps in a spasm. They shook, he teetered, and instead of holding up his weight they gave way, and he collapsed across Audrina.

He went still, body at war with itself. Heaving for air, quaking with lust. "I'm sorry," he gasped. "I—need to stop." Wincing, he rolled off her. Flat. Ironed to the floor, his arms a mass of fire as he looked up into the dark heights of the ceiling.

He had no right to touch her. He was a man without a future.

"But why must you stop?" She curled upward, the smooth line of her throat corded with tension. "I am not a virgin. You guessed, surely, after gathering the tale of my past relationship with Llewellyn."

He squeezed his eyes closed, praying that the pressure of his squinting eyelids would distract him from her trailing fingers, from the delicate cadence of her voice. Her lips almost touching the lobe of his ear. "Are you thinking to watch out for my honor, Giles? There is no need."

Her hands, sliding, questing, stroking . . . oh, he could have surrendered to her. He wanted to.

But he was not as improper as he pretended to be. He owed her the truth.

Wrists still twingeing, he caught her hand and laced his fingers with hers. "As a matter of fact, princess, no. You're a grown woman, so you'll have to see to your own honor. I'm busy enough seeing to mine."

Sliding his free hand over his jaw, he considered. Such a familiar shape, for now. One day his hands would not be able to follow the form. "Look, Audrina. I've got nothing to offer you."

"Indeed?" She guided their linked hands to his erection, still stiff and needy.

His face heated; good thing it was dark in the library. "All right, one thing. But if that's all I can give you, that's almost worse than nothing."

"You do not advocate well for your skill."

He smiled, and a bit of the terrible tension eased. "No? Well, I'm not trying to." He lowered their linked hands between their bodies. Side by side, like chess pieces put away in a box. "I have arthritis, Audrina. It came on while I was at university, while my mother was dying each day from the pain of it. For now it's in my wrists and hands, but one day it'll spread."

Her hand clasped his more tightly. "Are you certain?"

"Certain as I can be. I've been lucky so far. It hasn't gotten worse for a while, but it's only a matter of time." His own future had vanished with the terrible knowledge: The pain that racked his mother would one day lay him to waste, too. Better, then, to save himself any other pain. Anything else that might one day be lost. "So you see, there's no point in my having dreams or stars or whatever we called them. There's no purpose to pleasure."

Her thumb stroked his. "What about pleasure for its own sake?"

"It's done too soon, and it brings too much pain with it."

"You really are *not* advocating well for your skill."

"I'm not talking about sex. But thank you. Very kind." Almost impossible not to kiss her again at such a moment, for making him smile. "While I'm able, I'm trying to help my family with their dreams instead. And if I meet any beautiful princesses along the way, I'll be as good to them as I can."

"How nice for you to know what to do." She looked away. "I'm sorry. About your mother. About your hands. I—hope it's not true."

"I wish it weren't." He sat up and shook out his wrists. "I'm not looking for pity. If you try to give me pity, I'm taking my coat right back and I don't care how cold you get."

Her smile was watery, but she snatched at the discarded coat as he'd hoped she would. "You can try to take it back, but I will pit my weak little feminine wrists against yours."

"If it helps," Giles added, "I am physically uncomfortable and hate every scruple and better feeling that is telling me I mustn't keep touching you."

"It probably should not help, but it does." She paused. "Why did you kiss me, then, if you are so set against pleasure?"

"Why did you kiss me first?"

"Why did you kiss me back?"

They eyed each other. "We could do this all night,"

Giles said. *I wish.* "Answer on the count of three," he suggested. "One—two—three—"

"I wanted to," they both said at once.

Giles scrubbed a hand over his face. Stubble abraded his palm; he hoped it had not scraped her face. Throat. Collarbone. The hollow at the top of her breasts, just before the firm line of her chest went soft and rounded and . . . "Princess. Good God. If I could be paid according to how much I want to kiss you, I would have a fortune and my father and I would be able to leave England right away."

She sat up to face him. In her lap, she held his coat in tight-clamped fists. "I know you will leave. But if I want you to kiss me before you go, why will you not?"

Her eyes were fathomless. Giles had stared into the bottomless blue-green ocean during his Atlantic crossing, but he could not remember feeling this sense of sinking into unknown depths.

"Because I wouldn't—I don't—want to stop at just a kiss. And anything more would be . . ." *Too much to want. Too much to take.* He cleared his throat. "Done for the wrong reasons. Rightly, an ocean and about three hundred ranks of society belong between us."

She clutched his coat like a shield. "That might be a slight exaggeration. Remember, I am ruined. What is the value of a ruined earl's daughter? Is she worth more or less than an obedient commoner?"

"She's worth precisely one human being, just as an obedient commoner is. And neither of them should be talked about as if they are disposable." His shoulders felt bare under only the light fabric of his shirt. "Audrina, I don't grant much weight to your father's earldom or those three hundred ranks between us, or however many there are. But I know that people in

England do. And I can imagine what I look like from your viewpoint: a foreign-born commoner with a few skills I never use, a modest income, and a brick wall of a body and face. Even before you subtract a pair of reliable hands from the equation, I don't amount to much for an earl's daughter."

Her hands fluttered on the collar of his coat, then let it fall to her lap. "Are we to have an argument about who is worth less?"

"Not worth less. Worth—different." Twisting around, he retrieved a sheet of the gridded paper and the pencil that Audrina had laid on the telescope table. It was a stall, a distraction to give them both time to think. "Unless I've misinterpreted your hints—and if I have, let me apologize right now—you were implying that you'd give yourself to me."

She hesitated. "Yes."

"Yourself? Your true, whole self? Or some part of yourself that you think isn't worth anything because someone told you it wasn't?"

"My virtue was worth everything, or so I have been told." Her tone was lusterless. "Without it, I have little value."

Frustration boiled up within Giles. "Oh. So you're offering to give me something you don't care about? Or something you don't have anymore? I'm confused." The pencil skated over the paper, a dark slash of graphite. "Are you using me, or asking me to use you?"

He thought she might be offended by this question. He *wanted* her to be offended. But she only stared at him with those fathomless eyes. "Does the answer make a difference?"

Her voice was quiet, defeated, like the fall of a

dry leaf. It abraded him; it wrung him. Frustration vanished, and all he could think of was how much he wanted her not to say the things she was saying. Not to feel the emotions that threaded tightly through her words. Yet it was done; she said and she felt, and the pain behind her words sounded like a lifelong bruise.

"It makes a difference to me." He dropped the paper and pencil between them. Gingerly, he settled back again onto the shawl, taking care to keep his weight from his wrists. "If we choose to stop, surely that's worth something. Surely that means we're not using each other at all, if we stop because we think it's right. Because we both deserve better than being used. We both deserve better than something meaningless."

He wasn't explaining himself well to his own ears— because never, never, had a kiss felt like it held more meaning. Never had a kiss felt like it mattered more.

It mattered too much. He had meant what he'd told her: With numbered days, he could not allow himself that sort of pleasure.

"Is that what you think?" Her question was quiet.

"That's what I think, yes, but that's not what matters. What matters is that you have to live with people who are preoccupied by rank and reputation, and you have to know and obey all the rules that go along with that." He laughed, a low sound of disbelief. "You had to memorize the entire peerage, Audrina. You *are* an earl's daughter. We both live in the world we were born to. We're not better or worse, but we're . . . different."

Something about the night-quiet room unlocked

this honesty. The usual rules had gone dark. The usual barriers were invisible.

All except the ones they carried within.

In his peripheral vision, he saw Audrina fold his jacket, then reach forward. Grabbing the paper and pencil, evidently, because the soft graphite began to shush over one of the gridded sheets. "So for you, honor is a test of control?"

"Hardly. I'd never test myself on purpose. What are the chances I'd pass? No, you're the one who brought up honor, princess. I'm guessing it means something to you."

The pencil stopped its movement. "I do not know what it means to me."

"Maybe. But you must know what sort of behavior it's not."

"Yes." Her reply was faint. "Does reputation not matter to Americans?"

"Of course it matters. We're not heathens." He chose his words carefully, keeping his gaze fixed on the painted ceiling. "But a woman's good reputation doesn't come from not being alone with a man. All that does is tell me she's solitary. It doesn't tell me anything about what sort of person she is."

"What do you require to think well of—someone?"

"Would it be too imprecise to say I know it when it happens? Yes? Well—pluck, I guess. Courage. I admire courage."

"Oh." The pencil began shushing furiously over the paper again. "That is not unique. Everyone admires courage."

"Are you sure about that? Do you think the illustrious David Llewellyn does?"

"Ugh. No, I suppose he does not. He begged me

for a gift, then scorned me when I granted it to him."
She gave a harsh laugh. "I wonder how he and my
father are getting on. The subject of my shortcomings
as a proper English female might well occupy them
halfway to London."

"Then they'll be repeating themselves a lot."

"Flatterer."

"Not one of my skills, sadly. If I've said anything flat-
tering since entering this room, I can't remember it.
Maybe not since entering England."

A cloud passed before the moon, and he took that
as a sign to sit up again. She folded her paper, then
handed back his coat.

"Do we have to pretend this never happened?" she
asked as he stood and struggled back into the snug-
fitting coat.

"I'm not that good at pretending." He held out a
hand to help her up; her fingers brushed his only for
a pale instant. "I'll probably think about it all the time,
even when I shouldn't. Like when you're being show-
ered with dry evergreen needles, or when you're eating
soup at dinner—"

"Or when you gnaw on your lip as you glare at the
puzzle box," she added.

"Do I do that?"

With a nod, she looked up into his face. "We will
think about it. But we will also remember that it will
not happen again." The twist of her mouth was almost
like a real smile.

She left the library first. Reputation, for God's sake.
Reputation.

He admired courage, he'd said, and that she possessed in great amount. She had a regimented place
in the world, and she didn't know whether she fell

into step with it anymore. Yet she gave the appearance of marching along for the sake of the militant around her. Better to protect her winged heart than let others stone it.

How had Giles lost his? When had it fallen so heavy and low? He'd given up his hopes in exchange for his father's dream of gold and jewels. To protect his siblings; to live through them since he had no idea what his own life would be like.

The pain in his wrists had ebbed again, and he bent to retrieve the forgotten pencil from the floor. He folded Sophy's shawl, too, and placed it over the back of her chair before dousing the lamp and the candles.

It was only a matter of time before the pain came back. Yet in the meantime—ah, Audrina had tilted and shaken the world. She made him want to forget his dying hands. To have the right to hope, when all he should be thinking about was cracking open that gilded *himitsu-bako* and getting the hell back to Philadelphia.

It was too late for him to follow a star, but she made him want to forget that, too.

Chapter Eleven

Wherein a Drawing of Indeterminate Nature Is Created

For the next three days, the world felt like a caught breath. Outside, the sky dithered between grayness and rain, sleet and more rain. And within, Audrina waited—because now that something had changed, it seemed inevitable that more change would follow.

But for the next three days, nothing did. Long hours were spent in the drawing room, where fires were built up high and Giles sat at a tiny table pretending to work at the puzzle box. Audrina had stopped taking notes on his attempts, because by tacit agreement, his attempts had stopped being serious.

Because once he opened the box—whether it proved empty or not—there would be no reason for them to remain here.

It was just as well that she and Giles had not vowed to ignore their nighttime interlude. Though some of their conversation that night had been awkward, even abrasive, the parts that were not conversation had been very pleasant indeed.

But it was the conversation, especially, that Audrina could not forget.

Maybe it was this that caused the feeling of air still before a storm. Now that Audrina had skipped like a stone over the rings of Saturn, now that she knew Jupiter had moons and that stars came in different shades, England seemed small. London, longed-for London, was too close in some ways: Llewellyn and her father had probably finished their journey by now.

Richard Rutherford and Lady Irving had wreathed nearly everything that could be adorned with festive trimmings; Lady Dudley had fastened a sleigh bell about the neck of each dog. It was impossible not to be aware of Christmas, hurtling closer with evergreen and hummed snippets of carols and the notion of hunting for a star.

And that meant the time was drawing nearer for Llewellyn to ruin something: the Earl of Alleyneham's fortunes, Audrina's reputation, her sister Charissa's wedding to the Duke of Walpole.

Maybe all three.

Llewellyn must get money or he would cause a scandal: this, she knew. And she also knew that His Grace the Duke of Walpole would not tolerate such a humiliation. Not when he was stickler enough to ask Audrina to sit in as a chaperone during his every teatime call to his future wife.

But she knew one more thing: Charissa, dutiful daughter that she was, really loved the duke.

There was no denying that Charissa loved London society, too. She wanted to be a duchess and have noble babies and raise them to responsibility and fashion. But during a nighttime sisterly conversation a month ago, Charissa had admitted how she felt about Walpole himself.

"He never does anything wrong." Wearing her nightdress, she flopped across Audrina's bed, stretching out her limbs. "He's incorruptible. He's *good.*"

Audrina thought he was a prig, personally. "I do not doubt that he will make you a faithful husband." Which was true.

"I know he will," Charissa breathed. "A duke. To think a duke should choose *me.*"

She sat up, her long red-brown hair a floating tangle. Audrina fetched a hairbrush from her dressing table and began to draw it through her older sister's hair. "I am happy for you." *Brush brush.* "But you are quite good enough the way you are. He is lucky to be marrying you."

"Pfft. He could have anyone. There are far more earl's daughters than there are dukes."

"True, but only one of those earl's daughters is Lady Charissa Bradleigh. He's fortunate that you chose him."

Audrina tried to twist her sister's hair into a loose braid, but Charissa turned to stare at her over one shoulder. "Who would not? What is there not to admire about the Duke of Walpole?"

At the time, Charissa had been satisfied with Audrina's noncommittal gesture and a turn of the subject to her bride clothes.

But Audrina had an answer now. *If he had a sense of humor, I would admire him more. If he ever said what he ought not, but what was on everyone's mind, I would think him braver.*

If he kissed me, then stopped because he thought I deserved better—I would . . .

She would not know what to think. At the time, she had felt insulted; then ashamed. Unwanted. But this feeling had faded, and now she was less certain she had tried to do the right thing, or Giles the wrong one.

The household had fallen into a simple carousel of steps in their short time at Castle Parr. The Dudleys shuttled between the drawing room and the yellow parlor. Lady Irving and Richard Rutherford had become oddly fond of a passageway full of severed statue heads, though they popped into the drawing room at intervals for tea.

And Sophy remained in the library. Usually alone, though Audrina wondered if she wanted to be. She had been willing to share her telescope; eager for them to see what she saw, and to understand it.

Were it not for Audrina's dread, her feeling of helpless distance from her sister, she would enjoy the slow dribbling of these days. She liked the space of York, the high ceilings and the open land. The eager wind that knocked at the windows and the fires that seemed all the warmer for the cold outside. The dogs that roamed the house, toenails clattering across the finest marble floors.

In London, she was so used to carrying chaos about with her that she forgot what it might be like to set it down; to scrub her fingers through the wiry fur of a brindled hound, then laugh when it bounded off to join its friends.

The fourth day was a slow Sunday. Freezing rain had prevented the party from attending church. Giles and Audrina had taken their seats at the tea table in the drawing room, the puzzle box between them like a talisman.

She wanted to shatter that caught-breath feeling, to make the world around her hitch and heave. As she extracted a wood-cased pencil and several sheets of Sophy's gridded paper from a pocket, her voice was bland. "Just so you are aware, Giles, I am not planning to kiss you today. And I certainly will not permit you to kiss me."

His hands went still. She could not help but think of them as harbingers of ill health now—though they seemed flexible and fit enough.

Were she to allow herself to remember, she'd think them much more than that. Those hands had covered her with a coat. Had spread a shawl on the floor for her. They had cradled her face, skated over her clothing, and caressed her breasts.

"As a matter of fact, princess"—those same hands tightened about the puzzle box—"I wouldn't even try. Don't think about kisses, because it's not going to happen."

The pencil slipped from Audrina's fingers to clatter on the table, sending a chip of precious graphite flying.

"I'm telling you," he added, "don't think about me kissing you. Or you kissing me. Or both of us wanting to kiss each other so much that we argue over who gets to kiss whom first and wind up falling to the floor in a tangle of limbs. Kissing, naturally."

By the time he finished this speech, she was biting her lip so as not to laugh aloud.

"That's something that won't happen today. Just for example." He worked a penknife into a seam of the puzzle box, then eyed it with great concentration.

"And getting this puzzle box open is another example of something that won't happen today."

This time she did let herself laugh. What was the harm in a laugh?

Giles began nudging at panels of the box again; he coaxed a few of them to slide, beginning the process of opening the box.

Across from him, Audrina let her pencil travel across one of Sophy's gridded sheets. The lady astronomer used them for mapping out her observations, but Audrina wondered whether the page could be used to map something far more everyday. A building.

She had seized on the idea when talking to Giles in the library, when desperate distraction was needed from desperate thought. With all the freedom of being male, trusted by his family, and free to travel the world—how had he given up on doing exactly what he pleased with his life?

And what, for that matter, would she like to do with hers? Now that Charissa was to marry a duke, the other Bradleigh daughters might be more free for . . . something.

Or maybe not. Marriage or disappointment; this was what her parents expected of her. Such expectations were the habit of years. Audrina had battered at them, but had never been able to shake them. They only sprang back, knocking her about. Knocking her into the company of people she hardly knew so that she would not return to London an embarrassment.

But she knew these people now. And—she wavered. Wanting to be home; wanting to stay here. Blessedly free of her father's disapproval, Llewellyn's threats, her mother's well-meant suggestions for improvement.

She knew the freedom was false, temporary, but it beckoned nonetheless.

In silence, Giles worked at the box and Audrina began to pencil in a few unsteady lines. She would have found it easier to build a model with blocks or clay; rendering a three-dimensional structure into something flat was unfamiliar and odd.

Before she had sorted out more than a few shapes, Lady Irving slammed into the drawing room. At her heels, the smallest of Lady Dudley's dogs—a sweet-tempered russet mongrel named Penny—yipped and nipped at skirts of a bright paisley.

"Save me from your father, Rutherford," Lady Irving called. "He wants to decorate every head in the passage."

This sentence would have been unintelligible to Audrina a few days ago, but she now knew of both Castle Parr's corridor full of broken statuary and Richard Rutherford's fondness for adorning sculptures with evergreen leaves.

"What are you up to, girl? You're wearing an uncommonly mischievous expression." Lady Irving marched over to Audrina. Penny's short legs were a blur as the small dog followed, the sleigh bell around her neck jingling with every tiny step.

"Uncommonly? Do you really think so?" Giles said. "In my experience, Lady Audrina looks like that a lot. She has a devious and inscrutable mind."

Audrina ignored him. "I am drawing, my lady. You know how proper young ladies are. We can't bear to be idle."

"Harrumph." Lady Irving would no doubt have said more, but Richard Rutherford entered the drawing room just then. "Out of rosemary again," he sighed.

"A shame, because just one head lacks a wreath. Ah, son, there you are. Do you think mistletoe would make a good wreath?"

Lady Irving rolled her eyes. When she bent over the gridded paper, Audrina caught a faint whiff of something sweet and sharp. Brandy? "That," declared the countess, "is the ugliest brooch I've ever seen."

"Let me take a look." Richard Rutherford all but ran over, then looked disappointed when he saw Audrina's drawing. "Oh, I've seen far uglier than that. Remember, Estella, I've been looking at jewels for the last two months."

"You haven't asked to look at any jewels here," said Lady Irving.

"There's no need. The jewel here"—Rutherford made a little bow toward the table—"is the puzzle box."

"Am I," broke in Giles, "supposed not to notice that *you*, Father, just called *you*, Lady Irving, by your first name?"

"Too many pronouns," said the countess airily. "I don't have any idea what you're talking about, Rutherford."

"Oh, God," said Giles. "If I'm Rutherford, then he's . . ."

"Richard. So? A matter of efficiency."

Giles folded his arms atop the table, then buried his face in his makeshift fortress. A muffled voice issued forth: "I wish my ears had fallen off this morning."

"Son!" Richard sounded amused rather than dismayed. "What an irrational idea. Your ears would only need to have fallen off a few minutes ago." When he caught Audrina's eye, she saw laughter in his.

No sense in trying to save face when everyone seemed bubbling with good humor—or good liquor.

"Thus are my artistic dreams dashed," she said. "I meant it to be a drawing of Castle Parr, not a brooch."

The speed with which Giles sat up straight was astounding. "Let me see." Before she could move, he grabbed the paper from the tabletop. "Castle Parr . . . Huh." His brows knit.

"You don't like it."

"Of course he does," Richard Rutherford hastened to assure her. "I've known my son quite a while. That's the face he always makes when he's liking something very much."

"Rubbish." Lady Irving poked at the paper. "And if that were a brooch, that pointy bit would puncture someone's skin."

"But it's not a drawing of a brooch," Giles ground out. "Please allow that I can tell the difference between a drawing of a gemstone setting and a building, since I have been trained in both areas." He added a frown to his furrowed brow.

"*She* hasn't, though," pointed out Lady Irving. "So there's no shame in being confounded by the strange blobs on that paper."

Audrina snapped the paper back and folded it in half. "Point taken. I will never draw anything again."

"Allow me." Giles drew it from her hand and flipped it open again. "This gridded paper—it's interesting. I haven't seen it used before."

"Sophy said she makes it." Audrina made another grab for the paper, but Giles held it out of her reach. "Giles, give it back. I have been mocked enough for today."

"Surely you've heard me mock things and people enough for you to know that I'm not mocking you now," Giles said.

"Wait, wait." Richard folded his arms. "Am *I* supposed to ignore the first names being bandied around this table?"

"Yes," muttered Giles. "And yes, I think you could make a wreath out of mistletoe."

Now beneath the table, the little dog Penny yapped her approval. A hard nose bumped at Audrina's feet as Penny sniffed around, probably looking for biscuit crumbs.

Again, the drawing room door opened, and Lady Dudley ran in—white hair flying, a calico apron askew over her gown. "Where's my Penny? I need Penny. There's someone at the door and I need all the dogs." Catching sight of the little animal, she strode over to the table and scooped Penny up. *Jingle.* The dog rewarded her with an affectionate lick.

"Ah—is someone opening the door to whoever has arrived?" Giles asked.

Lady Irving hesitated. "I'll check. Lady Dudley, care to come with me?"

Penny yapped again, a sound of canine delight, which decided the matter. The older women left the room.

Richard made a V of his index and third fingers, pointed them at his eyes, then pointed them at Giles. "Puzzle box," he said. "That's why we're here." And then he, too, trailed from the room.

"There's more traffic through here than there was at the Goat and Gauntlet." Giles smoothed out Audrina's drawing, then slid it back to her and took up the puzzle box. "As though I don't know this is why we're here. In this castle, in Yorkshire, in England."

"It is why *you* are here." The caught-breath feeling in the room had vanished, replaced by heavy reality.

There could be nothing between them but teasing and a few Christian names, and suddenly she just wanted the whole damned situation to be resolved. Yes, all right; she liked Yorkshire. But she didn't belong here, and she wasn't supposed to be here. None of them were. "Do you want me to work on the puzzle box for a while?"

"Sure, try it out. I'm probably thinking too much about it. You might have better luck since you're not utterly tired of it."

So she was not the only one upon whom time weighed. Did Giles think of arthritis as a ticking clock, his hands the counterweight? Would it one day soon fall, rendering the clock useless? The gears of the human body were delicate and complex. Sometimes they ran smoothly for decades; sometimes they ground and locked far too early.

Such an analogy. This was what came of spending so much time with a man who wanted to build.

"Do you want some of this paper? To draw a brooch or a building, or both at once?" she asked lightly.

"No. There's no point." But his gaze lingered on the disproportionate lines she had drawn.

When Audrina picked up the puzzle box, she marveled again at its slightness. This fragile structure of gilded wood had waited for more than three decades for someone to open it. It could only have waited and survived so long in the hands of someone like Sophy, a little girl when she'd received it. Too young to question the gift, young enough to treasure it. Keeping it, but over time, not really seeing it anymore. Not trying to open it. Just safeguarding it until the right moment—the right people—came.

A prickle between her shoulder blades made Audrina shiver.

The wood was smooth as porcelain under her touch; its patterns danced and dizzied the eye. She tapped at the box, holding it up to one ear, but it sounded empty and dry.

Giles had worked some of the panels from their starting position, and Audrina slid them back, marveling at the intricate catch and grab. The pieces would not budge if pressed in the wrong order.

She shut her eyes, imagining how it must lock together inside. Not the two pieces of a paper spring, but something far more complex. Dowels? Notches? Tightly joined; each slight movement of a panel working free, bit by bit, from that inner structure.

When she opened her eyes, the puzzle box seemed to gleam just for her.

She hardly noticed when the drawing room's door opened again—but there was no ignoring Lady Irving's voice. The countess spoke in a hurry, her tone breathless with relish. "Rutherford. Audrina, my girl. You've got to come meet this woman who just arrived at the castle. Somehow, she splashed her way here on the most abominable roads, and"—Lady Irving drew a deep breath—"she's brought another puzzle box with her."

Chapter Twelve

Wherein the Clues Are Doubled

It was becoming a common occurrence for Lord Dudley to rap at the library door and inform Sophy of a visitor. She could not recall so many arrivals in the past year as there had been in the past week.

Where Lady Irving, the Rutherfords, and Lady Audrina had been expected, though, this new guest was a surprise. As Sophy gave her arm to her father-in-law—an excuse to let him lean his weight on her as they shuffled along, for he did not like to use a cane— she could hear the ringing of voices over the barking of excited dogs almost as soon as they turned toward the entry hall.

At the center of the grand space, Lady Irving and Giles Rutherford were arguing about the puzzle box. Lady Dudley was holding up a biscuit, and several dogs were perched on hind legs, panting for the treat. And Richard Rutherford and Lady Audrina were talking to the visitor.

"Miss Millicent Corning," murmured Lord Dudley in Sophy's ear. As they walked close enough for conversation with the new arrival, she was glad for his arm to clutch.

Millicent Corning stood several inches taller than Sophy, and she appeared a bit younger; perhaps thirty-five years of age. Old enough to take a bold risk with fashion, and young enough that it still looked well on her. Her gown was a lustrous deep red-brown, a watered silk that caught and tilted light, with an elaborately swaddled bodice of filmy gauze over black lace.

Her features were of unexpected lines: a long nose with a gentle swoop in it; a strong cleft in the chin. Deep-set eyes, dark blue under arched black brows. Hair glossy and dark and tidy as a folded-up raven's wing, twisted into an elaborate tiara of a braid into which a few clipped green feathers were tucked. Jeweled droplets hung at her ears, and a stark band of hammered gold draped about her neck, over her collarbone.

She was money and elegance, confidence and excitement. She looked like London and promise and hope, and Sophy had to look away. As Lord Dudley performed the introductions, Sophy studied the worn toes of her kid boots.

"Sophy is an abbreviation of Sophia, correct? So you are the owner of the puzzle box," said Miss Corning. Her voice was low and tremulous, as though a laugh wanted to bubble through its surface. "I believe mine is a twin to yours. Or to be more accurate, ours are both triplets to a third."

Sophy's head snapped up at this—and hers was not the only one. Everyone fell silent, so that the only sound echoing through the entrance hall was the panting of Felix the beagle, the soft crunching of Penny's teeth on a biscuit.

"There are three puzzle boxes?" Richard Rutherford was the first to snap the surprised silence. "What has made you think so, Miss Corning?"

"Because the inside of my puzzle box says it is the second of three."

More silence, into which Miss Corning lifted her brows. "I see this is unexpected news to you, as was my arrival. Dear me—I did send a letter ahead. Did it not arrive?"

"We've had no letters for days," said Lady Dudley. She tipped her head, snowy locks drifting over her shoulder. "But we take in strays when needs must. We've always room for one more at Castle Parr." Their dark eyes limpid, eight dogs followed the movement of their mistress's hand and stared at Millicent Corning, panting.

"You are so kind, my lady." The visitor's smile took in all of them: people, dogs, the cold marble underfoot, the rogue bits of greenery at mantel and doorway. When she looked in Sophy's direction, a tickle bothered Sophy's nose.

Damn. She turned away and sneezed. And sneezed.

"Sophy hates the dogs," Lady Dudley informed everyone. "They make her sneeze."

"I do dot hade theb." When Sophy wrested her cranium back under her control, her face was flaming, her eyes streaming. "Welcobe, Miss Cordig. I should like to see this puzzle box that is a twid of mide."

"In the library, maybe," suggested Lady Audrina. "We should all like to see it. Once Miss Corning has been settled."

"Of course, of course." Lord Dudley tottered toward

the guest and gave her arm a squeeze. "Lovely to have company. I'm sure I don't know what happened to your letter, but we're glad to have you all the same. Are you staying through Christmas?"

Sophy did not catch the visitor's reply as her father-in-law waved the butler nearer. With a few instructions, Miss Corning's belongings, maid, and person were escorted off to the upper reaches of the castle. Lord Dudley followed, making pleasant chatter.

Without the warmth of a surprise to keep them collected in the entry hall, the others scattered. Lady Dudley called her dogs to heel, then led them away. The Rutherfords, Lady Irving, and Lady Audrina fell into a hurried patter of conversation about the puzzle box—something about notes, and progress. As a quartet, they hurried to the drawing room to get the puzzle box.

My puzzle box. Sophy shivered within her snuff-brown cotton gown.

Few possessions mattered to Sophy. Her telescope, for the sake of her mind. Her spectacles, for the sake of her body.

And her golden puzzle box, for the sake of her heart.

As a child of five years, she had not known she was plain or awkward. Sophy's older sister—now living in Ireland with her third husband—was doting, and her sister's friend Lady Beatrix had been everything kind and beautiful in the world. Had Sophy guessed that the puzzle box was sent to her as Lady Beatrix's good-bye, she would not have accepted the gift with such delight.

But it did delight her, then and through the years. As golden as her own hair . . . wasn't. As lightly and gracefully made as her body . . . wasn't. Such judgments of form mattered little to a child, but they mattered a great deal when she grew into a young woman and felt herself awkward, out of step with the polite world in manner and inclination. It was a comfort to remember that once, a beautiful woman had given her a gift for being good enough just as she was.

She had assumed it was a sculpture. Some sort of *objet d'art*. As a mathematics-loving child, she had called it "my parallelepiped," which made her father smile and her mother shake her head in tolerant dismay.

These past few days, she had shared her telescope. Her parallelepiped, which held secrets she'd never suspected. And she had found that it was frightening yet comforting to share one's precious belongings and have others treat them with tender care.

Only her glasses remained to be shared. Perhaps Miss Corning would like to borrow them.

As she plucked her pince-nez from her nose, her cheeks flamed with heat. Another sneeze overtook her, making her ears ring—and then, shaking her head, she returned to the library to await the first news her puzzle box had yielded in thirty-five years.

With everyone gathered in the library, Sophy felt like the hostess of a party. The room was rather cramped for eight people—or maybe it was just that all eight people wanted to stand in exactly the same spot to look at the pair of puzzle boxes, now resting on the tabletop of Sophy's flipped-open secretary desk. Several lamps had been lit against the waning gray afternoon light, casting their glow over the boxes.

"Why, they aren't twins at all." Sophy felt self-conscious as soon as she uttered the words. But where her puzzle box winked and tossed light off its gilded frame, Miss Corning's puzzle box drank it in. The wooden surface was dark and glossy, its patterns darker still, and the whole of it was smooth as resin. A faint floral scent was noticeable if one bent close; it was built of the rosewood Giles Rutherford said his mother favored.

"Not all twins are identical." Miss Corning smiled. Then she took up her own parallelepiped and, with a neat flex and slide of fingers, began to move the invisible joints apart. Bit by bit, the panels worked open: one side, then another, then back to the first in a dizzyingly swift and intricate set of movements.

"She makes it look so easy," said Lady Irving in an extremely loud whisper. "How long have you been fussing with that golden box, young Rutherford?"

"Long enough," said Giles Rutherford, "to grant a *brava* where one is due."

Miss Corning gave a distracted smile. "Oh, I've had quite a lot of time to work this out. I inherited it about three months ago."

And then with one last press, it was done. In one slow, buttery glide, the smooth lid slid free and revealed the interior of the box. Empty.

"It's empty?" Richard Rutherford sounded surprised. "Is there not even a message?"

"There is indeed a message." Miss Corning grinned, a warm expression lit by the lamplight. And flipping over the lid of the puzzle box, she revealed its secret.

For a moment, Sophy's eyes crossed at yet another

pattern. Letters marched in a crowded gaggle over the inside of the lid, incised as though by a nail or blade.

"May I?" The elder Rutherford reached out for the lid.

"Please." Miss Corning handed it over.

Squinting at the tiny letters, Rutherford held the lid at arm's length to catch the best light. It was not much larger than his hand. "'Two of three. Sophia Angela Maria. Salvation from our enemies, and from the hand of all that hate us: To perform mercy to our fathers.'" As he read out the inscription, his voice caught and halted. "It's—like hearing Beatrix's voice again."

"Rubbish. Those aren't your wife's words," said Lady Irving. When silence followed, she snapped, "Are you all heathens? It's from the *Benedictus*."

"The *Benedictus*. From—the Bible?" Rutherford's brow furrowed. "I never knew it to have special significance to Beatrix."

"It's a song of gratitude," Sophy remembered. She had fallen out of the habit of regular churchgoing years ago, after her marriage to Jack, but the rusty memories of a devout youth squeaked free. "From the Gospel of Luke. Gratitude and prophecy and—and redemption." When seven faces turned toward hers, she could not help but stammer.

"All right, set that aside for now," said Giles Rutherford. "What could the rest of the message mean? Miss Corning, have you divined any meaning from it?"

With the lid set in the brightest circle of lamplight, they all looked down at it. Following the brief verse were several rows of gibberish.

ZWKIPXDDDILZDDPUHVDRLRGPHDZKXH
WHQ JQRWQRDWUGYDRHVDOHRORLWVF
WQFUNZXYQYWHUUKWVDKRDLRRDWXG
QURWUDKHZ

"A code of some sort, but a simple alphabet substitution didn't work," said that elegant lady after
the others studied the string of letters. "And so it
occurred to me that I needed to find the other two
puzzle boxes if I was to solve the riddle." Graceful
beringed hands splayed on the glossy wood of the
secretary desk. "I came into a fortune recently, upon
the death of a cousin. This box was among her effects,
and when I got it open—not without a great deal of
effort, I assure you, Mr. Rutherford—I was intrigued
by the message inside." She paused. "You see, my
cousin was called Angela. And in her childhood, she
was given this box by Lady Beatrix Newcombe, just
before that lady left England in hurried secrecy."

Sophy could not help admiring Miss Corning's gift
for the dramatic: that low, throbbing voice waltzing
over the words until they all danced through the story
with her. "My cousin Angela spoke of her sometimes,"
added the storyteller, "when I took this box down
from her shelf of keepsakes. She remembered Lady
Beatrix as a delightful woman, a friend of her older
sister. When the lady gave Angela this box, she said
she was doing so because she knew children had not
yet forgotten what was important, and that she knew
Angela would keep it safe."

"Yes." The syllable drifted from Sophy's lips like a
sigh. "Yes, exactly."

Miss Corning's deep eyes searched Sophy's face. "I

thought it a lovely story. But when I opened the box and saw my cousin's name along with two others, I realized it was far more than an old tale of kindness. It was a mystery."

"An adventure," interjected Richard Rutherford.

"Quite so." Miss Corning's puckish grin returned. "And so, being a woman of independent means and few personal ties, I decided to turn my hand to hunting Sophias and Marias. By searching through ancient family correspondence, I found reference to some of my cousin's friends. And to their families."

"And you found—me?" Sophy's brows knit. Was it always this hot in the library? Or cold; maybe she was cold. Her fingers felt clumsy, her feet ungainly.

"I found three Sophias, and then I hunted up their married names and present locations. I wrote to all of them, but the other two politely assured me they had never received a gift from Lady Beatrix Newcombe. I believe they also doubted my sanity, but *c'est la vie*." Her hands gave a careless flutter. "I was on the scent, so to speak, and if anyone knows how dedicated a hound is once it finds a clue, it should be this household."

Lady Dudley beamed.

"But I never received a letter from you." Sophy tucked her hands—bare of jewelry, even her old wedding band—beneath her folded arms.

"So I have learned." Miss Corning traced a few circles on the surface of the desk. "It was terribly precipitate of me to travel without hearing a reply. But I was eager to set out at once."

"From where do you hail?" Richard Rutherford, calm and kind as ever.

"Some ways east of here, at the northern tip of Lincolnshire. A hamlet called Barrow Haven that no one much has heard of, unless you are fond of brick-making. I lived with my brother's family, but once I came into some money, they thought I ought to hand it over to them. And when I disagreed, they thought I ought not to live there anymore." Spoken calmly, and yet there was something flat and terrible in the tone.

"So you—came here?" Sophy hated the hitch in her voice. Even less than her reeling mind did her throat seem to know what to do with so much new information.

"Well, yes. You see, it *had* to be you. You were the only other Sophia, and so you had to have a puzzle box."

"And if I had not?"

"Then . . ." Miss Corning paused. "Then I would have had to figure out what else to do."

"Well, you don't have to worry about that." Lord Dudley eased himself into Sophy's chair, his raspy voice full of delight. "Our Soph's got the puzzle box, you see, and you're welcome to stay as long as y'like. Good to have a bit of company about the place."

"More than a bit," grumped Lady Dudley. "Where will she stay? She shan't take the dogs' room."

"Of course not, dear," the viscount soothed. "The dogs sleep in the stable, don't you recall? You said yourself we'd plenty of room in the house."

"You've put me in a beautiful guest chamber," Miss Corning said. "I cannot thank you enough. Though I didn't mean to be, I'm a foundling on your doorstep until the weather clears. My coachman cursed me heartily for traveling in this weather, and on a Sunday, but you see—" She pressed her lips together.

"You had nowhere else to go." Lady Audrina spoke

up. The earl's daughter was a bit of a mystery to Sophy: proud and prickly, but with a curious mind—and sometimes, like now, flashes of soft sorrow.

"Nonsense, nonsense." Lord Dudley positively glowed, his white hair like a halo about his beaming face. "You may stop and bide here as long as you like."

Sophy could not recall seeing him so transported since Jack's death, and probably not since quite some time before. A long illness such as Jack's ground away at a family, so death came in tiny stages over endless attenuated time.

"How gratifying," barked Lady Irving. "But we've still got another puzzle box to open. You, Corning girl, do you think you can do that same trick with the golden one? No one here seems to know what to do with it at all."

Giles Rutherford made an incoherent sound.

"Shh," said Lady Audrina. Did she slip a hand within the crook of his arm? No, only a trick of the shadows; darkness split them apart even as Sophy squinted.

"I can but try," said Miss Corning. "If Mrs. Parr will permit?"

"Sophy," she corrected through numb lips. "Please, feel free." A deeper admonition than she intended. A deeper hope for herself.

Miss Corning followed the same set of movements she had used to open her rosewood box; this time Sophy counted forty-five slips and catches of the panels. Panels she had never realized her parallele-piped possessed until a few days ago, and now they were loosening under this stranger's touch as though her very fingertips were keys.

"That's done it, by God." Richard Rutherford

touched the golden lid as Miss Corning began to slide it free. "Sophy, will you open it?"

With fingers cold and heart a thunderstorm, Sophy freed the lid from the puzzle box. A neat little compartment was hidden inside, empty as they expected. Pulling in a deep breath, Sophy turned over the lid.

Again, dizzying letters were scratched in neat rows. Every head leaned inward, blocking the lamplight until they jostled into a better arrangement.

"I'll be damned," muttered Lady Irving. "'One of three. Sophia Angela Maria.'"

"'His mercy is from generation unto generations,'" Sophy read. "More of the *Benedictus*?"

"How should I know? I was fortunate to remember the first bit, you pack of heretics," Lady Irving replied. "Surely there is a Bible in here somewhere. We *are* in a library."

"I'll get one." Relieved to step away from the tight circle of faces, Sophy slipped to one of the familiar shelves. In brown, she would be as invisible as shadow itself. She had fallen into the habit with Jack in the dark days of his illness. What he did not see, he could not speak to. Could not touch.

The library held several Bibles; the first one Sophy laid hands on was an antique quarto in crumbling black leather. She carried it back near the desk, standing in the penumbra outside the lamplight. For a book of moderate size, it was heavy, the paper old and thick.

She handed it to Lady Irving, who rolled her eyes before accepting the book. "Must I be the voice of God? Well, if you insist." The countess flipped open the cover. "A Douay-Rheims Bible. My, my. Harboring Papist tendencies?"

"Harboring old books," said Sophy. "If you will, my lady?"

Lady Irving sniffed, then flipped pages. "Ah," she said after a few minutes of skimming. "The *Magnificat*. Richard, your Lady Beatrix had a fondness for the Nativity story."

Sophy could not imagine why Richard Rutherford looked sheepish. "Ah—so it seems, yes. How interesting." He cleared his throat. "And more of those coded letters?"

More indeed. Seeing a second set made the code seem even more impenetrable:

LLWVUKEGGBPBPKHSBLKBZOHBNHHWR
UDYLQDFHNZHRHQRHKKDKHYBDIJHLHS
RLDLRRRDGQUDRWQHUJIZGRIZGRDHXW
HHHFKRU

"Well, that's that," said Giles. "We shall have to find Maria's puzzle box or there will be no peace until the end of time."

"I believe, son," said Rutherford, "that I am being remarkably peaceful. Although, Miss Corning, I would very much like to know what you learned regarding my late wife's acquaintances named Maria."

"Of course," began Miss Corning, "I should be glad to—"

"Did she know Jack?" Lady Dudley's voice cracked with hope. "Did you ever find a letter with some reference to Jack? What do you know about Jack?"

Sophy shut her eyes.

There was a pause before Miss Corning spoke. "My coachman goes by Jack, and I know that he was annoyed at having to drive out today. But surely that is not whom you meant?"

Sophy hauled her eyes open.

"Lady D, we must be getting you to your room for a rest." The viscount spoke up. He shot Sophy an apprehensive look.

"Her ladyship refers to her son, John. My late husband. We called him Jack." For once this afternoon, her voice was clear.

"Ah." Miss Corning's oddly elegant features went soft. "You all have my condolences. It is difficult to lose a loved one."

"It was a long time ago," Sophy said. Not that that was so much a reply as an explanation. An excuse.

But why, or for what, she could not let herself think.

Chapter Thirteen

Wherein Giles
Does Not Throw His Fork

The subject of the puzzle boxes, the codes, and the identity of the unknown Maria occupied the party at dinner that afternoon until Giles felt he could have thrown his fork at the wall. Just two things prevented him from doing so: First, that there was every chance he would miss the wall and hit one of the enormous glass windows instead.

And second, the roasted widgeon was delicious.

Besides the widgeon, there was a beef tongue in red-currant sauce, potted shrimps, and a variety of vegetables. Broccoli, artichokes, and tender little lettuce leaves. Best not to throw the fork until the cloth was removed.

"Yes," Miss Corning answered Lady Dudley for perhaps the seventy-fifth time. "I wrote to all the Marias I identified through my cousin's correspondence, too. Only two remain from whom I haven't received a reply."

In dressing for dinner, the new arrival had exchanged the small feathers in her headdress for larger plumes. Enjoying having money and being a peacock for the first time; well, Giles couldn't blame her for that. If he found that someone had given his sister Rachel a fortune—and that someone else was trying to take it from her—he'd urge her to spend every penny of it however she wished.

Miss Corning had paused after her explanation; now she looked abashed. "I hope you do not mind, my lord—my lady—but I gave the direction of Castle Parr should either of the Marias wish to reply. I did not mean to presume by doing so, only I knew I should not be returning to my brother's household."

"Quite all right." Lord Dudley smiled. "We send a servant to the village for mail almost every day. Lady D, I haven't seen any odd letters arrive for a few days, have you?"

"Thank you, my lord. You are very good." Miss Corning's voice wavered a bit.

She must have traveled with everything she owned. No wonder she was so relieved the Dudleys were willing to take her in. But that seemed to be their way. It was a wonder they were so rarely visited; maybe their hospitality wasn't known. Giles had met a number of worthless hangers-on in London who would shoulder their way into any aristocratic household with which they had the slimmest of family connections.

"And you, young Rutherford." Lady Irving's black-smith hammer of a voice clanged at Giles's ears. "What are you going to do with yourself now?"

Giles stared at her. His stomach gave an uncomfortable twist.

Lady Irving waved her knife. "Now that Miss Corning has opened the puzzle box, of course. You've got nothing more to work on while you bill and coo."

"Oh, that." His stomach untwisted. "You're right, I need some new occupation. Maybe I could decorate a few of the statue heads in the antique passage." He snapped his fingers. "Wait a moment; I can't. Because *you* did that already while *you* billed and cooed."

"Son, really," said Richard mildly. "No need for such rough talk. You must feel free to decorate those statue heads all you like. The effect is pleasingly festive."

"Indeed!" Lord Dudley wheezed. "Exactly the sort of thing m'lady and I like."

It did not pass Giles's notice that his father had not protested the bit about billing and cooing. With a shudder, he drained his glass of wine.

No puzzle box. No jewels. Nothing but another mystery, and home seemed farther away than ever.

Much as he hated to admit it, Lady Irving asked a fair question. What was he going to do with himself now?

After dinner, the cloth was removed for syllabub and candied oranges and ginger. When the rest of the party seemed inclined to head into the drawing room for more tinkering with the puzzle boxes, Giles caught his father's arm and held him back.

"Father. Wait. I need to ask you something."

Richard looked delighted. "Of course!" Over Giles's shoulder, he waved on the others. "Go ahead, Estella. I shall meet you in a few minutes. Mind you don't start gambling without me." He chuckled. "Funny woman. She pretends to be so irritable, but you know, I think she's not nearly so bad as she wants everyone to believe."

"I wouldn't want to contradict a lady." Giles pulled out chairs for himself and Richard, waving off the servants who had come in to clear the table. "If she wants me to think she's terrible, I'm happy to do so."

"Oh, son." Richard chuckled again. Picking up a bit of candied ginger from its porcelain dish, he pointed it at Giles. "What's on your mind?"

Giles picked up a piece of ginger, too, rolling the sugar crystals between his fingertips. "It's our time in England."

"Yes?" Richard popped the ginger into his mouth. "My, that's tasty. Warms you right up, doesn't it?"

Ignoring this aside, Giles said, "We've got two puzzle boxes and no real information. What if we never find anything else? Without the lost diamonds, how will you set up a new shop in London?" He took a deep breath. "How will you care for the family? They need you, Father. They need you more than you need this . . . adventure." The word was so sour in his mouth that he crunched at the ginger root, sweet and fiery and sharp enough to make him squint.

Richard made a tidy stack of the candied orange peel, crossing one slice over another. "Are you certain of that? They're grown, Giles. You might be the eldest living, but you should not still think of them as children. Now, don't protest—you do think so."

"I do not." Giles bit his bottom lip, hard. He knew they were no longer children; they were scattering off to begin their own lives. Even his bosom companion, Rachel, had left the family home to live with an aunt. "That doesn't mean they don't still need a father's guidance."

"You asked me to wait to return to England—my wife's final request—until Sarah was engaged to be married, and I did. Now they're all building their own lives, Giles. All of them except you, and if you had your way, me. But don't we all deserve better than a dreamless life?"

"We support one another," Giles ground out.

"Support or shackle?" The smile disappeared from Richard's features, the smile that customers at his paper mill and shop liked because it made them feel that Richard cared about them and not only how much paper they ordered. Without the smile, he looked far older. Worn and tired. "Son, I love you, but you mustn't think I don't know why you're here. You didn't want to see the land of your mother's birth; you didn't want to meet relatives and old friends. You wanted to keep watch over me and make sure I didn't do anything reckless."

"I—"

"Don't worry yourself; I'm not angry in the slightest. You might grumble and grouch, but you do it out of love. And I wanted you to come along. Because whether you intended to or not, now you *have* seen your mother's birthplace, and you've met some of her friends. And now you know where I intend to live. Giles, I never wanted to work with paper. I always meant to be a jeweler. That's why I wanted you to do it so much—so you would know that it was possible."

He sighed, and the smile flickered back for a gray moment. "You want a father's guidance? Here it is. Go home, Giles. Go home whenever you're ready." Another chuckle. "Maybe we can work together. Your designs and my execution, what do you say? We could be the first trans-Atlantic jewelry firm the world has seen."

There it was, like a wall. A smiling, oblivious stone

wall with a mouth full of candied orange peel. For Richard to pursue his dream, Giles had to return. To be his proxy in America. "I don't want to work with jewelry, Father."

With an effort, Richard swallowed the tough citrus. "You may think so now, but you'll say something quite different after a few years working with paper."

"But I do want to work with paper," Giles murmured. Not for its own sake, but because it could hold folded dreams: the furled plans for a home or a warehouse or a shop or a church. Anything. Paper could hold the design of a future hope. Paper was a springboard.

Paper could become a spring. He smiled, thinking of Audrina's absent hand gestures that turned flatness into a toy. Thinking of Audrina's drawing of Castle Parr, which was nearly, tantalizingly close to what he wanted to do.

"You want to run the mill?" Richard's brows furrowed; dark brows so unlike Giles's features. "I'd be glad for your brothers to have the guidance, but I've never heard you say so before."

"You didn't hear me say so now, either." Not for the first time since arriving in England, he felt he was speaking a different language from the people around him. This was the first time he'd had that impression with his father, though.

He didn't want to pursue this stone wall of a conversation anymore. Richard was sure everything would work out, because . . . well, for no good reason. Just because he wanted it to. Because that was the sort of person he was: He could cross an ocean for an apprenticeship, then cross back with a marquess's daughter. Then cross it again for an *adventure*.

Really, Richard was right. Everything did seem to

work out well for him. Maybe because someone else was around to tie up the loose ends he left behind.

"What would you have done if I hadn't been here to open the puzzle box?" Giles tried to match his father's calm.

"But you didn't open it." With a smile, Richard topped his citrus tower with a curl of candied ginger. "Miss Corning opened it. And she'd have done that whether you were here or not."

"Assuming you were here at Castle Parr."

"Why wouldn't I have been? I'd have met up with Lord Alleyneham eventually, and he and Lady Irving would have directed me here."

"Not necessarily. Remember, Lord Alleyneham's family is unraveling on a precise schedule."

"They needn't be." And with a shrug, he indicated that he was done with the topic. *Simple as that. If they don't want to be torn apart, they needn't be.* Maybe he was right, but it was still infuriating. More so because Giles felt the same way about their own family.

"If you loved it so much in England, why did you ever leave?" Giles hardly expected an answer. It was one of those questions asked out of annoyance, the main purpose of which was to let the other person know how unfathomable their actions were.

Of course, Richard answered at once. "When it came time for a family, my best prospects were in America. I couldn't support a marquess's daughter in England."

"Why not finish your apprenticeship first? Why the urgency to start a family?"

Richard raised an eyebrow.

"Oh, good God," Giles groaned. "Are you serious?"

Richard raised his other eyebrow.

"The puzzle boxes with the bits about the Nativity— the elopement—Mother was with child?"

Richard tipped his head. "It happens to the best of us."

"Not if you don't—ack. Never mind. I don't want to hear any more about that."

Giles knew that two older siblings had been lost: a sister and a brother, not much more than babies when illness took them. He shouldn't have been the oldest child at all.

But he had never known before that his mother left everything she knew, including her own parents and the native land that valued her blue blood, for the sake of her child. A child who would never be accepted by the *ton* that had birthed her, because of its father.

Giles had thought her adventurous—and yes, she had been. But she'd been more than that. She'd been brave.

For the thousandth, millionth, infinitely numbered time, he looked at his hands. So much of him was a legacy from Lady Beatrix.

And she had left one last legacy in the form of these puzzle boxes. A mystery, an impossible adventure. Richard loved that nonsense. Maybe that was part of why Lady Beatrix had done it: She'd known that nothing would capture her beloved's imagination like a mystery.

But the answer slipped away like air. Always, there was another gasping step, and another. Giles was damned tired. His dreams were in pieces, scattered about Philadelphia and New York.

And York, too?

No, no. Nothing tied him here except a thread of

fascination with an aristocrat's daughter. Quite a family tradition the Rutherford men had.

An ancient dream was better than nothing, and he couldn't take that from his father. He couldn't break that spirit of adventure. In a way, it had given Giles life.

"I'm sorry, Father. I'll help you wrap this up. For Mother."

Then Richard could do what he liked. Giles's place was clear—and it was half a world away, picking up the pieces others had left behind.

After Giles left him behind in the dining room, Richard toyed a bit more with the candied citrus peel. He knew he ought to let the servants get on with their work. The rest of the party had long since found their way to the drawing room—and judging from the jingling heard through the open doors, at least one of the dogs was in there, too.

Good, good. Lord and Lady Dudley seemed to enjoy having company about, whether human or canine. But Richard wasn't quite ready to be a part of it. My God! The span of one day had brought him the solution to one puzzle box, then had introduced and solved another he had not known existed. Then introduced a third.

After three years' wait, this was the end of his quest—or the beginning of the end, at least.

Richard rather liked thinking of this time in England as a quest.

On a quest, he had traveled to England thirty-five years before, to apprentice to the watchmakers and smiths who created art in precious metals for Rundell and Bridge. His nation's independence was new and rough, and there were some things the English did better.

Ignorance was bliss, in some cases. In Richard's case, it had been. Because when he dared look at the marquess's daughter who called at the shop, she had looked right back at him. Her frank blue eyes, her freckled sunniness, her free laughter were irresistible to a young jeweler's apprentice who had no right to raise his eyes so high.

When Beatrix had agreed to marry him thirty-five years before, she had left behind the glittering court of King George; her sisters, brothers, parents, dowry. She and Richard had taken one another with nothing but health and hope and humor, making their way across an ocean. There he had assumed control of his family's paper mill in Philadelphia; they had built a comfortable fortune, had raised children and lost children, too.

Beatrix had still been young when the pains began; sharp in her hands at first, and only in the mornings. But then they spread to more of her joints, to more of the day, until she never had a moment in which her body didn't feel wracked and torn.

Though her health slipped away, she had never lost that wry edge. At the end, she had even laughed at death. "My love for you is not such a paltry thing that it can be dissolved," she whispered. Though their six surviving children surrounded her, Giles alone ducked close enough to hear along with Richard. "I could not bring a fortune to the New World, so I left it behind. Perhaps enough time has passed that you can reclaim it. My puzzle box . . ."

Giles had found the item to which he believed she referred: a neat creation of wood that he and his younger brother Alfred had fitted together with bated breath and careful hands. Puzzle boxes had been a tradition with her family, Beatrix had told them, ever since her Dutch ancestor had traded with Japan and brought back treasures never before seen.

"No," she'd breathed. "In England. You must find it in England."

Giles had thought it madness. A fool's quest to cross an ocean. But what was foolish about believing in Beatrix's last words? At that moment, she'd told them the most important thing on her mind: She had wanted to see to it they didn't lack for anything.

The loss of Beatrix had faded over the past three years, a wound knit and scarred over. A happy marriage left a permanent mark on a man. Richard was glad Giles had come with him, no matter the reason. Being apart from all of his children at once, he would miss them as though part of his world had gone silent.

Richard was determined to see Beatrix's wish granted, to give their children a fortune beyond paper-mill dreams. Paper was as nothing, flat and dull, compared to the luster of the unknown. A mystery. A puzzle. An adventure!

One diamond parure wasn't enough to change all their lives—but it was enough to begin with.

And he and Giles were two-thirds of the way to finding it.

A smile slipped over his features, comfortable as being wrapped in a blanket before a fire, and he rose to join the others in the drawing room.

Chapter Fourteen

Wherein Sheep's Guts Hail Souls Out of Men's Bodies

For the next four days, Audrina had nothing to do but wait.

Oh, she actually had much more to do than wait. Now that the puzzle boxes had been opened, there were also codes to play about with. Audrina wrote the letters on slips of paper, and she and Giles arranged and rearranged them atop their familiar table in the drawing room. There were far too many Q's to make any sense of the message, which they both realized almost at once, but it was pleasant to sit together, to talk and not kiss and to talk about not kissing.

She also had many things to try not to think of, such as whether Llewellyn was threatening her father or her sister, or whether Walpole might have called off the wedding entirely. She knew nothing, nothing at all, of what was passing in London.

It was an agony and a relief at once—and with relief came guilt. The feelings warred, with relief being defeated day by day as the wedding grew closer. Four days before Christmas, and Audrina's every emotion was heightened.

Lady Irving wandered into the drawing room, intercepting Lord Alleyneham's footman as she did. "Ah, Jory. Is that the post you've got there? Glad to see the mail's getting through again. I know we're at the end of the earth here, but the Royal Mail shouldn't be stopped by a little thing like that."

After handing over his fistful of letters, Jory straightened his wig. "Yes, my lady. Right you are."

Lady Irving meandered over to Giles and Audrina, who had just spelled D-O-G with her letter slips in a vain attempt to feel some sense of progress.

"How sweet, Rutherford. Are you teaching each other to read?" Lady Irving flipped through the letters with narrowed eyes.

"*Au contraire*, my lady. We've put together this little primer for you. Since it seems you can't read 'Lord Dudley' on a letter that's clearly not for you." Giles's smile was a predatory affair of bared teeth.

Audrina had to smile at what was an undeniably amusing—if rude—reply, her feet fidgeting in their slippers at his quick defense of her. She could like him far, far too much.

Or was this kindness at all? Did he see her, again or still, as weak? How could one tell? She had few examples on which to base a guess.

"Aha!" Ignoring Giles's response, Lady Irving pulled free one sealed paper and dropped the rest of the post on the floor. "This one's for Miss Corning. How about that, Rutherford? News at last."

She shoved the paper in Giles's face. A twitch in his jaw was the only sign that he did not enjoy this experience. "Yes. I see that clearly. Thank you. Shall we notify her?"

"If I don't find her in three minutes, I will open this letter myself." And in a cloud of scarlet and blue, she whirled and left them.

"A letter for Miss Corning." Audrina met Giles's eyes. Her heart picked up its pace; somehow, she had become invested in this hunt she had joined only as a happenstance. "Shall we go see it read?"

"We certainly cannot let my father and Lady Irving read exciting news without our steadying presence." He held out a hand. "Princess."

This was only a game, which made it safe. And therefore it was safe for her to lace her fingers in his as they followed Lady Irving from the room.

After scooping up the fallen post for Lord Dudley, of course.

They found Miss Corning in the library, where she was paging through a novel. Sophy was, as usual, jotting something at her secretary desk. Both women regarded the arrival of the letter as unexpected, though as Miss Corning noted, "A York postmark. This one had not far to go."

She slit the seal and skimmed the lines in a few seconds. Then, with a trembling smile, she extended the letter to Sophy. "We've found our Maria—or actually, her daughter."

It took seventy-five years, or so it felt, before the letter made its way from Sophy to Lady Irving and Richard Rutherford, through the Dudleys, and finally to Audrina and Giles.

The note was brief, dashed off in a hasty clotted

hand with many abbreviations. The paper was so cheap and thin as to be brittle.

Dear Miss Corning,

My mother passed on last yr, but I blv she was the Maria you seek. I inherited a sandalwd box frm her. Shd you wish to buy it, I will be at the Goat & Gauntlet on Dec. 23. As you are in Yorkshire, I hope this will be conv.

Yrs & c.
Mrs. Dan'l B—— (Kitty)

The last name was an illegible thread.

"'Should you wish to buy it?'" Richard Rutherford said. "Of course I'd like to buy it, but how could she sell such a treasure?"

"Is that what caught your attention?" Giles folded up the paper. "I'm more startled by her reference to the Goat and Gauntlet. It's not as though I've had fantasies about returning there. Is it the *only* inn in all of York?"

"No, but it is the northernmost one. Perhaps she wanted to pick a place convenient for us."

"But—the twenty-third?" Lord Dudley shuffled to a chair near the library fireplace; Sophy hopped up to ease him into the seat. "No, you had much better tell her to wait a few more days. The box has waited all these years. Could it not wait until after Christmas?" His voice was plaintive; his heavily veined hands gripped the arms of his chair tightly.

The Rutherfords looked at one another: father and son, so different in appearance, but with identical expressions on their faces. *I hadn't thought—well, maybe—if it's all right with you* . . .

"No, my lord." Audrina spoke into the fraught pause. "I am sorry, but it cannot wait even a single day more."

She said this not for their sake, but her own. Each day that fluttered by left her more distant from Charissa, her chance of returning to London more impossible. From a post-house, she could make her way back to London somehow: either with the Rutherfords, or Lady Irving, or even a hired maid.

Sophy was the first to reply. Her pince-nez hid her eyes, but her mouth was an understanding curve. "Well, then, we shall have to celebrate while you are all still here."

The contrast between Audrina's most recent London ball and her last evening at Castle Parr was so extreme that they seemed almost on different planets. This was Saturn, maybe; soft and beringed as she had seen through Sophy's telescope.

Her favorite part of a ball was mixing, dancing, laughing, making it seem as though she was everything proper and delighted—and then slipping away for her own secret purpose. Once upon a time, with Llewellyn. More recently, she had fallen into the habit of leaving alone, just to see if anyone would notice and come looking for her.

No one ever passed this test.

Tonight, she felt no urge to slip away. She sank into the moment, this warm evening gathering in the drawing room where she had spent so much time. It stabbed at her with pain and spice and sweetness, knowing that it would soon end. That she needed it to end. And yet while it lasted, it was good.

Giles had said pleasure that ended in loss was not worth the having, but he was wrong. If that was the only sort of pleasure one could have, it was worth whatever price must be paid.

A day had passed since the arrival of Mrs. B's letter, as they had taken to calling it. In the morning, the Rutherfords, Lady Irving, and Audrina would follow the road south that had led them north so recently. Miss Corning, invited to accompany them, declined with a sideways smile at the trio of Sophy and Lord and Lady Dudley.

"I have been invited to stop here for a while," she said. "And I am glad to do so. Now that the hunt is in your hands, I feel much more reasonable about the matter. I shall never get over the embarrassment of arriving here unexpectedly, though everyone was so kind."

With Sophy taking notes on the movements required, she opened a puzzle box. "Good to have a record," said Lady Irving. "You seem to be the only one who knows how to work these things."

Giles rolled his eyes, but made no reply as he finished copying out the writings inside the gold and rosewood boxes. "If we find the third, we shall send word at once."

"I would miss you all very much," quavered Lord Dudley from his seat near the hearth, "save for the fact that you're still on the same adventure." Giles made a choking sound, which the viscount seemed not to hear. "And so it's not really like you're going, is it?"

"Not at all, my lord," said Audrina. "We shall think of

you with great fondness." How different his eagerness was from her own father's impatience. But perhaps if Lord Alleyneham spent years in York with little or no company, he would manage a smile or two at the sight of a new face.

"Who will play this game with me?" Lady Dudley held forth a chessboard.

"Chess?" Lady Irving lifted her brows. "Not I. Can't wager on it."

"You could," said Rutherford, "but it would take a great deal of time to finish one wager. Unless—you could wager on which piece was to be taken next. Or the first to take some number of the opponent's pieces!"

Lady Irving looked approving. "That's not bad at all, Richard. Are you sure you aren't a member of White's? You have a more devious mind than I gave you credit for."

"No, *I* will play chess. No one else can play." Lady Dudley clutched the chessboard close, her expression confused.

"Now, Lady D, I'll be glad to play chess with you." Her husband's voice was gentle. "You just pick out the pieces you'd like to use."

The viscountess took from her pocket several crumbled biscuits. Once the viscount had set out the chessboard on a loo table, she set a crumb on each of the sixty-four squares.

"Very good, Lady D. You make the first move."

She handed a bit of biscuit to her husband. "Shall we ring for tea?"

Lord Dudley's shoulders sagged; his back seemed to stoop. Such loneliness as Audrina had never seen, made all the more palpable by being in the middle of a bright group. In his twilight years, his wife was slipping away, and the best way to keep her comfortable—her pack of devoted hounds—drove his daughter-in-law into stuffy-headed isolation.

A wild urge seized Audrina, to offer, *I'll stay; I will stay with you all.* But a life lived entirely for someone else was no lingering solution.

She did what she could for the moment. "Please allow me to ring for it, Lady Dudley," she said. "And if you'll permit it, I would be glad to pour out."

When the tea tray arrived, Audrina arranged cups according to each person's preference. It was a familiar ritual, with a sleek economy of movement and manners that soothed even before the first sip of tea was tasted.

Audrina extended a cup of tea to Richard Rutherford. He was gazing into the fire, and it took him a moment to blink back to the present.

"Thank you, my lady." His smile was as warm as the tea she had just poured out for him. Much more polite than his son, who had scrutinized the tray for a long minute before declaring he would prefer coffee, after all.

The fact that he'd done so with a wink made no difference.

In some little-used chamber of the house, Sophy had located a guitar, and Miss Corning seated herself near the tea things and began tuning the old strings one tentative twist at a time.

Her modishness surpassed even Audrina's, who wore whatever Lady Irving's maid had deemed acceptable for—as she presumed—a wild young lass trying to run off to Scotland. This included punishingly thin muslins and plain cottons, along with a few velvets for much-welcome warmth. Miss Corning was garbed in a dull-gold bodice trimmed in shocking white ermine, over a round gown patterned in lustrous browns and reds. Pearls clutched her neck and ears, and as she plucked at the strings of the guitar, bringing it into tune, she could have stepped into or out of any London ballroom.

"There, I think we'll be able to make a song of it now." Her thumb brushed each string in turn, setting them to humming. "What shall we sing first? 'Coventry Carol,' or 'The First Nowell'? Or 'Here We Come A-Wassailing,' while we're all full of hot beverages."

Lady Irving turned to Rutherford, all false innocence. "Do you know those songs in the heathen reaches of the world, Richard?"

"I can't answer for the heathen reaches of the world, but we know them quite well in Philadelphia."

And so one after another, they sang the old carols. Their voices lifted, more well-meaning than musical. Lord Dudley's voice was a rasp, and Lady Irving merely spoke the words. The Rutherfords both had pleasant warm baritones, though, and Audrina had a serviceable alto. Miss Corning and Sophy had the only truly good voices: Miss Corning, a contralto, and Sophy's a dark soprano that threaded harmonies about the others.

It felt like home, like family of a sort that Audrina had never had. To take a moment to pluck at vibrant gut strings, to sing together a fond wish: *love and joy come to you . . .*

Had anyone ever bothered to wish that for her before? Had she paused to wish that for anyone, even herself?

When her gaze wandered to Giles, his hair gleaming

like a new penny in the candlelit room, her heart gave a heavy thump.

She hadn't left all her chaos behind in London after all. There was a fair bit within her soul, and every time she looked at that wry, rough-hewn face, the chaos gave a tumble and a heave, longing to reach out.

Lady Dudley bobbed her head to the music, enjoying its lilt with sleepy-lidded eyes. When the final strum of the guitar vibrated into silence, she opened them wide. "Lovely." The word sounded odd on her lips, as though she hadn't pronounced it for some time and wasn't sure if she had said it correctly. "That was—lovely."

Rutherford beamed. "I do believe this is the first time we've all been in harmony with one another."

Lady Irving folded her arms. "I hate puns."

Giles lifted his brows. "Ah, the moment has passed."

Audrina caught Lady Irving's gaze. The countess's mouth was pinched and tight, as though she wanted to smile but regarded the expression as beneath her dignity.

No, the moment had not passed. The moment was just beginning.

"Your mother-in-law is not well." The voice startled Sophy out of her drawing of Ganymede, the scarred gray moon of Jupiter. She had not heard anyone enter the library; she had thought the household gone to bed hours ago after their festive song.

Sophy set aside the paper and squinted up at Miss Corning. "Her body is strong." Excuses, excuses. The refuge of the cowardly.

Lady Dudley had faded slowly for years, so slowly it seemed like nothing but ordinary forgetfulness when she asked the same question twice in a day. Then it became twice an hour; over and over, lost in her own mind. And Sophy studied the stars through her telescope to forget the wounded woman right outside her door.

She had always used science to forget the world.

Removing her pince-nez, she struggled to her feet. Somehow a shawl had got wrapped around her ankles.

"I'm sorry to bother you, Mrs.—Sophy," said the taller woman, a pale column of silk and grace, all blurry about the edges. "It is none of my affair, and I see that you were working on something. I have interrupted you."

"Don't give it another thought. The world doesn't lack for drawings of Ganymede."

A pause. "The youth from mythology?"

"No, the Galilean moon of Jupiter." As though she would be drawing that scandalous tale, the youth abducted by Zeus because of his beauty. Zeus took what he wanted, male or female.

Sophy's cheeks went hot. "I'm fond of astronomy. I have a telescope." She gestured vaguely, as though Miss Corning could possibly have overlooked the gleaming brass tube by the library window. "Winter is the best time for looking at the sky because the nights are long and so often clear."

Though any time was good for turning the scope away from the earth. She had never found answers here—though Jack had offered one, for a while.

"It is a beautiful instrument," said Miss Corning, trailing across the room to look at the telescope more closely. *Millicent. Strong and brave*, the name meant. Sophy's own name meant *wisdom*. Ha. "My brother owns one that is not nearly so fine." Moonlight caught her plumes, granting her a feathery halo. "Please, you must call me Millicent after giving me the favor of your own Christian name."

"I do not prefer to be called by my husband's surname," Sophy said. "But thank you. I should be glad to call you Millicent."

Millicent inclined her head. "Truly, I am sorry for your loss."

"There is no need." The polite demur again tripped easily to her lips. "It was long ago."

Long ago, yet she could never forget it.

Jack Parr had seemed the answer to Sophy's prayer—*please, please, Lord, let me fit in; let me be like the other young ladies.* The ladies in graceful silks and sweet floral perfumes, ladies of soft curves and bell-like laughter. Beautiful faces, beautiful in form; so beautiful that Sophy's mouth felt dry when she was flung into their company.

Jack found her standing thus at the side of a ballroom and twirled her into a dance. It was impossible not to smile at him.

No more than a week later, he told her of his plan. Were they to marry, they need never be pursued again, or pursue someone for whom their heart was not inclined. They could conduct affairs in private—though such affairs were, of necessity, very private indeed.

Sophy was slow to realize the import of his hints: Theirs would be a *mariage blanc*, never to be consummated. Instead of a true marriage, it would be a shield against gossip. An alliance. He had recognized in

Sophy a heart that, like his, beat out of time with the rest of society.

He was the first to do so. Even Sophy had hardly put a name to the impossible longings of her nature. There was such a fine line between *wanting to be like* and *wanting to be with*.

"Yes," she had agreed as soon as his intention became clear. "Yes, I will marry you."

And so had begun several lovely years of friendship away from the peering eyes of London. At Castle Parr, Jack was blithe and reckless, but so happy in his daredevil tendencies that it was impossible to worry. He was indestructible. He could make anyone laugh, anytime. Even Sophy.

Sophy was not in the habit of laughter, and she had fallen out of it again after his injury.

What a relief it had seemed when, after being thrown during a match race on unbroken colts, Jack returned home uninjured. He had struck his head and lost consciousness for a few minutes, but soon was standing and laughing with friends.

Not for long, though. Within a day, an apoplectic seizure shook him. Then another a week later, and then they came more and more frequently. Each one took a little more of Jack away, leaving a dark and bitter stranger. A violent man whom she knew not at all and to whom she would never have given a single dance, much less her hand in marriage and her deepest secret.

Lady Dudley took in the first two dogs at about this time. Sophy bought a telescope. It came to be a comfort spending the long nights not alone, but with the bright lights of planets, of dying stars like Aldebaran and of the twins, Castor and Pollux, who made sure the other always had company.

For brief moments, Jack returned—her dear, sunlit friend. But she could almost hear thunder in the distance. His departure was always sudden and swift, a lightning bolt. Often she was struck.

She forgave him readily, for he didn't know what he was doing. Until one day he taunted her: *Unnatural. Unwomanly. Not fit to be any man's wife.*

That was when she knew he was truly gone. Their alliance was ended, and she was alone.

"What I am, you are, too," she had told him. In the resulting rage, Jack broke her arm. When he was restrained, he thrashed so hard that he broke his own.

His parents could no longer deny that their son was beyond control. He never returned to Castle Parr, though a few years later he made one final trip to the churchyard. There, he seemed to have found peace.

But that had been almost a decade ago. So many years. Sophy's arm had knit well, and there was no physical sign of how he had hurt her.

"It was a long time ago," she said again, forcing herself to look up into Millicent's perceptive blue eyes.

"I see." Millicent tipped her face up, moonlight limning her features. "It's nearing Christmas; have you found a new star in the heavens?"

"I've found many that are new to me." Sophy resettled her pince-nez on her face. "But what good is that? I don't think any of them are new to the world. Everything has been charted."

"Maybe it just means that salvation can come from any number of sources. I never expected mine to come from strangers after my letter went astray." Millicent touched the scope's tube, tentatively, as though the cold brass startled her. "Do you like searching the stars for their own sake? As long as what you find is new to you, then it's as new as though it was never seen before in the world."

"The search is all I have," said Sophy.

"It's all I thought I had, too, until I arrived at Castle Parr."

Sophy had to laugh. "Nonsense, Miss Corning. With a fortune and independence—"

"Ah, but those came at the cost of all the family I had left in the world." Millicent's smile was brittle. "It is sobering to know one's exact value. I confess, I'd rather hoped to be thought priceless."

"I am sure that you are." Sophy bit her lip.

Millicent hesitated before she spoke again. "While I am staying here, would you mind if I came into the library some nights? If you care for music, I could bring the guitar."

Love and joy come to you . . .

The promise and pain of Jack had been a long time ago. A long, long time ago.

"Thank you," said Sophy. "I should like that very much."

Chapter Fifteen

Wherein the Clues Are Trebled

The usual tangle of half-packed bags, forgotten items, and prolonged good-byes delayed the travelers the following morning, and it was almost noon before they finally set off in Lady Irving's carriage. Lizzie and Jory, the servants, preceded in the Rutherfords' hired carriage with the array of trunks.

Audrina was not prepared for the damage a week of difficult weather could wreak on Yorkshire roads. Absent was the macadam of London, the punctilious care to smooth any path on which wealthy feet might walk. The drive back to the Goat and Gauntlet took hours longer than the drive away from it, on roads of such rutted misery that Richard Rutherford was not the only one fearful of disgracing himself with illness. All the while, the sky seemed to spit and cry with frustration, alternating between drizzle and a heavy rain that dropped like marbles.

The days were at their shortest, and before they

caught sight of the yellow-gray building blocks of the York walls, early twilight had blanketed the world and the moon had risen. *Waning gibbous*, Sophy would say of the moon.

The thought of Sophy and her telescope, offering a look at unimaginable places beyond, brought a watery smile to Audrina's face. *Gibbous* again, as though no time had passed since she had looked through the telescope and imagined a world that wasn't worth more, but was . . . different.

So different, she hardly knew its form. And the only person who might help her trace it was someone she could not have. Someone who would leave and go back to his dutiful *shoulds* until his life wound down.

At last, the post-house they had been so eager to leave beckoned them back, the lit windows on the ground floor winking at them like an old friend. A chill wind swung the Goat and Gauntlet's sign until it was a blur, but there was no mistaking the building that had last swum into Audrina's awareness through a laudanum spell. When the travelers piled out, the innkeeper and his wife welcomed them with some relief.

"Pleasu' to have you all stay." Their host, who introduced himself as Joseph Booth, took wet wraps with an anxious look out of the window. The public room into which they had trooped was almost empty.

Bathsheba Booth performed a neat curtsy. "Everyone's trying to get home ahea' of the weather. A powerful snowstorm's comin' in tonigh', so says the mister's knee. And his knee weren't never wrong abou' snow an' such. Better than a almanac, so 'tis."

The couple matched as well as any set of chess pieces: both barrel-shaped and simply clad, with strong limbs shaped by constant work. Her graying hair was tucked under a mobcap; his was cropped short about a balding crown.

"We shall require the use of your private parlor," said Rutherford. "And a simple meal, with—"

"Is anyone awaiting us?" Lady Irving broke in.

"We are to meet a Mrs. Daniel . . ." Audrina trailed off, not knowing the surname for which to ask.

"A Mrs. Daniels? No one by that name, m' leddy." Bathsheba Booth tipped her another curtsy. "No one waitin' a'tall, to tell ye true. If soomeone coomes for ye, I'll shoo her righ' up."

Audrina blinked her way through the bouncing Yorkshire accent. "Thank you, ma'am. That will be very good."

When the quartet entered the inn's private parlor, Audrina recognized its simple form from endless days ago. Just being in the room reminded her of being afraid, tired, fuzzy-headed, helpless.

A fool.

She lifted her chin. There was nothing so frightening about a room, after all. It was not as though it contained corpses and ghosts. It was a low-ceilinged space with a gently uneven wooden floor, a mullioned window, and a large table. A cloth of gratifying cleanliness had been laid over the table, and Mrs. Booth—eager to give her wealthy guests every courtesy—promised to send up tea *and* coffee, along with what she vowed was a *loovely* shepherd's pie.

Once the travelers were braced with hot beverages and hearty food, a variety of reactions began to leak forth.

"Damned wild goose chase." Lady Irving poured something from a flask—*where* had she hidden a flask?—into her tea. "Jaunting off to a post-house on the say-so of someone whose name we don't even know."

"I didn't note you making this complaint earlier," said Giles. "My lady."

Her ladyship sniffed. "Because we were all far too busy trying to keep our innards under control."

"Vulgar," said Giles. One of the countess's favorite words—when applied to others, that was. Audrina could not help but smile, and after a moment, Lady Irving nodded her approval.

"Can you build up the fire a bit, son?" Richard rubbed his hands together. "This chill cuts right through the walls, doesn't it?"

Giles poked up the fire, but to little effect. "It's because the window lets in a draft. I noticed and cursed it the last time we were here."

Audrina marched to the window. "Is that all you did? I can do more than curse it." She struck the warped sash with the flat of her hand. When this resulted in nothing but a stinging palm, she allowed herself one glare at the window, and then considered its size.

"Hmm." She unknotted the fabric fillet that laced through her hair. A long, thin rectangle, it was the perfect size and shape for pressing into the gap about the frame. "There, problem solved. Once your hands and feet warm, you may thank me."

"I'll thank you now," said Giles. "I can only hope that if I'd had a pretty cloth sort of thing in my hair, I'd have thought of stuffing it into the window."

Did he linger over the word *pretty*? Did he trace the tumble of her hair with his eyes? Audrina touched the tangled curls, feeling somewhat undressed with her hair down.

Fortunately, a distraction arrived in the form of a knock at the parlor door. When the person was bade enter, a bedraggled woman opened the door. With a sigh of pleasure, she stepped inside. "Ooh, this is nice and warm."

When she closed the door behind her and turned to face them, she revealed herself to be much younger than Audrina had expected, perhaps twenty years of age. Her belly showed noticeably pregnant beneath her too-thin cloak. This visitor had got a soaking outdoors, but her exhaustion seemed to run deeper than one tiring walk. Her skin was pasty and translucent, and the shadows under her eyes were purple-dark.

"You've brought the puzzle box?" When the young woman nodded at Lady Irving, the countess said, "What's your name, girl?"

"Kitty. Kitty Balthasar." She shook her head. "Mrs. Balthasar." Tilted it. "Mrs. Daniel?"

"Too many names for one person," Lady Irving replied. "Though I suppose you're collecting names for two now. Even so, pick something and stick to it, girl. Not Kitty. It's better suited to a pet than a human."

The wan face took on a bit of color. "I can't help what my father named me." Her crisp accent belied her coarse and simple clothing. "If you have a dislike of my name, you'd best talk to him."

"I'm old and I'm rich and I'm bored, so don't think I wouldn't consider it. But"—Lady Irving gestured toward the window—"the weather is terrible, and the innkeeper says snow is coming. I'm not going to hunt anyone down in that mess."

"Oh!" Kitty's thin hands crept to cover her mouth. "Oh, Daniel—I didn't tell him I was coming here. I wanted to surprise him with the money, if I could get some."

"He'll be surprised, all right, to find his wife gone when he gets home from the day's labor," Lady Irving said drily.

Audrina stood and took the younger woman's arm. "Do come sit, Mrs. Balthasar, and have something hot to eat and drink." Kitty's dark-haired fragility reminded Audrina of her sister Petra. A drifting soul, she was far better suited for the warmth of Italy, where she had lived and studied art for the past year.

Kitty would probably thrive in a warmer clime, too, but for now, a warm beverage would have to do. It was pleasant to—well, not to mother her. That sounded odd for someone only a few years younger than she, someone already married and with child. But to elder-sister her, maybe. To introduce her to everyone in the room, to fix her tea just as she wished, and ease her into a chair that caused her to sigh. "Thank you, my lady. This babe's been kicking me something fierce all day. It feels good to get off my feet."

"When you feel quite ready, Mrs. Balthasar," said Richard Rutherford, "we would like to see the box you inherited from your mother. Maria was her name, wasn't it?" He pronounced it in the proper English way, with a long *I* vowel.

"Yes, sir." After one more sip of tea, Kitty set her cup aside with a look of regret. "It's in my cloak, if—"

"Please, remain seated. I'll get it for you." Giles was on his feet in an instant, grabbing the wet cloak from the hook near the door. He carried it to Kitty, where with a murmured thanks, she pulled an oilcloth-wrapped package from a deep pocket.

"Who wants it? You, sir?" As Giles draped her cloak over the back of a wooden chair to steam dry before the fire, Kitty extended the small parcel in Richard Rutherford's direction. "Or should I send it to Miss Corning? She was the one who wrote to me."

"We will all take a look, if we may." Richard's calm voice seemed to reassure Kitty, and she handed it to Giles to be unwrapped on the table amidst the leavings of their dinner.

This was how the end of the Rutherfords' quest would come, then. Not with a fanfare in an elegant setting, but with a rain-soaked cloth beside a half-eaten shepherd's pie. Audrina had to smile at the thought.

But when Rutherford unwrapped the parcel, Audrina's smile fell away. "Why, it looks nothing like the other two."

Judging from the expressions on the others' faces—ranging from dismay to confusion—they, too, had been expecting a box of glossy, intricately patterned elegance. Though obviously still of foreign make, Kitty's box lid bore not a carved pattern, but a clean and curving inlaid image of a snow-covered mountain behind a wavering sea. The wood was of a yellowish hue, and the front face of the box was adorned with false book spines, seven stacked side by side.

"Is that from Lady Beatrix?" Audrina asked.

"I am almost certain," Rutherford said, "that it is. This is a characteristic Nipponese design of which I saw prints, long ago. It's called a *ruiji* box, if I recall rightly. Something to do with the false books across the front." When he picked up the small box with one careful hand, a rattle sounded from inside.

"There's something in there?" Lady Irving craned her neck, as though the box would spring open at the sound of her voice.

"I believe the rattle we're hearing is the key." Rutherford shook it gently. "It's hidden behind a moving panel, as is the keyhole."

"So your son's notes on Miss Corning's puzzle box won't help us a bit."

"*His son*"—Giles sounded testy—"can figure out a thing or two on his own, though *his son* is quite willing to let you have a try."

"I'm not done eating." Lady Irving forked up a bite of what must have been cold-as-rain shepherd's pie, because she grimaced when the food touched her lips.

"Do you know how to open this, Mrs. Balthasar?" Audrina turned to the puzzle box's owner.

"No, I never tried. My mother told me there wasn't anything in there, and she never put anything in it because it was so tiny. It smells good, though, doesn't it?"

Giles bent over the box in his father's hand, inhaling. "Sandalwood. Audrina, would you care to see?"

He plucked the box from Rutherford's hand and gave it to her. Audrina's hands closed around a solid of surprising weight. When she breathed in, a woodsy aroma stung her nose, followed by a powdery, spicy note that made her blink, unsure if her eyes were watering.

"Do you want to buy it?" Kitty spoke up. "I didn't know it had a special name. Does that make it worth more money?"

"To the right buyer," Rutherford said quietly, "it

would be worth a great deal. I would like to try to open it, if that is all right with you."

"It's all right with me." Kitty reached for her teacup. "But if it breaks, you will pay for it?"

"Money, money," said Lady Irving. "Goodness, girl, can't you think of anything else?"

"I'm sure I could if I had more of it." Kitty drained her tea, chasing the last drop with her tongue. "Me and Daniel—we just got married, because of the baby. And I've been poorly, more and more with every month." The deep shadows under her eyes stood out like bruises.

She's afraid. What was it about this simple room that brought such fear to young women? Or no, they were already afraid, and in this plain, isolated parlor there was no distraction from the fact. Kitty's knotted hands, her frailty, her secret attempt to gain a little money—it all made sense. She was afraid—no, she was *terrified*—that she might not survive.

Audrina knew nothing about this particular fear, but she knew about being afraid and pretending not to be. She smiled at Kitty as she would have at Charissa, were her fluttery sister here. *Take your time. It's all right.*

Kitty pulled in a slow breath. "I thought if the box is worth something, maybe you would want to buy it. And that would be a nice Christmas surprise for Daniel. It would help, a little, in case . . ."

"In case of need," Giles finished the sentence when she could not. "Because babies need so many odds and ends."

"Well, let's see what we have." Richard Rutherford began to slide seamless panels in a way that had become familiar to Audrina. "Giles, would you care to do the honors?"

Giles had seated himself next to his father, and he was pressing his hands against the hot metal of the coffeepot. "Go ahead, Father." As he held the coffeepot, his brows knit; pain rising or easing, Audrina wasn't sure.

Her scalp gave a prickle, and she hastily twisted back her unbound hair and slung it over one shoulder. Likely his hands were just cold. Not everything was a symbol of disaster.

This different style of puzzle box came apart more easily than the other two. Fewer pieces squeaked their protests, and eventually Richard slid aside a panel that revealed a hidden compartment. From there, he extracted a small key, and a few more minutes' work with the false book spines exposed a keyhole.

"Three of three? Anyone want to place a wager?" Lady Irving said as Rutherford fitted in the tiny key.

"No, thank you," he said with great calm, and Lady Irving's mouth slammed shut.

Just as the box opened.

Inside, the fragrant wood was covered with chiseled letters, just as the other two boxes had been.

"Three of three," breathed Rutherford as he skimmed the letters. "Sophia Angela Maria."

"You all should have taken the wager," Lady Irving whispered loudly.

"What else does it say, Father?"

"Several lines of mixed-up letters. But before that, 'Now Thou dost dismiss Thy servant, O Lord, according to Thy word in peace.'"

"Because my eyes have seen Thy salvation." Kitty rose from her chair with a hitch and a shuffle.

"You know this?" Giles asked.

She blinked at him, her expression puzzled. "Well, yes. *Nunc dimittis.*"

The Canticle of Simeon. Her memory prompted, Audrina could recall it now. The song of praise from the man who had wished only to live long enough to see the infant Lord. A quotation for an eagerly awaited baby.

All three boxes held quotations from the Nativity story. But why? And what in heaven's name—if such a figure of speech could be permitted at the moment—did the scrambled chains of letters have to do with anything?

They all gathered around the tiny box, the dinner forgotten. Silently, Audrina read a string of letters as nonsensical as those from the first two boxes:

UHLRBVQQQDOHBYBDUWWXOQDDSFLB
UOLVHOGPRRQQKDOHFWULYRGXOUYK
GHLUKGQBOHDHXIPHDKWLWUUONUUR
UYWHJKVUWWH

"We could think about this for ten years and never get anywhere," said Lady Irving. "You know, the same amount of time young Rutherford took about opening that golden puzzle box."

Giles's hands fell from the coffee urn with a thump.

"Or," continued the countess more loudly, "we could turn this over to my niece Louisa. Lady Xavier, that is. She has a head for puzzles like no one else I've ever met."

"It's too much to hope that she's in York." Nevertheless, Richard Rutherford sounded as though he did hope.

"She isn't. But she will be in London after Christmas for . . . the wedding. Ahem. You know."

"My sister's wedding," said Audrina. "It is a happy occasion. We need not act as though it is otherwise, and we certainly need not treat it as a secret." Her smile was more hopeful than it would have been only a moment before. For if the Rutherfords wanted to go to London, she could accompany them. Perhaps they could leave in the morning, even travel over Christmas. They might just make it back to the city in time.

In time for what, though? For Audrina to wed Llewellyn? Impossible. To hand over to him a fortune her father did not have, in exchange for silence they did not know if he would keep? Impossible again.

"I must be getting home," Kitty said. "If you've seen all you want to. Mr. Rutherford, is the box worth a—a pound to you?" She bit her lip, as though embarrassed to have asked for such a sum.

"Mrs. Balthasar, I'd be a villain if I bought it from you for less than twenty," said Rutherford.

Kitty's eyes widened, and she clapped her hands together—but Richard held his up. "I'm afraid you cannot be going home right now, though. Look at the turn the weather has taken."

As one, they turned to the window. A window that was newly glassed with ice, and against which snow was battering in a furious white fist.

"I am sorry, Mrs. Balthasar," he added. "But we are all quite snowbound. Mr. Booth's prognosticating knee did not lie to us: There will be no leaving this inn for days."

Chapter Sixteen

Wherein a Vegetable Is Clothed

"A parcel arrived for ye, m'lady." Mrs. Booth extended a paper-wrapped package to Audrina when she entered the otherwise-empty public room the following morning. "Las' mail coach to get through before the snoo blocked the roods late las' night."

"A parcel was addressed to me here?" How odd. It was far too soon for any forgotten item to be sent from Castle Parr.

Oh. Perhaps it had been sent by her father? No, that was illogical. He could not know where she was.

Her fingers fumbled on the twine about the parcel. *Steady.*

Audrina thanked the hostess, who tipped her a polite curtsy and went back to wiping off tables. Their small party had all risen at different times and breakfasted simply and separately. Mrs. Booth had sliced ham enough for a dozen guests, though the bread was running low.

Not that anyone else would be arriving to eat it today. Overnight, it looked as though the Almighty had slit His down mattress over the world. The snow had fallen in great fluffy flakes, piled high over the ice and slush that had plagued them during the previous day's travel. Today the road was not only impassable, but invisible.

Trapped.

No. She had been more trapped before than this. She was safe. She was all right.

With a deep breath, then another, she seated herself at a table in the corner to open her parcel. It was a flimsy, tiny thing—and as soon as she pulled back the paper, she saw why.

There lay a silk ribbon and lace garter, embroidered in purple and gold with her initials. Unmistakably one of her most personal belongings; unmistakably one of the pair filched by Llewellyn with the help of Audrina's former maid.

A note was enclosed with it:

One more where this came from. One more is all I need.
December 31.

The snow outside seemed to be piled upon her chest: heavy, freezing, choking. For a long moment she could only stare at it while her brain whirled with useless *hows* and *whys*.

She rewrapped the garter and pressed at her eyes with the heels of her hands. All right. She knew why: Llewellyn wanted to make her think of his threat. To feel desperate at the reminder of the ticking clock. Maybe even to be more willing to marry him. Anything to save her family the humiliation, the ruination, of the otherwise-inevitable jilting by the Duke of Walpole.

She lowered her hands with a thump. That was the why of the parcel. But how had it come to be *here*? Did Llewellyn think she had never left?

Turning it over, she studied the postal stamps. The garter had been sent not from London, but York itself.

A prickle between her shoulder blades made her shift in her seat. He couldn't be here. Behind her. He wasn't. She knew that, and yet . . .

With a quick twist of her head, she looked out through the row of mullioned windows that faced the main road. Nothing. No one. Just deep, unbroken snow. And no one was staying at the Goat and Gauntlet save their party and Kitty.

He must have had someone else post this for him. Once he reached London with Audrina's father, Llewellyn would not have slipped away again; not if he could catch the ear of a duke. How much was it worth to him to be brother-in-law to Walpole? Far more than Audrina's dowry, probably. Certainly far more than her father could pay.

Rain had turned to ice had turned to snow, and she had never felt so far away from where she ought to be.

Another deep breath. There was little she could do about that right now. Little to pass the time; little to take her mind away from the impossible.

Little, but not nothing. Her father wasn't here to tell her to stay out of the kitchen this time. She could make something, could do something worthwhile, no matter how small.

"Mrs. Booth." She pushed back her chair and stood, addressing the publican's wife, who was still wiping tables at the other end of the public room. "Would you permit me to bake something in your kitchen? Bread for dinner, or some sort of Christmas pastry?"

Mrs. Booth's mouth made an *oh* as she straightened up. "Well, now, m'lady, that's a righ' generous offer. But I shouldna like you to go to any trouble. Especially with it bein' Sunday an' all." The older woman looked doubtful despite her polite words.

"We must have bread, no matter the day. I was taught by the Earl of Alleyneham's favorite cook." She disliked using her father's title at this moment, but it had the intended effect of smoothing the doubt from Mrs. Booth's sonsy features. "If my baking fails, I will certainly recompense you for the supplies used."

Aha. With the magical combination of nobility and money, the doubt was entirely gone. "M'lady, I should be deligh'ed. Thank you. On Christmas Eve, why no' have as much good things abou' us as we can get?" Mrs. Booth bobbed a curtsy.

Audrina's ear was adjusting to the soft patterns of Mrs. Booth's Yorkshire dialect. "As you say, why not? I assume the weather will keep some of your employees at home, so perhaps this will ease the load on those who are here."

With a hand at the small of her back, the publican's wife admitted that only one maid and the stableboy lived in. Though she did the cooking herself, the baking was usually done by a kitchen maid. "She an' the others who work here don' live far, but they won' be able to get in today with the snoo as deep as your chin."

This was an exaggeration on the level of at least one human torso, but Audrina made a sound of sympathy. "You have not much help today for such a

grand place as this. As soon as I stow my parcel, I will
get right to the kitchen."

Another curtsy. "Once my maid, Jeanette, finishes
her work, she migh' be able to give you a hand wi' the
baking."

Scooping up the paper-wrapped garter—she felt distaste at touching it, though it was her own belonging—
Audrina raced up the stairs to her bedchamber, the
same one in which she had stayed the night of her unexpected arrival in York. Her breath came more
quickly than it ought after such a short flight.

The fire had been banked, but a nudge with a
poker turned over coals hot enough to burn the
parcel paper and Llewellyn's note. It was a tiny triumph to watch ash eat the terrible words and crumble
them to nothing, though she would not forget them
so quickly. Eyeing the garter, she considered throwing
it in the fire, too, but settled for stuffing it into her
trunk along with a few other oddments that Lady
Irving's maid had not unpacked. It was *hers*, for God's
sake. There could be nothing wrong with having it in
her chamber.

Right. Wiping her hands on her skirts, a cotton
print of thin brown and blue stripes, she closed the
door on that morning's unpleasant surprise and went
in search of the kitchen.

It would be on the ground floor, she knew. As
Audrina checked one doorway after another for the
right room, she heard male and female laughter mingled. Across from the servants' stairs she found both
the kitchen and the source of the laughter.

The kitchen was a comely room, similar in its trap-
pings to the kitchen from which Audrina had once
been chased at Alleyneham House. The whitewashed

walls were bright, with light slanting in from large windows next to which were arrayed gleaming tin-lined copper utensils. At the center of the space stood a huge wooden worktable and a laughing Giles Rutherford and Kitty Balthasar.

Audrina peered past them to see what they were looking at. "Is that a vegetable marrow?" She squinted at the large green gourd. "Wearing a diaper?"

Giles turned first, his grin still in place. "Audrina!" He sounded so pleased to see her that she couldn't help grinning back. Not that it was difficult to enjoy the sight of a big, broad red-haired man with a sweet scoop of a dimple.

Kitty matched their smiles. Though dressed in the same print gown as the previous day, she looked much less bedraggled and fragile. "Mr. Rutherford told me he had a houseful of younger brothers and sisters. I was never around a baby before, so I'd best figure out how to care for one before my own's born in another two months."

"So he taught you to put a diaper on a vegetable marrow." Audrina held up a hand. "No, Giles, there is no need for explanation. It makes perfect sense. What else would you use? After all, an apple or a sack of wal-nuts wearing a diaper would be ridiculous."

"To be strictly accurate," Giles said, "it's not a diaper. It's one of Mrs. Booth's finest napkins, so don't tell her."

Kitty laughed again, one thin hand resting on her great ball of a belly. "Oh, Lady Audrina, I'd no idea the cloth had to be folded so many times. Only imag-ine the disaster if I hadn't learned."

"It would indeed be a disaster for your clothing." With a little wave, Audrina took an apron from a hook, then slipped behind the pair of them to the far side of the kitchen. "Carry on with your diapering lesson; do not let me stop you. I am searching for the pantry."

Holding on to the cloth about the wizened, bulbous old vegetable marrow, Giles flung out an elbow. "It's that way. Step across the corridor, right at the corner of the building. That's where we found the marrow."

He turned back to his task, and as Audrina passed through the doorway into the scullery, she heard him add, "Once it's nicely folded, you can tie it around the baby's waist, like a little sash, or fasten it with a pin." After a moment: "No, not a hairpin! Good Lord, Kitty. You'll pop the baby like a bubble. Use a spring pin."

Kitty's laughter sounded again, much like a bubble itself. Audrina's step faltered. *This is what he's like with his sisters. This is what he gave up to come here.*

America seemed farther away than ever.

But the pantry, as Giles had promised, was quite close, and it was there that she must turn her thoughts. Resolutely. Immediately.

Although a small room tucked behind the servants' stairs, the pantry and larder were cleverly arranged to use every bit of wall space and even some of the awkward triangular space beneath the stairs. Wooden shelves of jarred and preserved foods, a butter churn, apples and root vegetables in barrels, wheels of cheese, cones of sugar.

Cold nipped her nose, and she tied the apron on over her gown in a hurry. She would come back with a measure once she decided how much bread to make. While the dough rose, though, perhaps a treat? It was too late by a month to start on a Christmas pudding, but she thought she could remember how to make apple tarts. With mulled wine, that would give their evening a festive air. She piled a dozen apples into her apron, then, shivering, darted back into the kitchen.

Kitty had gone, and Giles was removing the makeshift diaper from the vegetable marrow. "What are your plans for the morning, princess?"

"I told Mrs. Booth I would bake something."

The smile that spread over his face was warm and secret, quite different from the mischievous look he'd worn with Kitty. "Will you really? Good for you. No one to chase you from this kitchen."

"There's no one to work in this kitchen at all today, except for Mrs. Booth." Audrina hitched up the apron to the level of the huge wooden table and let the apples roll out. "And me."

"And me, if you like."

"You? Really? It is even worse for a man to work in a kitchen than an earl's daughter."

"Then we won't call it work." He winked at her. Shrugging free of his coat, he added, "You've got an apron as big as Yorkshire, but I have to protect my clothing somehow. Can you find me a knife? I'll start peeling those apples."

"But your hands—" She bit down hard on the end of that phrase.

Giles shot her a Look as he hung his coat on the apron hook. "My hands are fine. They've been well-rested for a few days and they're not too painful. Nor are they clockwork machines whose life winds down. I can use them even if they hurt."

Audrina found him a small paring knife and herself a larger one. With the urge to avoid his gaze, she made herself tip up her chin all the higher. "I did not mean to insult you, Giles. Only to let you know that I don't want you to be hurt. Not for something so frivolous as apple tarts."

I care about you. But now I am embarrassed to have revealed as much.

"That's a compliment indeed." He set the knife tip near the top of one apple, then sliced free a long, tidy curl of blush-red peel. "But if there's anything worth hurting one's hands for, it's an apple tart."

It's fine. We don't have to talk about it anymore.

So much of a conversation bobbed below the surface.

As Giles worked on the apples, Audrina tried not to be obvious about watching his arms flexing within their shirt sleeves.

Instead, she made herself familiar with the kitchen. The floor was made of large flags of native stone. One wall was taken up by a fireplace large enough to roast a calf, though fortunately a modern oven was set into the brickwork. Clean sand scattered about the hearth would catch drippings and ash. An ironwork rack held bowls and serving dishes and—aha!—the blobby leavings of the last baking, well covered in flour to preserve it for leavening the next baking. Thank goodness. Audrina had a vague idea of how to start a loaf from a dirty-gold slurry of yeast, but this would be much easier.

As she collected what she needed, she felt Giles's gaze following her—though every time she looked at him, he was studying another long curl of apple peel as he sliced it free. "You know, princess, you don't have to make bread any more than I have to peel these apples."

"Why are you peeling the apples, then?"

"Why are you making the bread?"

"Because someone needs to, and I know how."

"Likewise." He looked up, one eyebrow arched.

"Oh, stop it. If you want me to praise you, just say so."

He considered his handiwork: five neatly peeled apples in a line, with seven more to go. "Yes. I would like you to praise me. I'm doing an excellent job and I want you to know it and prove to me that you know it."

Her mouth quirked. "You are doing an excellent job. I know it. Thank you."

"And now your turn for some praise. Thank you for doing the baking. It's kind of you."

The thought of the garter hidden in her chamber—a frail scandal in the making—weighed so heavily that she could only shake her head. She counted out fist-fuls of flour, then set them to rise in a bowl with warm water and a lump of the leaven-dough.

His knife went still in apple number six. "What, you can thank me but I can't thank you?"

"It's not worth thanking me," she mumbled. "I needed something to do. I am not making bread out of kindness."

"Just the apple tart, then?"

She ignored him, covering the bowl with a cloth and setting it at the corner of the wooden table nearest the fireplace. There the air was pleasantly warm, and the leaven would rise until tomorrow morning. Then she could finish mixing the dough, and they would have fresh loaves for Christmas. For dinner today they would have to make do with the remainder of yesterday's bread.

She picked up the larger knife, along with the first in Giles's line of peeled apples.

He took the stem of an unpeeled apple between

thumb and forefinger, rolling it in a gentle arc before him. "I wonder if you know anything about gratitude, princess."

Chock. She split the apple in half with a determined blow of the knife. "No more or less than any woman in my position, I suppose."

"And how much is that?"

Her head snapped up. "Don't you have apples to peel?"

"I can peel and talk at the same time." Something in the blandness of his smile reminded her of his unflappable father. "So. How much is that?"

Chock. She quartered the apple. "I don't know. Not as much as I should, probably. My parents never bothered to hide that they wanted a son, and I did not think I had much to be grateful for as the youngest of five daughters."

He began to peel the next apple. "Nor I as the oldest in a large family. The weight of expectations is pretty heavy."

"Is it better to be burdened with heavy expectations, or none?" When she met his blue eyes across the table, something within her quailed.

"I don't know." He slipped free one cuff link, then the other. After tucking them in his waistcoat pocket, he rolled his sleeves up his forearms. "With the former, someone's sure to be disappointed. With the latter, maybe they already are."

Cold sunlight picked out the golden hairs on his forearms, corded and firm with muscle. His strong fingers handled the knife with dexterity. Such hands were made to create beauty in gold or bricks—or out of nothing but an apple peeling.

A shudder shook her at the memory of those fingers

caressing her breasts, cradling her face as though she was worth more than she had ever imagined. *The sort of person you are, you need never change.*

How had he described her worth? Worth *different*. Not more or less. Just . . . different.

She was different from the docile daughter her parents had wanted her to be; she was certainly different from the son they would have preferred. She was different from the grateful whore Llewellyn seemed to think her.

But what was she instead? And what place was there for her in the world, if she was not what her parents or suitors wanted?

She shook off the question. "There is no *maybe* about the disappointment inevitably involved in expectations." *Chock*. The knife made a satisfyingly determined sound on the wooden table.

"Oh, I wouldn't say it's inevitable. I expect these apple tarts to be delicious."

She pressed at her temple with the back of her wrist, then cut another apple. "That is hardly a credit to me. If someone shows me what to do, I can repeat the process. I'm not unobservant. Nor unintelligent."

"So you tell me what you're not." He leaned forward across the table. "Can you say it the other way 'round? 'Giles, I am observant. Giles, I am intelligent.'"

Chock. "Giles, I have apple tarts to make." She pressed her lips together so they would say no more; she fixed her gaze on the table so he would not see her eyes grow damp.

"That's all you have to say? Really?" When she didn't answer, he said, "All right, have it your way." One last apple, peeled with perfect neatness, rolled across the table into her field of vision.

"I didn't have to peel the apples, princess. But I wanted to. I wanted to help you and spend a few minutes in your illustrious presence." She heard his footsteps cross the flagged floor, the shush of cloth as he pulled his coat from the hook. "Why do you do the things that you do?"

She waited, still and poised until he left. As soon as she was alone, she wiped her eyes on the apron, then went back to slicing the apples.

Chock. Chock.

With Giles gone, there was no satisfaction in the sound.

Chapter Seventeen

Wherein Lady Irving
Removes Her Turban

"Christmas Eve," said Estella, Lady Irving, "should be spent sitting before a fire large enough to melt one's eyebrows, drinking brandied chocolate strong enough to melt everything else." She extended her hands to the fire in the private parlor.

"What is the present state of your eyebrows?" Richard poured out a cup of something hot from a service the inn's maid had just brought in. Estella did not see a flask anywhere; this was unlikely to be spirituous. Damn.

"Unmelted. Sadly." She drew her chair closer to the fire; any more and she would be sitting on the coals. Midday light filtered gray-blue through the pebbled-ice surface over the window. They seemed glassed away from the world, and in a prison of glass there was no warmth. No escape. "Aren't you anxious about being trapped in this inn?"

"Should I be? Will that help melt the snow so we can set out sooner?"

She glared at him. He smiled. "Thinking on it won't make a difference, Estella. You said you knew how we should go on once weather permitted. We shall put the code into the hands of your clever niece Louisa. Until then, let us try to enjoy ourselves." He handed her a teacup full of something suspiciously brown and syrupy-looking.

"What is this?"

"Coffee." Hitching his trouser legs up at the knee, he seated himself across from her. "I made it very sweet for you."

"Because I'm so bitter?"

He took a sip from his own cup. "No. Because that's how I like it best, and you told me you didn't care how you took your coffee."

"When?"

"A few days ago, at Castle Parr. When that footman, Jory, brought us refreshments while we were wreathing all those statue heads."

"Oh." The cup warmed her fingers. "I didn't realize you'd remembered that." One tentative sip won her over. The smell was almost acrid, but the taste of it was liquid heat, liquid sugar. "That's not half-bad."

"High praise." He reached up to set his cup on the mantel, then settled back into the chair with drowsy eyes. Such calm and peace; he made the simple wooden chair look like the softest-cushioned fauteuil.

How dare he be so calm when she was worried? How could he feel so peaceful, so unaffected by her, when her fingers tingled every time she caught sight of him?

She ran her fingers over the paste gems on the front of her aquamarine turban. Brightness. She must remember that. "So. When you get to London, you think you'll find some jewels and set up a shop of your own."

"Half-right. I have no idea where, or whether, I will find my late wife's jewels. But I *will* set up a shop of my own. I've already found the perfect spot in Ludgate Hill, not far from Rundell and Bridge."

Was it the American accent that made him sound so certain? Where the London accent tripped and twirled, his speech rolled over consonants like a gentle boulder. As though to speak something was to make it happen.

Oh, it wasn't just the sight of him that drew her. It was the sound of him, too.

But her contrary habits had been formed long ago. "London society is devoted to Rundell and Bridge—not just for jewelry, but for silver and gold plate. An American competitor is sure to fail."

He opened his eyes: deep blue about a ring of brown. "But that is not what I am at all. I've no thought of competing with them on their terms."

Estella snorted. "That can hardly be called business. All right, what sort of gewgaws will the fashionable young ladies of London be wearing next season?"

"Oh, you probably have a better idea of that than I do. More influence, certainly."

"Where is your pride? You'll never take the *ton* by storm unless you are far haughtier."

He chuckled, eyes crinkling at the corners. "Haughtiness works for some, but I don't think I could manage it. I'll do business in my own way. A different way."

"And what way is that?"

Rubbing a hand along his angular jaw, he considered. "If I love a piece, it will show. And that enthusiasm will make it sell."

"All right." She took a sip of her bittersweet coffee. "Sell something to me so I can see whether you've the skill to back up your claim. Try to sell me . . . oh, how about my turban?"

His dark brows knit. After a pause, he said, "If you'll forgive me, I do not love your turban. I don't think I could sell it."

She flailed for a place to smash down her coffee cup. With no table at hand, she had to settle for draining the cup and slamming it back into its saucer.

Cursed man. He looked not the slightest bit abashed. "Why do you wear such—things?" Left out was the adjective *dreadful*, but Estella heard the space of it, unuttered but unmistakably there.

"Because I can. I can do and be and wear whatever is offensive, and people have to accept it because of my rank and age and fortune."

"I'm sorry to hear that."

"I have horrified you." Disappointment mingled with bitter triumph; she had known he would falter eventually.

"No, not in the slightest." He folded one leg up, resting the foot on the opposite thigh. "But it sounds as though you don't like the things you do. Or be or wear, if that's the way you put it. And that's what I'm sorry to hear."

Estella occupied the next moments with the careful drawing of breath. Air seemed thick, too thick to enter her lungs without great ragged pulls.

"Where it peeks from the edge of your turban, your

hair is quite a pretty color," added Richard, calm as ever. "A true auburn. My late wife called hers auburn, but it was red like Giles's."

He spoke this as he would any fond memory, with a light matter-of-fact smile teasing his lips. When he mentioned his wife, his grief seemed neatly folded away like a favorite old silk.

Estella had never grieved for her husband. No, after her marriage, she had grieved only for herself. The late earl had made her wealthy, but he had been careless and lecherous, his young wife a pretty toy with which he played whenever, however he wished. There had been no purpose to seeking harmony with him; no reason to strive to better herself. A hard shell grew over her heart, so quickly that it was brittle.

She like the idea of a softer strength, like Richard's folded-away memory.

"Did you not like your wife's hair?" She shaped the words carefully. Naked feeling was far more unseemly than a naked body.

"Of course I liked it. It was part of her." His surprise was no more than a ruffle on the surface of an untroubled pond. "But maybe she didn't, since she called it by another color. Do you not like your hair? Is that why you cover it with turbans all the time?"

"No, I wear turbans because I'm too vain to wear a lace cap. You call my hair auburn, but it's mostly gray. I'm old, Richard."

"Do you feel old?"

"I *am* old." She was a great-aunt. Her sixtieth birthday loomed less than two years away. Fifty-eight; it seemed impossible that she should be fifty-eight and trundling about northern England. Fifty-eight and sitting beside a handsome man, wondering why he asked her so many questions. Not liking the questions, exactly, but not wanting them to stop.

"But how do you feel?" Richard was looking at her, really looking, as no one had for decades. That warm brown ring about his pupils pulled at Estella; though she had drunk all her coffee, her throat had gone dry.

"I feel . . . different."

He smiled, all warm eyes. "I like different."

She smiled back. It was an uncertain expression that had to crack its way through the shell about her. When it reached her lips, it wobbled—but it was there.

Unfolding his legs, he slapped his hands onto the flat of his thighs. "As long as we are at our leisure, how about a game of cards or chess? You may name the stakes."

Her heart beat a little more quickly. At some point, she had stopped feeling cold. "Cards, then."

"Cards you shall have. Wait here, please; I'll go find a deck."

As soon as the parlor door closed behind him, she removed her aquamarine turban. Scrubbing her fingers through her short-cropped hair, she woke and eased her tense scalp, then replaced the turban.

After all, she liked it. And Richard liked her. Or he liked her being different, or feeling different, or—well, maybe it came to the same thing.

The turban was not heavy to wear, no more than a few ounces of cloth and paste jewels. But she felt as though a much greater weight had been lifted.

* * *

Giles could not resist. He brought the poor wizened vegetable marrow into the public room after dinner. "Here's our Christmas decoration. It's green, at least."

It was worth the horrified looks on Mrs. Booth's and Lady Irving's faces to see Kitty and Audrina laugh.

Mrs. Booth had concocted a simple but tasty dinner. Every person in the inn, from countess to stableboy, tucked into meats and pickle and potatoes, washed down with ale and a mulled wine that Giles strongly suspected Lady Irving had fortified with distilled spirits.

With the main dishes set aside on empty tables, the motley group handed around bowls of nuts, dried fruits, and the apple tartlets: perfect palm-sized pies of sour-sweet apples and a buttery crust, with a snow of sugar atop.

"And for tomorrow," said Mrs. Booth, "we'll all enjoy a nice Yorkshire Christmas pie."

"If it's as good as this apple pie, I look forward to trying it," said Richard.

"It might be as good, but it won't be anything like," said Mrs. Booth. "Lor' bless you, I forget you're not from aroun' here. Though how I should forget with your odd accent, I can' imagine."

"It must be our charming personalities," Giles said. "People get so distracted by our delightfulness that they forget everything else."

Someone kicked him under the table, and he smothered a curse.

"A Yorkshire Christmas pie," said Mr. Booth, hitching at his suspenders with an expression of pride, "has five kinds of bird stuffed wi'in each other, all inside the tastiest crust you can imagine. Oh, and there's a rabbit in there, too, isn't there, Mrs. Booth?" At her affirmation, he added, "Mrs. Booth made it two days ago so it could age properly in the larder."

"Age . . . properly?" Richard made a valiant effort at enthusiasm. "Well, that will be a pleasure to try. I'm not sure I could even think of five kinds of bird."

"Oh, go on." Mrs. Booth laughed. "Who's for chestnuts?"

Somehow, this question marked the dismissal of the servants. The lady's maid melted off, and the overworked live-in, Jeanette, began to clear the dishes. "Jory will help," said Audrina, and the footman moved forward at once.

Giles felt as though he ought to stand and help, too—but then Mrs. Booth shoved a bed warmer into his hands and tasked him with roasting chestnuts. He surrendered himself to the distraction of scoring the smooth wedge-shaped shells, steadying the long-handled pan over the flames, and shaking them around every few minutes.

But as he crouched before the fire, a twist at his heart caught him by surprise. Audrina, laughing as she passed the plate of tarts, her tip-tilted eyes the shade of . . . of . . . damnation, he had no idea. Trees or leaves or something like that. It was a dark-green color like something richly alive.

Not that he could see the color from this distance. But he knew their color, all the same.

This was indeed an adventure, though Giles had hardly wanted to admit it to himself. At some point, after being wet and cold and puzzled, after teasing and embracing and staring at the stars, they had become friends. More than friends. Their whole party was knit, and there was nothing to do right now but be together.

The joy of it was almost enough to gild the ashen awareness of departure. Soon, it would come. All pleasures must end. They would leave the inn, they would leave York. He would leave England.

Time was the villain, even more than the threats of David Llewellyn or Lord Alleyneham. Where it had once dragged for weeks across the Atlantic, then northward across England, now each hour slipped by too quickly and each day raced. Every night, when Giles folded himself into yet another too-short bed, he thought of dark hair and a voice that turned every sentence into blank verse, and he wondered how he had ever found the strength to stop kissing her.

He shook the pan, roughly this time, and one of the chestnuts gave a pop. How long had he been holding this pan? Drifting through thought? Minutes on end, for the chestnuts had begun to roast. The smell of them was scorched and sweet and savory all at once, a smell that worked its way through Giles's body with a comfort like heat itself.

"Who's for chestnuts?" With an echo of Mrs. Booth's words, he stood and shook the pan in the direction of the diners.

Kitty dumped the walnuts from a bowl. "Pour them right in here!"

Giles tipped the bed warmer, scattering out the hot chestnuts as a maid would usually dump out the coals. Kitty set upon them right away, hissing as she pulled free the hot shells and the fuzzy inner skin. She handed the first one to Giles. "To our roaster, with thanks."

With a smile, he bit into the mealy nut. The smell was far better than the taste, but a chestnut could taste like dirt and he would still be glad to roast it for the sake of that heavenly warm scent.

Kitty handed him another, and he tossed it in Audrina's direction. Her hand snapped up to catch it, quicker than a blink. She looked, bemused, at the nut in her hand, and then at Giles. "Thank you."

"Good catch." He lifted the remainder of his chestnut to her, a half-eaten toast. She smiled, accepting this silly praise as she would not take his thanks earlier.

Unaccountable woman.

He liked her. Oh, how he liked her. It was a promise and threat at once.

Only when he reached his bedchamber that night did it occur to Giles that his wrists and hands had not hurt while he was roasting the chestnuts. Balancing that long-handled pan for minutes on end—he'd felt fine.

His hands still felt fine. He tested them, flexing his fingers and wrists, fearing a twinge. It came, along with a prickle of numbness at his fingertips, but it was slight.

He could write a letter to his sister Rachel tonight. Before he left America he had promised to write her every week, and it had been too long since his last letter.

But there was so much to say that, once he lit a lamp, and gathered writing implements, he had no idea how to start.

I don't know if you would love it here, he could say. *You would miss the sun as much as I do. But the moon . . .*

He had never known the moon could be so near. So big and imperfect and yet still reliable.

No, no moon, because then he'd have to explain the telescope, and *then* he would have to tell Rachel about Audrina, and what the devil ought he to say about her? That she was brave? That she was wounded and ungrateful? That he envied the promise of her life, but thought the circumstances of it a gilded cage?

That he couldn't imagine staying in England, nor returning to America and leaving her forever?

He recalled how bitterly Rachel had cried when he and Richard left Philadelphia. How even before their carriage rolled out of sight—with Rachel and Aunt Mathilda waving wildly—he had felt the weight of being gone, of traveling into an unfamiliar world, like a stone on his chest.

The divide between Giles Rutherford and Lady Audrina Bradleigh was as wide as the Atlantic. Yet when she was as near as the next chamber, it was almost impossible to recall this.

No, no sun. No moon. He would not write to Rachel about that.

You would love seeing Father so happy. He could tell her that instead.

He filled a page about the code in the puzzle boxes, the differences between each box. The three owners: *Mother gave these gifts to the girls who were precious to her.* Lady Beatrix had doted on her daughters, probably even more than her sons.

When he had filled the entire sheet, he wiped the pen and sifted through his papers for another blank page. He came across one of Sophy's gridded sheets.

For drawing a map of the sky—or a brooch, or a building, or a building that looked like a brooch.

Hmm.

He could send Rachel a drawing of Castle Parr. She would enjoy seeing where they had stayed.

And he? He would enjoy drawing the place where he had forgotten himself, so briefly and sweetly. And then he would send the memory of it far away from him.

Chapter Eighteen

Wherein the Ordinary Is Unacceptable

Eight days until the wedding; seven, perhaps, until Llewellyn sent the dreadful parcel to the Duke of Walpole.

Audrina hoped to distract herself from this thought in the kitchen of the Goat and Gauntlet. The leaven had risen nicely overnight; it was pale and bubbly and sticky as paste. With the help of the Goat and Gauntlet's live-in maid, the exotically named Jeanette, she worked cup after cup of flour into it, then added warm water and salt.

Jeanette was a raw-handed slip of a young lady, with a light-brown tangle of hair tied back under a sensible dark kerchief. "This is a nice change from doin' the fires, foor once. You'll tell me if I'm mixin' the dough righ', m'lady?"

Her thick Yorkshire accent was a creamy lilt that took on the rhythm of her kneading hands. As flour blended with leaven, a look of delight perched on her delicate features.

Audrina shared the feeling, muddled and distracted though she was at the moment. It felt good to shove at something, to remold it. To make something new.

But it was not enough to still her whirling, wondering thoughts.

What was Christmas in London like for Audrina's family? Was the stuffed goose being put into the oven, to be eaten crackling-crisp for dinner?

Had Charissa bought a gift for the Duke of Walpole? She had wondered whether that would be proper, but Audrina had left London—had been taken from London—before her elder sister came to a conclusion.

Were the earl and countess at church right now, their eyes roving the tall nave of St. George's in anticipation of Charissa's wedding? Or was Llewellyn meeting with Audrina's father to work out a settlement? *Blackmail*; such an ugly word. She hated the idea of Llewellyn profiting from lies. She hated the idea of him profiting at all from what had been private.

Whatever the London Christmas might be, Audrina would have been barred from the kitchen. Cooking and baking was not romantic work, she knew. It was brutal and tiring and endless. But just once, just for once, she had a task to finish. Even though pushing at such a great quantity of dough made her hands hurt.

Which, of course, made her think of Giles.

"Jeanette." Audrina hesitated.

"M'lady?"

"Did you ever know anyone with arthritis?"

"Ooh, yes indeed. Me grandmam had arthi'is soomthin' terrible. Gave her the divil of a time findin' woork wi' them hands."

"When she was young?"

"No, m'lady. It coom on when she was oold, p'raps sixty. She 'urt when she woorked 'ard, but she also 'urt when she di'n't woork a'tall."

"So rest did not help her." Audrina shook her head. "There must be more than one type. Some people get it old, some get it young."

"Can't say, m'lady. I never heard of anyone gettin' it young."

"It happens. Sometimes. But how does one *know* if it's arthritis at all, or—something else?" *Something that would not strip away one's hope for the future?*

Jeanette lifted one shoulder as she pressed at the dough. "That'd be a job for a doctor, wouldn't it?"

"I suppose it would." She tossed a reassuring smile to the maid. "No matter. I was woolgathering."

She was spattered with flour; Mrs. Booth's capacious apron was daubed with sticky dough. But no matter how vigorously she mixed and kneaded and punched and shoved at the dough, she couldn't stop *thinking*.

"M'lady? How loong do we mix the dough?"

Audrina blinked. The great mass of bread dough lay in a sad blob over the surface of the wooden table. "Oh, dear. Ah—until about three minutes before it looks like this."

With a sigh, she used the back of her dough-sticky hand to push back hair that was threatening to fall loose over her forehead. "All right. Let's add a bit more flour, a little warm water, and work the dough gently into a ball." If it rose again, they would have fresh bread for dinner. If not, they would have to eat it as crackers.

Jeanette carried out these instructions with smooth efficiency. Setting the hopefully rescued dough at its corner near the fire, the maid then promised to tidy up. With thanks, Audrina stripped off the apron and wandered into the public room.

Lady Irving had just descended the stairs, and the countess cast a gimlet eye over Audrina. "You've got flour on your face and you look like a wet cat."

"I have no idea what that means." Audrina swiped at her face.

"No, the other cheek. It means you look tired and miserable, my girl. You need a distraction."

"I probably do." She swiped at her face again.

"Well, come and play cards with Richard and me. He only bets chicken stakes, but he's not altogether terrible. I've come in search of a new pack because I suspect him of throwing the ace of spades into the fire."

"How devious."

"A bit, at that. There's hope for him." The countess's mouth crimped tightly at the edges, which Audrina knew to mean *I can hardly contain my delight, though I regard that as a sign of weakness.*

"I had best leave you to your own game." Kind of the countess to offer, but she and Richard Rutherford would better enjoy their distraction—whatever form it might take—as a solitary pair.

Leaving Lady Irving behind, cursing and clutching at her turban as she searched a sideboard, Audrina mounted the steps.

Last time she had been here, she'd wished for time to flit forward. Now she wanted it to drag. She was too far away from London, and her head was too full: her distant family, the endangered wedding; Charissa's happiness and the Duke of Walpole's stern demeanor; the puzzle boxes and their codes. The Rutherfords' inevitable departure.

Had she been able to lay down these worries, this snowbound sojourn would have been a respite. For these few days, Audrina had been just that: herself. No parties or falsehoods, no barbs from a disappointed parent or lover. Just good humor, and a bit of work, and—and Giles, who wondered why she did the things she did. Who told her she need not change who she was.

Intoxicating thought.

Already the snow was soft and heavy from sunshine upon it, and the unfortunate stableboy had been tasked with shoveling paths from stable to carriage house, from entrance porch to road. If the skies stayed clear, tomorrow the travelers would be on their way.

She was studying her boots as she mounted the stairs, each polished tip ink-black on the smooth stone-plated treads. *Bump.* At the top of the staircase, her head collided with a wall.

Which proved not to be a wall at all, but the chest of Giles Rutherford. Nicely clad in a waistcoat checked in dark blue and green.

"If you want attention, just say so." He steadied her with a gentle grip on her upper arm. "No need to put your balance or your fancy coiffure at risk."

"I was woolgathering." Her cheeks warm, she used this excuse for the second time within a few minutes.

"About wanting attention?"

"Ha. No." *Maybe. Yes.* She wished she had stepped into the retiring room to clean her face and set her hair to rights.

He stood aside and let her precede him into the corridor. "Did you get the bread pummeled into submission?"

"More than you know. Jeanette and I beat it so much that it might not rise at all. But if it does, we'll feast on fresh bread this afternoon with our Yorkshire Christmas pie." A thought struck her. "Were you about to go downstairs? If so, I warn you, Lady Irving will offer to play cards with you. But under no account must you say yes, because then you will have to watch her flirt with your father."

He made a mock grimace. "That's not something I want to witness, though I'm sure they're having a pleasant time. No, I was coming in search of you."

"Why?"

"To see how you were doing."

"Oh. I'm—fine." Again, she dashed a forearm across her face. Did she look as disheveled as she felt within? She'd had not a moment to compose herself, although a moment would hardly be enough.

"I don't mean to imply that you're lying," Giles said thoughtfully, leaning against the plastered wall, "because that would be rude. But if you're *fine* on Christmas away from your family, with as many worries as have been jostling for space in your head, then you must have turned into an automaton."

"Not an automaton. I am merely a proper English lady of good breeding." She held up a quelling hand. "I know, I made it easy for you to compare. 'What is the difference?' Ha ha. Let me pass, please."

"Pass whenever you like. I've shoved myself against the wall so I'm not in your way. And no, I would never make that comparison in regard to you." He folded his arms. "For one thing, you're not as proper as you pretend to be. For another, I know there's a big difference between not showing a feeling and not having one. And so no, I don't think you're fine. But if you want to act like you're fine, that's your business."

She could not trick those blue eyes; she did not want to. And yet there was so much to say, or hide, that speech was impossible for the moment.

She shook her head.

His expression softened, mouth in a sweet quirk. "Come with me, princess."

The corridor made a leftward jog, then extended straight to the north face of the building. Passing by the bedchambers flanking the corridor on the left, Giles opened a door on the right. "After you, dear lady."

Audrina entered not a squat, dark bedchamber—scandalous thought!—but a great square ballroom that soared to the inn's rafters, slicing through the attic story. The floor was oiled and painted a glossy brown; the ceiling in imitation of marble. Two rows of windows broke the outer wall: the lower of normal dimensions, the upper ones smaller to tuck under the roofline. Molding framed these stacked windows, striping the light-colored walls with chestnut brown.

"Fancy, isn't it?" Giles said as the door closed behind them.

Quiet. Pressingly quiet, like wind in one's ears muting all other sound, and empty. A puzzle box with nothing inside, but there was no guiding message scrawled on its inner surface.

"Look, we're by ourselves now." Giles seated himself against the far wall, across from the windows. "If you want to talk about what's making you all twitchy and shy, fine. And if you want to just sit here and not worry that someone is going to try to extort money from you in a game of whist, or make you eat a pie made of five kinds of bird and a rabbit, that's all right, too."

Audrina hesitated. She should—she wanted to—she ought to—

Damn it all. She wanted to sit next to Giles.

So she walked over to him and did just that.

The ice that had coated the windows yesterday had fallen, heated by the sun. A cold but clear light filtered into the great room.

"Giles, is it possible . . ." She chose her words carefully. "Could it be that you do not have the same ailment as your mother?"

"That would solve a lot of problems, wouldn't it?" His expression was wry. "I've often thought so. But no, it came on right about the same time hers got very bad. Pain in the wrists and forearms—it's unmistakable."

"Jeanette told me her grandmother had arthritis in her hands, and that it never got better with rest."

"Different people feel it differently, I expect." His tone was light, but its tenor was unmistakable: *That's enough.* "I can leave you alone if you like." Already, he had rolled into a crouch, ready to stand.

"No, stay. Please. I would like the company."

He searched her for a long moment, eyes clear and piercing. The scrutiny was awkward yet pleasurable, a slow sweep of blue that made her insides clench and heat. She could not break the gaze, and yet to look at him for so long was a type of nakedness she had never felt before.

"All right." He settled back into place beside her, close enough that his coat sleeve brushed the long sleeve of her gown. The fine hairs on her arm prickled. Her throat felt dry.

"We shall be leaving tomorrow, I think." Her voice echoed with false brightness in the high-ceilinged room.

"In time to get you back to London for your sister's wedding." Giles folded one leg into a careless triangle and slung his arm over the top. The icy sun paled his skin against the dark green of his coat. "That's what you've wanted, isn't it? To get back to London?"

"I want my sister to be married. Once she is, Llewellyn's threats will not matter."

"They'll still matter to you."

She clenched her fists in her lap, wishing for a shawl to worry at. "Maybe. Yes. But that is not the most important thing right now. Protecting my sister is."

"From Llewellyn's schemes? Or from that duke she's going to marry?"

"Decidedly the former. If Charissa fears anything about the duke, it is that she may not enchant him as much as he enchants her." Blithe Charissa desired her wedding day's arrival with single-minded delight. They was no room for any anxiety in her mind, except a pleasurable flurry of nerves about pleasing her stiff-necked betrothed. "She . . . loves him," Audrina added as though it were an afterthought.

When of course it was everything. *Loves*—a word of only one syllable, yet so weighty it was almost impossible for Audrina to pronounce.

For now, Charissa was happy, and Audrina must make sure her own actions did not endanger that feeling.

For that matter, their elder sisters Romula and

Theodosia were happy, too. Quieter than Charissa or Audrina, once they had been scarred by smallpox, they were content to abandon society for a country life with men who loved them.

And then there was Petra, the fourth daughter, who had expressed such a strong desire to study art in Italy that she had retreated to her room, crying, for days on end. Finally, the earl and countess had let her go. For a year they had received chirpy periodic letters from her, and even a painting the previous Christmas.

Petra had found happiness, too.

That just left Audrina, sitting on the hard wooden floor of a ballroom in a York inn.

"Charissa. Audrina." Giles ticked the names off on his fingers. "Petra. And who else?"

"Romula and Theodosia are oldest."

Giles whistled. "Your parents certainly didn't give you ordinary names."

"They did not want us to be ordinary."

"What's so bad about ordinary? Ordinary is the way most people live."

"That alone makes it unacceptable." She stretched out her legs, keeping her focus on the glossy toes of her boots. Blinking too often by far, but there was no help for that. An occasional tear must leak out with these words. "And yet I am just like everyone else, Giles. There are five of me within my own family. I could do nothing that had not already been done first or better. So I could only do things last and worst."

"Not worst." He spoke low and gently. "Different. I guarantee you none of your sisters has done anything like what you've done over the past week or two."

She could make no response but a tight smile. Tense, to hold in feeling that trembled like a plucked guitar string. *Love and joy come to you . . .*

A man like Giles could only have come from a family where he was loved enough to stretch, to go his own way and come back. A land where buildings were new and snow scrubbed the sky clean and blue and white. None of these gray winters, these gray people in ossified buildings.

Maybe he was not her equal by birth, but she was not his by behavior. She was the one who had been foolish and weak and tricked.

But he had never held that against her. *She* was the one who had chosen to dwell on it. She had agreed, meek and tired, to stay away from London. She had let her father tell her she was not welcome at a family wedding. That she was an embarrassment.

Because she believed him. Because she had put her trust in the wrong person, and he had betrayed her, and therefore she deserved to be punished.

Once upon a time, maybe, there had been bravery in secretly doing what she ought not. Oh, what a clever girl to take a lover. To slip from the house to call on a scandalous friend. Oh, how cunning and sly to do these things and smile demurely over dinner, no one the wiser.

But there was no such thing as a secret. Any interaction—from conversation to intercourse—involved at least two. Though she might guard her tongue and her speech and her behavior, that other person had the power to make a different choice.

Had power over her.

And now she was eaten by the idea that no one on earth was proud of her, not even herself. To be different was to be unacceptable. To be ordinary was to be unacceptable.

To hold oneself at a chilly distance was intolerable, but to mingle with servants would never do. To bake was improper; to be idle was insufferable.

She was familiar with every negative prefix the English language had to offer, but she did not know their converse. What to put in their place? How to fill the gaps in her time and her heart?

"No," she said quietly. "None of my sisters has done what I have." None of them had wondered like this. None of them had needed to.

Giles Rutherford seemed to like her the way she was. Not as a reflection of her family, or a purse to be dipped into. As fellow travelers, they were on their own, divorced from the outside world.

But the world waited. It crouched outside the snowbound inn, with the sharp claws and teeth of rumor and ticking time. It would tear apart Charissa's wedding, and that would tear apart their family.

So what was Giles's opinion worth if she knew he was wrong?

And if he was wrong about her, why was it so reassuring to be near him? To breathe in his scent, soap and starch and something sweet, like sugared coffee or a stolen apple tart. To study the map of freckles over his cheekbones; the thin slice of a scar through his lip, permanent proof of his devotion to a younger brother. To admire his hands, his strong-fingered, broad-palmed hands, and to want them tracing every line of her body.

Not worse, he had said. *Different*.

Maybe different was better—or could become so.

The air between them was thick and vibrant as crystal.

"Giles. Will you come to my chamber?" she asked.

Eyes closing, he took a deep breath; a breath that looked as though it hurt him or scoured him clean. She could not tell which, and her heart tottered, ready to fall into despair or delight.

When he opened his eyes, they looked like a warm summer sky. "Lead the way, princess."

Chapter Nineteen

Wherein Giles's Hands Could Carry the World

As soon as the bedchamber door locked behind them, Audrina understood why she had requested the same room she had stayed in two weeks ago, when first arriving at the Goat and Gauntlet. It was for the unspoken hope of a moment like this: to replace the shame and fright of *locked away from* with the delight of *locked away with*.

She turned from Giles to remove her boots, feeling nervous and powerful at once. It was an unlikely setting for a seduction, this simple, clean bedchamber with a small desk and a privacy screen—and a pencil post bed, covered in a pale piecework quilt that seemed, in its elegant jumble of patterns, an apt reflection of Audrina's feelings.

The walls were blue as Giles's eyes; the fireplace of

white-painted brick. It was like being in the sky, unmoored and free.

But this was hardly a moment to go flitting off into fancy. This was a moment for locking the door. Building up the fire. Pulling back the counterpane on a bed that seemed very large. A cocoon of crisp sheets and heavy bed-curtains.

This whole journey was a cocoon, and soon enough she would have to leave it and stretch her wings. For now, though, she was wrapped in lost time, and when she turned back to Giles, tall and solid and smiling, he cradled her face in his hands.

Gently, he brushed her lips with his, then pulled back to look at her. "When I said I was not going to kiss you, I couldn't bear for that to be the end of the sentence. The word *yet* always followed in my thoughts."

"Yet you seemed so determined not to."

"I had to be very determined indeed. When a beautiful, brave, curious, passionate woman wants to kiss a man—well. It seems like the best thing in the world."

"What's different this time? Are you going to stop?" She covered his fingers with hers, holding his hand to her cheek. "Tell me now if kisses are all you want, or if you want to stop."

"I never wanted to stop." His thumb traced her cheekbone. "The difference this time is why we are doing it."

"What it means." Her voice was quiet over the desire that began to flow and pool, liquid within her.

"Yes." He seemed to look deep into her, sifting through her every thought. But she could not read his, and what it meant to him, she did not know. Again, she wanted to lose herself. To let the outside world fall away with its troublesome past and future; to live only in the pleasure of the moment. But it *was* different this time, because she chose him as her partner: not because he was at hand, but because he was Giles.

When he kissed her again, she rose to her toes to meet his lips. A deeper kiss, and she threaded her hands through the short silk of his hair to pull him closer. Sipping, tasting, a pressure of lips melting into a sweet clash of tongues. The heat of his mouth on hers made winter fall away.

Was this wrong? Too much or not enough? She couldn't ask what passion meant to him; not now. Not when she was all stammering need, halting and wanting and hoping. She did not even know what she hoped he would say.

So they kissed: deep kisses that made wetness slick between her thighs, gentle ones that made her strain for more. Laughing kisses as his mouth danced over her cheeks and nose; then demanding kisses that crushed their bodies together until she could feel his solid shaft, pressed between their bellies.

When she sank down from her tiptoes, breaking their link, he was breathing as hard as she was. A hot flush colored his cheekbones. God bless the complexion of a redhead, which proved he felt as much desire as she.

"We must get you undressed," she said. It was the work of two to tug free his boots and strip off his heavy woolen coat. His cravat, he untied with steady hands and a slight smile as she watched, hungry for every fraction of skin exposed.

Then he worked free his cuff links, smooth jasper set into gold.

Audrina smiled and laid them on the wooden desk

for him. "When you removed these in the kitchen yesterday, I had a treacherous urge to take them away from you so that you couldn't put your sleeves back down."

"You liked that, did you? I never guessed at the time. I took off half my clothes in that kitchen and you didn't seem to turn a hair."

"Yes, well—I'm not as proper as I seem."

"I am delighted to hear it." He made a great show of rolling up his sleeves, of rolling his hands to make the muscles of his forearms jump and flex. "Look at that. Do you find yourself overcome by lust? I'm not the slightest bit tempted to put my cuff links back on."

"Are you tempted to take your shirt off?"

He blinked. "I *like* this improper mood of yours." Within a minute, he had unbuttoned and removed his waistcoat, then tugged off the braces of his trousers.

Audrina caught hold of one and tugged it toward her. "Is this a handle for retrieving a Giles?"

"He is fair and fully caught, my lady." With an *are you ready* look, he pulled free the tails of his shirt. Audrina gave a quick, breathless nod, and at last, he bared himself.

Well. Half bared himself. But it was more of a bare man than she had ever seen before. Her dark fumblings with Llewellyn had been quick, relegated to slivers of time and corners of dark rooms. More pleasurable for the knowledge of their forbiddenness than the intimate acts themselves.

This felt like a different act entirely, though, with an intimacy never imagined. Facing him, she drank in the sight of his firm, rangy frame: golden hairs dusting the chest; strong lines of collarbone and shoulder, of pectoral and rib. His trousers slipped at the waist, granting a glimpse of a delicious angle of hip.

In a giant step and swoop, she sprang to wrap her arms around him, tightly, surprising a laugh from him. Oh, he was so big and solid and warm that she felt she could lean on him forever.

But he was not for leaning on, and she was not for leaning. This time was for being together: the pleasure of the moment, taken and given and shared. Equals, right just as they were.

"Take off the rest of your clothing," she murmured against his chest. "Please. I want to look at you."

"You said 'please.' My, my. The world has tipped on end."

She turned to the desk. Locks of hair began to tumble as she plucked free one hairpin, then another and another, laying the metal pins in a neat pile beside his cuff links. "You make me sound so impolite."

"Not impolite at all, princess. No, the world tipped when you told me what I'd wanted so long to hear."

"That I want to look at you?"

"That you want anything from me within my power to grant. That you want something from me that can please you. You—for your own sake, because you know I think you are worth pleasing."

This, she supposed, was why he would say yes now. Why they could claim one another in intimacy, not a fleshly transaction.

"I am worth pleasing," she said, "and so are you."

He turned his head away; the muscles of his shoulders bunched and shivered. He would not argue with her at such a moment; he would not refuse pleasure offered and sought. Not now, though she caught him glancing at his hands with some trepidation.

"You are," she repeated, and she knew what to do. "Come, sit by me."

She crossed to the bed and sat upon the neat white sheet. When she patted the spot next to her, he did as she asked. And she took his hand.

Not for holding in quiet peace. No. She was going to turn this hand from pain to pleasure. Cradling it palm up in her hands, she sank her thumbs into his palm and pressed. Spread. Stretched the skin and the sinewy muscle beneath.

His legs shifted, still clad in their trousers. One bare foot twitched.

"All right?"

He made an incoherent sound low in his throat. This seemed adequate permission to continue.

So she pressed again, working her thumbs into the tender heel of his palm. Pressing inward with her own hands, then tugging out, to flex and bend every one of his troublesome joints.

Pleasure can be found where you least expect it. That was what she wanted him to know; that was what she now believed. Had she not been drugged and tossed in a carriage, she would not be here now, working her fingers between those of a kind man, a great stone who let everyone batter themselves against him and who denied himself the shape he most wanted to carve out.

Who asked her what she was worth, but put no price on it. Who wanted her to see the moon and stars, not because he gave a damn but because she did.

She understood him, as though they had known each other a long time ago and only just met again. As though they'd each been waiting for someone to see them—not as better or worse, but as different. Different from how she ever thought she might want to live or be.

She was coming to love that word, *different.*

Or—*was* it the word she was coming to love? Might it instead be a love for the person who had first seeded her thoughts with that word, where it flowered?

How could one tell the difference between love and need?

She shuddered off these thoughts, refocusing her attention on his hands. Lavishing attention on each in turn, she rubbed the fingers, rolling and stretching them one by one, pressing at the skin between fingers and thumb. Each tug and movement pulled a small sound of pleasure from him: a whimper, a moan. Sometimes just a choked-off groan, his eyes shut. "Yes," he said, and her nipples went tight against the inside of her stays.

When she found the hollow at the base of his palm and worked at it, up his wrist and into the base of his forearm, his head began to sag. "Audrina. Lord."

"Are you all right? Are your hands hurting you?"

"My hands," he said in a ragged voice, "could carry the world if they needed to."

"That won't be necessary." Her mouth curled with delight. "Try this instead." And she placed his hand on her breast.

He jerked upright in an instant, all languor forgotten. They worked quickly together to strip her bare of gown and stays and shift. She crouched on the bed, nipples hard in the cool air of the room. There was no shyness; not with Giles facing her, his expression warm as he stroked her gently, up and down the sides of her rib cage, as though learning the shape of her by touch.

But she wanted to touch, too. "I like to make things,"

she said. "Paper springs"—she danced her fingers up his inner thighs, still clad—"and terrible drawings"— she clutched at his thighs with a hard, flat palm—"and delicious things." She stroked the long length of his erection through his trousers.

"You're going to *make* me finish before I even get my clothing off. Is that what you want to make?"

"The first part, yes. I want you to finish. But I don't understand why you still have anything on."

"I have no idea." He slid from the bed, yanked off his trousers, and rejoined her within a few seconds. His whole body was large and tight-corded, all solid angles and lean lines, with faint freckles on his skin as if he'd been spattered by sunlight. The copper-gold hair of his chest trailed down, turning dark as bronze about his shaft, long and thick.

Had she thought the room cool? Her skin felt hot, tight; her folds slippery.

She remembered what he could do with his hands, how just the gentle plucking of his fingertips on her nipple had cleared her mind of every thought but *more.* But his mouth—oh, that mouth. Just as it so often teased her with words, now it tormented her with touch. Tasting and pulling, a deep undertow of pleasure that made her wetter, more eager. Somehow she had climbed atop him, rolling her hips against the hard line of his thigh.

He eased himself back, lying flat on the bed. His other leg nudged between hers, spreading her wide over him. "Is it all right if we do it like this? The view is beautiful. I could not ask for better."

"My view is more than fair, too." Kneeling above him, she eased him into her inch by inch. The pleasure of taking him in, that slow slide of heat and hardness, was made even better by being able to watch his face. By seeing his eyes fall half-shut, an expression of ecstasy over his strong features.

Neither of them had words for the moment they were fully joined. It was completion, a togetherness that made Audrina's heart twist. She was not brave enough to hold his gaze; it was too deep and raw. And so she folded herself over him and began to move.

She had never felt such sensations: closeness and power and vulnerability at once. The thrust and slide of their bodies, the pressure of his hips against her pleasure spot, and his hardness within—already, this was shockingly intimate. And then he eased her upward on his chest, so his tip worked the entrance to her passage with a greater friction, the sounds of wetness an erotic background to the tight-coiling pleasure.

In this new position, she was raised over him, her fallen hair making a curtain over them. He brushed it aside, lifting his head to catch one of her nipples in his mouth. Raggedly, she worked herself over his length while he palmed her breasts and tasted and nipped, and she was tightening at both ends, so many points of pleasure at once, until she unraveled with a gasping cry.

"Oh, my Lord. Oh, Giles." She sank onto him in a boneless, pleasured heap.

"Not a lord. Just a commoner," he teased—and he thrust once, twice, more, then pulled free with a groan. Heat marked her thigh, and she realized he had spared her the risk of a child.

Had she thought, she would have asked him to do this. But she hadn't thought; she had only wanted.

"Thank you," she murmured against his chest, and she meant it for so many things.

"Wisest, I thought," he said, his breath still coming quickly. He stretched down an arm for his fallen trousers and found a handkerchief in a pocket, then reached to clean them off.

And then they settled: she atop him skin to skin on chest, breasts, belly; his arms wrapped about her. Perspiration had dampened them both, and on her back it dried cool where his touch did not shield her. "I know this can't happen again," he said. "I wasn't strong enough to say no this time."

Her thundering heart began to quiet. Yes, she had known this, too. And yet: "Why is *no* the answer that takes strength?"

His arms tightened; she welcomed the crush. "Because I wanted you so much. You—Audrina, with the bruised courage and ready laugh. Who bakes things and makes things and . . ."

Deeply, she breathed him in and let her lids flutter shut. "All I wanted to hear was that you wanted me. That's reason enough." A thought struck, and her eyes flew open again. "But why was that not reason enough to say yes?"

"Because I can't have you. Between the two of us, you're the one with more choices. You could live in the country, you could return to London. You could marry." His embrace about her loosened, one hand stroking her back.

"If I have so many choices"—she trailed her fingers down the spring of his ribs—"then you must allow that I chose you. Today. And that that means something precious to me, just as any other choice would for a woman with so many."

"Today, yes. But I know my own limitations. I know I'm not the sort of man you want for the rest of your life. And so the fact that we have only today is—difficult for me." The gravel in his voice revealed the truth of these words, though his face turned away.

A small gesture, but it made her feel as though she were twisting alone in the wind. Bracing her hands on either side of him, she pushed away from his chest and slid to the sheet beside him. "You are more maudlin than I ever imagined."

He cut his eyes toward her. "I'm good at hiding it."

"And why should you not be the sort of man I want?" She was asking far too many questions, but she was desperate for the answers. She and Giles seemed far more naked now than when their bodies had been joined, and she drew the sheet up over them. Any little shield would help cover the terrible bareness that made each word so difficult, so essential.

Heedless Giles. His expression told her she had, at last, asked a completely ridiculous question. "Why should you not want me? Because I'm an American with no future."

"Is that all? Your mother married one of those. Well—an American with a future different from anything she knew."

"You would marry me? You would leave everything you know?"

She raised herself onto one elbow and studied the stern lines of his face. "Are you asking me to?"

"No, I don't have the right."

"But if we didn't come from separate continents, would you ask me to?"

A deep breath made the sheet rise and fall over his chest. "And if I didn't have to work for my living, and if my hands were healthy, and—"

"No. I did not ask you all of that. I asked you if you would want to marry me—if we could."

His laugh was short and bitter. "Would I want to marry you? It's something I want so much that I never even dreamed I could dream it. But I don't get the things I want, Audrina."

"I am not a thing." The furious heat of a few minutes ago was cooling, leaving rawness behind.

"Marriage. Marriage is a thing. Not you. You are a marvelous person." His forearm jerked up to cover his eyes. "If there's one thing I've done right since arriving in England, it was that sentence. Saying that sentence."

Oh. Well. "I—like that sentence."

He lifted his forearm from his eyes, capturing her with a sapphire stare. "Do you believe it?"

"I want to."

"And why should you not? Who decides what you're worth?"

She shook her head to dismiss the heat prickling at the corners of her eyes. "No, Giles. *I'm* the one to ask the awkward questions."

His gaze turned to the ceiling. "There are awkward questions enough for both of us."

"What is your own answer to who decides what you're worth?"

"Me, I suppose. I decide that."

She mulled this over. "Yes, that makes sense. You are the one who has decided you cannot have the things—or the people—that you want. You are the one who has decided that because your future may be crimped, you need not bother with the present."

"And you? You have decided to seek pleasure at the expense of the future."

Her shoulder was beginning to ache where she had braced her arm, and she let herself sink back to the bed. "I think it is clear neither of us had the future on our minds when we came into this room."

"Yes," he said faintly.

"And that should be enough. A pleasure, taken and left behind." Her throat closed. They were side by side, so terribly distant, as though an ocean already lay between them. "When the snow melts, we will go our separate ways."

"It was always inevitable." There was something careful about the hard angles of his voice.

After this, there was no point in staying together. No point in pretending that resting her head on his shoulder might be a comfort, or that lingering was anything but attenuated agony. No point in pretending that they weren't both ready for him to dress and leave.

For such a quiet sound, the closing of the door reverberated through her whole body.

Because it *wasn't* inevitable that they go their separate ways—or at least, not because of circumstance. No, nothing made it inevitable but they themselves. But if Giles could not see himself with a future, how could he treasure the present as building toward it?

For the first time, Audrina saw her own reckless wanderings not as courage, but as cowardice. If nothing was serious or permanent, then nothing could really matter. No mistake would be lasting, no hurt would strike to her heart.

But this did. This did.

She was ashamed; not because of what she had done, or with whom. She was ashamed because of *why*.

Who decides what you are worth?
Everyone. Everyone but me.

She dashed an impatient palm across her damp lashes and began to dress.

Once upon a time, Giles had told her that she did not need to change the sort of person she was. But this was wrong. He gave her credit for far more bravery than she felt, and maybe for more than she possessed.

She could love him for that alone, if she allowed herself. But they both deserved a love granted on a firmer foundation than gratitude—and fear, relieved fear, that this was the end, and that their snowbound affair could be perfect in memory without dreary reality to ruin the fantasy.

Chapter Twenty

Wherein Advice
Is Freely Dispensed

The following morning, Audrina and Kitty stood on the entry porch watching trunks being loaded into carriages. Sunlight, warm on their faces, had continued to gobble snow from the roads, and the heavy slush remaining over frozen mud was thought to be passable.

"I can hardly believe it's been less than three days." Kitty tugged her cloak more tightly about her rounded body. "It feels as though I've been gone from my Daniel forever. But if I had to be trapped with someone, my lady, I'm glad it was with your party."

"Thank you, Kitty." Audrina caught her elbow to help her down the steps; the Rutherfords were planning to take Kitty home before continuing their own journey. "It was a pleasure to meet you and to learn with you how one diapers a vegetable marrow. I do hope you will be well. Will you write to me when the baby comes?"

Kitty bobbed a curtsy, setting both of them to fighting for balance on the steps. "Yes, of course. What would your direction be?"

Now, that was a good question. Would she want to stay in Alleyneham House with her parents? Would she be banished to one of her father's country estates? She could not imagine what lay at the end of this journey home, or even if there would be a home at its end.

"You'd best send the news to Lady Irving," she decided, giving Kitty the countess's direction in Grosvenor Square.

But Kitty wasn't listening; she was watching a bundled figure trudge toward the inn. Every fiber of her fragile body tensed. "Is that—" Then she uncoiled in a great spring of delight. "Daniel! Daniel!"

One hand bracing the small of her back, she navigated the final step and the yards between them with surprising speed. "Daniel!" She and the bundled figure embraced one another side to side, Kitty tucking his arm about her shoulders as naturally as though they were made to fit together. A quick flutter of low explanations followed, then Kitty led her husband back to where Audrina stood. "My lady, might I present my husband, Mr. Balthasar? Daniel, this is Lady Audrina."

Daniel Balthasar was a stocky, sturdy young man with dark hair and a deeply tanned face. He did not seem to want to let go of his wife to shake hands, so he bowed. Kitty crouched along with his bending arm, laughing.

"I am pleased to meet you, sir," Audrina said. "I

hope you were not too worried about your wife in her absence."

"I've been worried about Kitty for a while, m'lady, and tha's the truth. Fair sick when I foun' her gone, though I know she's a smart woman and wou' get a safe place to stay ou' of the weather."

"Oh, Daniel!" Kitty looked up at him with wide eyes. "And you'll never guess what I've done. Sold that puzzle box from my mother for twenty pounds!"

"You never!" The weather-beaten face of Daniel Balthasar transformed. "You've a magic touch, my loove. Twen'y pounds?"

"It's true! I've got it in my pocket."

Her husband planted a great smacking kiss upon her cheek. "Glad I am of it. We'll have the bes' doctors for you, Kitty dear, so you and baby will be well."

A dusting of snow must have blown into Audrina's eyes, for they would not stop watering.

The Rutherfords trudged over then, their carriage packed first. "We'll drop the pair of you at your home," offered Richard as he shook Daniel's hand. The Balthasars were too wise to decline this offer, and probably too cold.

Mr. Booth tugged his forelock in farewell, and Mrs. Booth bobbed curtsies all around. "Wha' an honor it was to have you all here for Christmas," she said. "I never had sooch fine crackers as what you made, Lady Audrina. If you're ever in York again, I hope you'll stay wi' us."

Audrina made some noise that probably represented assent. After Giles had left her bedchamber, she had fallen into a blue-deviled fit and forgotten to return to the bread in the kitchen. There it puffed and puffed and fell, and by the time she recalled it, there was nothing to do with the dough but make ship's biscuit and apologize.

Lady Irving arranged payment for them both, as Audrina had no money with her. The Rutherfords, too, settled their bill. And then there was just the farewell, looming like a thundercloud. No longer would they be traveling together: The Rutherfords intended to race back to London, pushing their lightly laden carriage to make the journey in three days over the terrible roads. If all went well, Lady Irving and Audrina would also arrive in three days—but just in case, Lady Irving penned a letter of introduction for Richard to take to Lady Xavier, the countess's clever code-solving niece.

"I expect we will see you in London." Giles stood before Audrina. His posture was stiff and over-formal, as though he were uncomfortable in his own skin.

She was, too, now that he had seen all of hers.

"I expect so." Audrina clipped her words off tight and kept her expression still, so it would not wobble or betray her.

He looked at her for a long moment, then with a nod of farewell, he left.

She hoped against all likelihood that they would not meet in London. Everything would be different in London: the crush of society, the demands of propriety, the disappointments of her parents.

Maybe *different* was not her favorite word after all.

The world would do nothing to bring Giles and Audrina together, and neither of them could bridge the chasm between them.

As she climbed into the carriage, she overheard Richard Rutherford behind her: "You wouldn't dislike the idea, would you, Estella? Think of me as a sleigh bell."

"Making noise long after it has ceased to be pleasant?"

Rutherford chuckled. "Bringing cheer to the wintriest days."

Audrina took her seat, peering out the carriage window, just in time to see Rutherford kiss Lady Irving's hand.

She flopped back against the hard horsehair squabs. Just now, their bright stripes offended her eye. When Lady Irving and her maid Lizzie climbed in as well, Audrina pretended to be asleep, and they pretended to believe that she was.

For three long days, the carriage cut southward toward London. At every inn where they changed horses or stopped for the night, Audrina contrasted their surroundings with the Goat and Gauntlet. Whether more lavish or less, nothing caught at her quite like the thought of that blue-walled room. Or the parlor, wherein she had left her fillet tucked in the window frame. Even the room in which Llewellyn had been locked up held a charm in memory for her. For that night, she had known he could not touch her.

It was safer to confine her thoughts to architecture. To think of people was too difficult, and for most of the journey, Lady Irving had let her keep her silence. The countess seemed to be mulling over many things, too, which Audrina guessed were related to that kiss on the hand from Richard Rutherford.

On the fourth day, at last, they drew near London. For the night, Audrina would stay with Lady Irving at the countess's Grosvenor Square house. Darkness was falling, the moon no more than a fingernail in the sky. *Waning crescent*.

She wondered how Sophy was doing. And Miss Corning—was she still at Castle Parr? How badly Lord Dudley had wanted company in his great lonely house over Christmas. Giles Rutherford was not alone in not getting the things he wanted.

By the time the lamps of London began to split the evening, Lizzie had drifted into a doze. Lady Irving poked her, and when the maid did not budge, she turned to Audrina. "Look here, girl. I've let you keep your silence, but I'm not going to keep mine anymore. Before we settle back into London, you need to know: There's no shame in changing one's mind."

"I have not changed my mind about anything, my lady," said Audrina, caught by surprise. "Or—wait, perhaps I have. What is the right answer?"

Harrumph. "A good try, but I'm not going to answer that for you. You're breaking your heart over your Rutherford and you're both too proud to say so."

Was this a broken heart, this feeling that the world was gray and endless? Before this month, she had thought the world too small. Now it stretched huge, with spaces that could not be spanned. "Nothing kept us together except a journey neither of us wanted to take."

"Wrong, wrong, and wrong." The countess's voice rose, and Lizzie stirred. Once she settled back into her slumber, Lady Irving added in a furious whisper, "Nothing *brought* you together except a journey neither of you wanted to take *at first*. By the end of it, you were glad for it, weren't you?"

Audrina opened her mouth to reply, then thought better of it. "Um."

"Blushing. I thought so. I can tell even in the dark."

The countess looked smug. "As to what might keep you together, that's up to you. But you can't blame the weather, or that stupid sot of a Llewellyn, for the fact that you left York in my carriage instead of theirs— nor for that pining look on your face. Like a child watching someone else eat an ice."

Why she had wanted to ride with Lady Irving, she didn't know. "We have all had more than enough ice lately, my lady. But I thank you for your kindly meant observations."

Lady Irving harrumphed again but did not press the matter. Likely she wanted to mull over her own romantic possibilities. This was all well and good for her, a widow of independent means and infinite opinions. She could fit in anywhere, molding any circumstance to her formidable will.

Not everyone could do so. The young, the unmarried . . . the ruined. Giles's mother had fled across an ocean. *He would probably prefer that to our staying in England besmirching his good name,* Audrina had said of her father.

Because she knew what it meant to be told to come back to London betrothed or not at all: Her father found her to be a thumb mark on the glossy surface of the family. One way or another—by marriage or by absence—she was to be buffed away. An unprofitable investment, and an unnecessary one now that Charissa's union with the Duke of Walpole seemed ready to yield such impressive results.

When had they all got into the habit of thinking that Charissa was worth more, because she was obedient and a duke wanted to marry her? Was Giles right, that Audrina thought of people as worth more or less depending on their rank? Or how much they cleaved to proper behavior?

Lamplight slipped in stripes through the carriage window; the streets widened into the familiar groomed avenues of Mayfair. Tomorrow she would call upon Charissa and explain what had happened, because she was quite sure her parents had hidden the truth of her sudden absence. Another of those thumb marks on their varnished life.

Audrina knew her error now, and it was not slipping away from a ballroom for stolen kisses, or even surrendering her virtue. Not taking a lover or hiding her heart. No, her error had been in laying her trust on someone undeserving.

And as Charissa was worth the truth, so Audrina hoped her sister would find her to be worth forgiveness.

The sort of person you are, Giles had told her once, *you do not need to change.* But this was too generous. Her courage had been false, testing others to make them prove how much they cared.

How much did she care, though?

She had cared enough, in the quiet of a Yorkshire inn, to ask Giles if he was willing to marry her. She cared enough for her sister to lay out the full truth. Asking for help, for forgiveness, was what allowed a problem to be solved.

Yes, she cared enough to think that both of these relationships were worth pursuing, worth setting right.

And that must mean she, at last, was deciding what she was worth, too.

"Lady Irving," she said as the carriage rolled to a halt before the countess's home. "You are right. I was glad for the journey."

* * *

"Are you going to marry again?" For the first time in the four days since they began their journey back to London—four long, muddy, tiring days—Giles asked the question of his father.

It was easier to talk of Richard than of anything that might remind Giles of Audrina. Like the moon, or the puzzle boxes, or an apple tart. Bread that failed to rise. A strip of folded paper. Cuff links and hairpins. Dressing or undressing.

He knocked his head against the carriage window.

Only when Richard spoke did Giles recall that he had asked a question. "I never thought to until very recently. But yes, if I can persuade Lady Irving that I would be better company than bearish solitude, I think it would suit me well. She's funny, isn't she?"

"Lady Irving?" Giles lifted his brows. "Funny isn't the word I'd use for her."

"No, maybe not funny." Richard rubbed at his chin. "Like a great grouchy tiger, all teeth and claws—but for all that, a cat who thrives on warm fires and coddling."

"So she's a bear and a tiger and a cat. Quite the menagerie you hope to set up."

"After raising six children, I'm capable of taking on any sort of menagerie." Richard leaned back against the forward-facing seat, sinking his chin to catch Giles with a *tell the truth* gaze he hadn't employed in some years. "Do you mind the idea? I hope you will not. No matter what lies ahead, a remarriage would not re- place or erase my life with your mother."

"No, no. I know that. Building a life with someone else would be . . . different." The word hurt, and he tried again. "It will be an adventure for you."

Richard smiled. "My favorite word. Thank you. And what about your happiness?"

Giles waved a hand. One of those cursed, damned hands. "Don't worry about me."

"Spoken like someone who has no children. I have done nothing since your birth but worry about you. In a loving way, of course. Wanting the best for you. Your safety, your health."

"About that." Giles flexed his hand, then drew in a deep breath. "Father. I—have what Mother had. My hands—it's been years, and . . ." Against the sadness that pooled in his father's eyes, words dissolved.

"Giles, no."

"Yes. I'm sorry." Why was he apologizing when he was the one who hurt? Or was it instead a feeling: *I'm sorry for this. I'm sorry for us.*

I'm sorry for me. He would never have told Richard at all, except that his heart hurt as much as his hands, and that was entirely too much not to speak of.

"How can you be sure?" Richard asked. The same question Audrina had asked; the same thing he himself had wondered at first.

So he explained: the long months at university, when the pain had grown beyond ignoring; the flares of agony that came with overuse. How it spread into palm and forearm, how his wrist weakened and burned until every design, every line he drew, had to be considered before he put his hand through the pain of creating it. How he had consulted a physician—and when the man offered to cure him with leeches and galvanic shocks, he decided to stumble through on his own.

As Giles spoke, Richard leaned forward: first just a slight bit, with the rocking of the carriage; then fully, a triangle with elbows propped on his knees and a smile growing on his features.

"Your hands have hurt for years?"

Why this should make his father smile, Giles had no idea. "Yes."

"Just your hands, and mostly at the wrist? Not your knuckles or feet or knees?"

"Right."

Richard let out a breath as big as a collapsing hot-air balloon. "What you've got—Giles, I truly don't think it's arthritis like your mother had."

Giles stared at his hands. As though to prove his father wrong, one wrist shot hot pain up into his forearm. "Why do you say that? After what it has done to me?"

"Because of what it has *not* done to you. Your mother soaked her hands in hot water every morning, and she had to brace herself to get out of bed because her feet hurt so badly when she first stood. Every day, it was like that, starting from when she was younger than you. None of you children are showing signs of that, thank God."

"Then what is it instead?"

"That I can't say. But if it hasn't gotten worse—if it sometimes gets a bit better—maybe it's an injury rather than an illness."

Not. Arthritis.

Not arthritis? He had lived with the certainty for—oh, seven years now. It had shaped his entire adult life.

Maybe it's an injury rather than an illness. An injury that never healed? What sort of injury could one cause by doing detailed work with one's hands?

"Maybe." His thoughts seemed locked in a wary

circle. "Maybe. I could consult another physician while we're in London."

"Good. Yes. I think that would be wise." Richard sighed. "You never said anything. All these years, you never told any of us. What a burden to bear."

"Mother was already so ill, and whenever I came home, you were so glad for the help—"

"Giles. Son. I was glad to see *you.*" In the shadow-dim evening, Richard looked worn and sad. "I should have known, when you never pursued a career you'd given years to learning. I should have guessed that something was wrong."

"Something *was* wrong. Mother could hardly move."

"Yes, but even so. She would not have wanted me to overlook any need of one of our children. And I wouldn't—don't—want that either." He shook his head. "Did she know what you thought?"

"No. I wanted to spare her that."

"And who were you sparing by never becoming an architect?"

Giles's jaw clenched. "I still got to design things."

Richard's expression looked—disgusted? It was difficult to tell in the wan light of the crescent moon and the scattered street lamps. "Buildings and jewelry aren't the same things at all."

"The process isn't completely different." Even to his own ears, Giles's excuse sounded thin. "Parts fit together into a harmonious whole, and materials are calculated."

Richard folded his arms. "Do you love it?"

"I . . ."

"Tell me right now if you love it. Do you love designing jewelry?"

"I . . . no. You know that. I've never said I loved it."

"True. That's true. Do you love something else more?"

Green eyes. Black hair. Curious and proud. Afraid but never wants to admit it.

Beautiful, within and without.

"Something, Father? No—not a thing."

"Someone, then." Richard's posture relaxed. Again, he rubbed at his chin: his *let me think about this* gesture. "Well, then. I have to ask you again: Who are you sparing by not pursuing what you want?"

Damned difficult question. He seemed to be surrounding himself lately with people who tossed that sort of thing his way.

But he thought he might be coming to an answer.

The problem was never what ailment he had, or—blessed possibility—thought he had. The problem was in how he had reacted to it. Instead of glutting himself on a purpose, on a rich and interesting life, he had bided his time. Herding the behavior of others, wanting to make himself indispensable.

But no one needed him. He wasn't indispensable. Richard had found the puzzle boxes, and Giles hadn't opened a single one. His sister Rachel missed him, but she loved many people. And Audrina—she had the money and health to do many things with her life, just as he'd told her. She need have nothing to do with Giles.

And that was all right, after all, because *need* was entirely different from *love*. Need was a parasite; love was a choice.

Richard cleared his throat. "You always seem embarrassed when someone notices what a good man you are, Giles. But I've noticed. It's nothing to be ashamed of, to be a good man." He smiled, that expression that settled so comfortably over his features. "You meant well, I think, by setting aside your dreams. But no one who loves you would want that of you."

"No," Giles agreed. "No, you are right." And these words, freely given, felt like the unlocking of a chain.

It would take courage to gather up the pieces of a long and complex future. How would it fit together? He could not imagine what form it might take. But a man building a future could ask a woman to share it.

If that woman were the expected sort of earl's daughter who wanted a life of rank and privilege, she would say no. But if she were a different sort of earl's daughter—if she saw possibility in everyday items and liked to transform them—then an undecided puzzle of a future might appeal to her.

He hoped. Hoped, like a wound soothed.

His fingers ached—not only from within, but to hold a pen and unleash a long-throttled vision.

So many details. Good God, how could there be so many details involved in one wedding? It wasn't as though he was unused to details; he—Roderick Francis Matthew Elder, Duke of Walpole, Earl of Carbury, Baron Winterset—had overseen a flourishing dukedom for nearly a decade.

With distaste, Walpole set aside the latest note from Lady Alleyneham. It was unseemly for her to ask his opinion of the future duchess's garments: whether he thought there ought to be three rows of lace at the hem of the wedding gown, or four. He could not possibly be supposed to care. The wedding gown was of interest to him mainly in its removal.

He clamped down tightly on that thought, which was also unseemly.

December 30. Only two days more, during which his future mother-in-law would likely assault him with all sorts of irrelevant queries. He pinched at the bridge of his nose, head aching just thinking about it.

He permitted himself the tiny pleasure of tossing Lady Alleyneham's note into the fireplace. This was a sensible act, for there were too many papers on this desk to allow one more to add to the clutter. And though some of his bride's relatives might display regrettable conduct, Lady Charissa herself was perfectly correct.

He returned to his work, making quick progress through reports and correspondence. During these late afternoon hours, much of polite society dined before their frivolous evening's amusements. Walpole worked.

He did not make a habit of seeing callers at this time. It was a notable trespass, therefore, when his butler rapped at the door to announce a visitor.

"A Mr. David Llewellyn, Your Grace," intoned March. "I endeavored to send him away, but he insisted his business would not wait. He says, Your Grace, that it is a matter of your personal happiness."

"My personal happiness." Walpole's brow furrowed. He could not imagine what the gentleman wanted. He, the duke, had had little to do with that family for some months, though they remained acceptable associations. "All right, March. You may show him in. Ten minutes, no more."

But he wound up listening to Llewellyn for far longer than that.

Chapter Twenty-One

Wherein the Outcome of the Ducal Wedding Is Endangered

The Earl and Countess of Alleyneham were in the habit of attending early services every Sunday. Audrina hoped they would not break their routine simply because one of their daughters was absent and the other was to be married the following day.

On the last day of 1820, then, she sneaked into her family's London home like a burglar. And maybe she was one, at that. She was stealing a space in this house—or rather, stealing it back.

Once settled into the Egyptian parlor, that fashionable horror so beloved by her mother, there was nothing to do but wait. Armored in gold brocade, she occupied herself by writing a few notes at the black-lacquer desk footed with Sphinx heads. To Sophy and Millicent, to give them the belated news of Kitty's puzzle box. To Lord and Lady Dudley. To Kitty and her Daniel. Even to the Booths, a thanks for their hospitality. All the members of the ragtag family that had collected: an eddy of people, swirled together by mysterious currents, before the tides of time and distance broke them apart again.

As she was sealing this last, she heard the sounds of her family's return. First the carriage door, then the front door, the butler's smooth greeting. Her mother's scattered speech, audible only as a pattern of sound, and then a great growl from her father.

Ah. He must have learned of Audrina's presence.

She had only time to straighten her notes and stand before the earl burst into the room. His square face was a ruddy brick of temper, his hair a wild white halo. "You have dared to return. I should have expected this. Is it"—his voice remained low and calm with apparent effort—"too much to hope that you are properly betrothed?"

Audrina waggled her ringless hands at him.

There was a delightful power in not needing anything of him. Oh, she would rather have his approval than not. But she didn't *need* it. "I returned, Father, because I want to attend my sister's wedding."

"Disobedience!"

"No. Desire." The earl grew still more red, so she added, "I do realize that my behavior reflects on you, as the man in whose household I was raised. But the behavior for which you have faulted me was not mine."

She had done many things for which he might have faulted her, had he known. But he didn't need to know the windings of her heart. He had already decided: *Your departure and your guilt are the same.*

Her anger flared to match his own. "Besides faulting me, do you realize what else you did? You took your chance to be shed of me. You left me in York, when I wanted only to come home. You traveled home with a man who had carried me off against my will. You chose him over me. You chose reputation—appearance— over the well-being of your own daughter."

As she spoke, his mouth made a hard, flat line; his eyes and brows were the color of cold metal. There was no breaking through. The heat of her anger might as well dash against a stone.

A stone could not grow or change. It could not become anything else; it was stuck. Her flood of anger began to ebb. "You abandoned me, Papa," she continued in a clear voice. "And now I am glad for that. I made the best of it—more than the best—and now I know two important things. I know what I am capable of, and I know the limits of your heart."

The earl had left behind his cane, and now he seemed not to know what to do with his hands. He folded his arms, opened his mouth—then closed it again, picking up a carved jet statue of a jackal from a marble-topped side table. "I . . ."

In the painful silence, a servant tapped at the door and announced a caller. "A Mr. David Llewellyn to see you both."

Audrina and her father made identical sounds of disgust. This was more than Audrina had been prepared to take on at once; strength quailed.

No. She was capable of this. This time she was awake, alert, and in possession of all her faculties. She could also lay hands on a penknife, if it came to that.

Not that it would. Llewellyn was a coward.

Before the unwelcome caller was shown up, the earl seated himself in the room's largest, most forbidding chair. "Keep silent, daughter, and leave this to me."

"If that seems wisest, I will." Audrina sat again in the writing desk's chair. "But the last time I kept silent and left matters to you, you gave in to fear and I was the one sacrificed. I shall not be treated that way again." The hard wooden back of the chair lent her strength, and she added, "By the way, my lady's maid should be let go without a reference, if you have not already seen to that."

"Because?"

Did it matter so little to him? "Because she allowed Llewellyn to bribe her and drug me." Confusion knit her brow. Someone else must have sent the garter from York before Christmas. Llewellyn himself? She did not know when he had returned to London. "Father, did Llewellyn stay with you all the way back to—"

"Ah, what a pleasure. *What* a pleasure." The familiar angular face of David Llewellyn beamed at them from the doorway. Cursed man. He was impeccable in wool and velvet, silk and linen, glossy boots and pomaded hair.

She wished quite desperately for a different man to enter: one with short-cropped red hair and battered boots. Not that Giles had any reason to call upon her.

"The pleasure is all yours, Llewellyn," Audrina said crisply. "Do sit. Let us get this over with quickly."

The earl cleared his throat.

"Have you something to say, Papa? Please do. Or do you simply require tea? I should be glad to ring for some to be brought to you. Not to Mr. Llewellyn, though, since he is clearly not here on a social call." She realized she was almost enjoying herself. Both men were goggling at her; she could not tell which of them was more surprised by her speech.

Good. Let them feel off balance for once. They had both betrayed her.

The earl was the first to recover. He turned to Llewellyn, who was now seated on a bench with figural ebony legs, a seat that Audrina knew to be most uncomfortable. "You're here to settle up, aren't you, pup? Let's have the garter and then we'll talk."

Llewellyn recovered his fanged smile in an instant. "*Talk* is exactly what I'm here to do, my lord. There will be no need for negotiation. You see, I spoke to the Duke of Walpole about this unfortunate situation . . . yesterday."

The earl fist's convulsed on the arms of his chair. "You foul little cheat!"

For once, Audrina agreed unreservedly with every word her father said.

Examining his fingernails with a careless air, Llewellyn tossed back, "Come, now. Would an extra day have made any difference? You never intended to turn over a penny to me. I had to look after myself."

Through gritted teeth, Audrina ground out, "*I am the one who decides what I am worth.* You had no right to set a price on me. I did no more than you to be ashamed of—and in fact, much less. I would never force someone to do anything against his or her will. Why should my family be punished and you rewarded?"

He chuckled. "Naïveté doesn't suit you, my little apple tart. We both know men rule society and men make the rules."

"Make the rules, yes," she said. "But women enforce them. Lady Irving will stand at my side. I hope that my sister will, too." She could not take for granted Charissa's help, since her elder sister had so much to lose. Her own reputation; her much-longed-for marriage. The completely conditional good opinion of their parents. Audrina did not know whether Charissa would judge this too much to risk, but she herself thought it too much to ask.

"How should a man be judged if he is looking out for himself?" A low voice rang out from the doorway of the parlor.

"Walpole!" Lord Alleyneham hoisted himself to his feet.

Audrina rose and bobbed a fractured curtsy. "Your Grace, I did not realize you had arrived."

"And would such knowledge have changed what you said?"

Audrina searched the severe features for leniency. "No, I suppose not. Though for my sister's sake, I could wish that I had not mentioned her."

"As a matter of fact, I have just spoken with her and your mother. I have had Lady Charissa's opinion of you from her own lips." By all rights, he should have handed off his ivory-headed cane when he'd entered the house, but Audrina had noticed he liked to keep it with him. At the moment, it advanced ahead of him across the room—rather like a knight carrying a lance, ready to joust at any moment. "Imagine my displeasure when I learned that Mr. Llewellyn possessed your . . . personal belonging."

"I did not give it to him, Your Grace."

Llewellyn snorted.

Audrina pressed her lips tight; held her chin high. There was really nothing more to be said than that. If appearance was all that mattered to him, as with her father, she was just as guilty despite—in this matter— her innocence.

"It does not matter if you did." Closer and closer,

the duke advanced. When Audrina dared look away at Llewellyn, a sly smile was beginning to cross his features.

Until the duke spoke again. "It would be just as wrong for him to betray a trust as it was for him to fabricate a scandal."

"I assure you, it was not fabricated, Your Grace." Llewellyn made an unctuous bow.

Audrina's face went hot.

"Was it not?" The duke lifted his stern brows. "It was Lady Audrina's idea, then, to hare off to the northern wilds and miss Christmas with her sister? Don't answer, Llewellyn. I should like the lady's reply."

"It was not my idea. No. Your Grace." She had an odd sense of unreality, as though the duke were toying with her. She clutched at the dignity Llewellyn seemed determined to strip from her.

"I asked a question earlier"—the duke swung his cane from an extended forefinger—"which neither of you has taken the opportunity to answer. But perhaps I caught you by surprise. I shall ask again. How should a man be judged if he looks out for himself?" *Thump.* The end of the cane smacked the carpeted floor heavily. "Even at the expense of others who may have less power than he? My response is that he is unworthy of the name of gentleman, but perhaps you have a different reply."

Disbelief and delight warred in Audrina, making her unsteady. She cast back a hand, supporting herself on the smooth edge of the lacquered desk. "I think that an excellent answer, Your Grace."

"And you, Lord Alleyneham?" The duke was all calm curiosity.

"I agree, naturally. Of course." The earl's face had gone a mottled red again.

"Very good. Lady Charissa, I might mention, also agrees. There remains only to solicit your opinion, Mr. Llewellyn. And it is?"

Llewellyn froze, clearly torn between bone-deep respect for the aristocracy and an even deeper desire to salvage some profit from the situation. "One must think of the scandal, Your Grace. A scandal can never be desirable."

"The scandal of canceling a wedding would be as nothing compared to the scandal of marrying into a family of whom I do not approve, I grant you that. However, I do not have to admire and adore everyone in this family. Only my future wife." Walpole fixed his gaze slightly above their heads. In a bored tone, he said, "I wonder why people are so certain that my mind can be easily swayed by personal revelations. Let me offer one of my own: I love Lady Charissa Bradleigh."

"Your Grace!" Audrina and Llewellyn both gasped at once, though no doubt for entirely different reasons.

The duke shook his head. "All of you forgot to account for that fact. I want to marry her. What could stop us, save her own disinclination?"

A laugh bubbled up from Audrina's chest. "That, Your Grace, you need not worry about."

"So she assures me." For a flicker, the distant eyes met Audrina's. "She sees the best in me. It is a lovely characteristic. I wish to live up to her vision."

What was there to do but curtsy? And grin. And— just a little, let her heart throb with a wish that someone would say the same of her.

But she and Giles saw each other too clearly for

that, and they had said far too much that could not be taken back.

The duke granted Audrina a sliver of a smile. "As we are to be brother and sister, Lady Audrina, I do wish you might call me Walpole."

Again he addressed Llewellyn. "Now, do you have Lady Audrina's item with you, or shall I accompany you to your lodging to retrieve it? I am most reluctant that you should benefit financially."

"I do not have the item of which you speak. It is being held by an associate."

"An associate?" The earl's tongue unlocked. "What associate? Damn it, man, this has gone on long enough."

Flip flip flip: The pieces came together in Audrina's head, neatly as one paper spill being wound around another. Llewellyn had told her in York that he did not have the garters—and one was sent from York upon their return from Castle Parr. There was every chance, then, that someone in the party had been bribed. And knowing Llewellyn's way with servants and a pocket full of silver . . . "It's Jory, Father. The footman. Your footman. He and Llewellyn must have worked this whole plan out ahead of time." Her nails bit into her palm. If a fierce expression could wound, Llewellyn would have been in mortal peril from several directions at once.

What is a person worth? A question that should be asked about everyone. Not only men, not only the spotless, not only nobles. Jory had been sent racing to York as though he were property. Yes, he was paid to do his work, but how had he been treated in the course of that work?

Guilt cast a shadow over her indignation.

"Is this true? Your accomplice was my own footman?"

Lord Alleyneham asked of Llewellyn, whose hesitation was confirmation enough. "Jory will be relieved of his position at once. And I shall see to it that he—"

"Papa, let us leave it at that."

Her maid and Jory had taken payment to help with Llewellyn's crime. This spoke to their character; it was their choice and their fault.

But it did not speak well for the household that two of the servants had been so readily bought. When this mad assortment of callers had departed, she would ask her mother who looked after the treatment of the servants, and how long it had been since the servants received a pay raise.

"What should we do with Llewellyn, then?" The earl's question, miracle of miracles, was directed at Audrina as well as the duke.

"Invite him to the wedding, perhaps?" The duke gave his walking stick a neat spin about his hand.

Audrina considered this startling idea. "His attendance would indicate that our family was on proper and correct terms with him. That might be an effective way to keep his repulsive schemes a secret."

"Indeed, Lady Audrina," the duke agreed. "And I do not think it a bad thing for him to be reminded of the massed power of your family associations. London society is a closely knit world, and I should be distressed to learn that he chose to prey upon the reputation of another female. Perhaps after the wedding he would care to visit the Continent for an extended time."

"I am *right here*," insisted Llewellyn with commendable poise. "And I ought to be consulted in—"

"No, you ought to be jailed." *Thump* went the walking stick onto the carpet again. "Consider yourself fortunate if you are not. Now if you will all excuse me,

I have a great many details to attend to. I shall see you at the wedding tomorrow."

Audrina curtsied as the duke made her a bow of farewell. "Your Grace, I count myself fortunate to have such a brother-in-law as you."

"Walpole," he reminded her with a hint of a smile. When he reached the doorway, he snapped his fingers. "There is one small detail—or rather two—that I neglected to mention. Our fascinating chat about the Continent reminded me."

Llewellyn made a rather interesting sound of strangulation.

"Alleyneham," continued the duke, "I arranged some weeks ago for your fourth daughter to attend the wedding as well. I do hope she will arrive today. Please give her my fondest regards. You see, all of Lady Charissa's relatives are welcome at the occasion of our marriage. They may choose to come or to stay away, but none shall I revise out of her story."

And with a final flourish of his cane, he was gone.

Easing herself back into her chair, Audrina released a deep breath. "Well."

"Good Lord," added her father.

There really didn't seem to be anything more to say than that. Except: "Nicely done, Charissa," she murmured. She had underestimated the duke. She should have credited her sister's undeniably generous heart with more sense.

Llewellyn bounced up from the wooden bench on which he'd crumpled. "I'll just be going, then, shall I, and . . ."

"Get my garter," said Audrina. "Go get it from Jory and bring it to me. *Now.*"

He was gone so quickly, he did not even close the door behind him.

There was no question in her mind that he would obey. On her own, her wishes had been easy for him to dismiss, but she was not on her own anymore. She had a family. Still. Somehow.

Gratitude, golden as a puzzle box, welled up within her.

"I am sorry you have been through so much trouble, Papa."

"You have been troublesome, I'll not deny it. But now that all's done, I'm not sorry myself."

A wry smile curved her lips. She had not meant to apologize for her own actions, yet he had heard her express fault. Oh, her stern father; he was entrenched in his own rarefied world.

"I want my daughters to have good lives." His words were halting.

"I know, Papa." Indeed she knew. This meant *I want you all to have lives that reflect well on me and your mother.* What parent would not? His limitation was in the fact that he was not able to see beyond this. To imagine that a good life might be . . . different.

Ah, that golden gratitude. It was beautiful, but it was not complete. There was a piece missing precisely the size and shape of Giles Rutherford.

A heap of coals tumbled in the fireplace.

"I have some letters to send, Papa." Audrina stacked up the notes she had penned earlier. "Would you give them a frank?"

"Hmm? Oh—yes. Certainly. Have them put on my study desk." The earl looked like a tired old lion, hands steepled and head bowed.

A knock sounded at the front door, a story below the front-facing parlor. "The duke again?" *Giles?*

When the door opened, a murmur of voices succeeded—and then Lady Alleyneham's cry of delight, so loud it traveled up the stairs. "Petra! Oh, my dear! My darling Petra!" And then a long silence, followed by: "You have brought . . . a baby?"

Audrina and her father locked shocked gazes. "Two details." Her voice was a croak. "Two details the duke neglected to mention."

Chapter Twenty-Two

Wherein the Code Is Decoded and the Cipher Deciphered

The Rutherfords swooped up Lady Irving before driving to Hanover Square to call on her niece, Lady Xavier. Both the countess and Giles's father were convinced that the young noblewoman would be able to decipher the coded letters of the puzzle boxes.

For Giles, this visit was more a matter of doggedness than actual interest. The savor of the outing had been lost when Lady Irving informed him that Audrina would not join them, as she had "already gone home to knock a few heads together."

He supposed this was a good thing. Certainly it sounded like a brave action. But he would have rather seen her than not, to put the matter mildly.

Once within Xavier House, their hostess greeted the trio warmly. "Aunt Estella, I hope you had a happy Christmas. What a pleasure to meet you, Mr. Rutherford.

Mr. Giles Rutherford." Lady Xavier was a tall woman—perhaps as tall as Audrina—clad in blue, with dark hair and eyes of a deep brown.

She looked the proper young matron, but the room in which they met her was more unusual. Over the past two months, Giles had been within numerous aristocratic town houses and country estates. Never had he seen a space quite so lived-in as the drawing room of Xavier House. Not that it was ill-kept in the slightest; its walls were covered in heavy textured paper in warm golden shades, and a thick-piled antique carpet stretched almost to the edges of the room.

But then there were the books. Books piled on every table. Books balanced atop an embroidered cushion on the sofa. There was even one tucked under Lady Xavier's arm as she made her curtsy of greeting. Each and every one of these books was bristling with tiny slips of paper.

"I mark the place," explained Lady Xavier. "When I find something interesting, or when I leave off reading aloud to the earl, and then again when I leave off reading on my own."

The earl entered the room then, a dark bespectacled man with a blanketed bundle in his arms and a harassed expression on his face. "Oh, hullo, Lady Irving. And I suppose these are the Rutherfords? Good to meet you all. Louisa, his young lordship is finally asleep, but if I put him down, he'll wake up and scream until the house falls down."

"Babies." Lady Irving rolled her eyes. "Dreadful creatures. Always needing something." Giles noticed she was reaching for the tiny bundle even before she had finished speaking.

As soon as the lightly snoring infant was taken from

him, Lord Xavier yanked the spectacles from his face and stuffed them into his waistcoat pocket. "So. Lady Irving said you had a puzzle for Lady Xavier to consider?"

"A delightful one," confirmed Richard. "Three coded messages that might—no, must—surely be related to one another. They were found inside three puzzle boxes. I have the third here." He produced the *ruiji* box that had until recently been Kitty Balthasar's, and Giles handed over his copy of the text found within the first two puzzle boxes.

Lady Xavier's brows knit as she skimmed Giles's paper, then turned the small *ruiji* box over in one hand.

"Let's all have a seat," suggested the earl. "Except for you, Lady Irving. If you let that baby wake up, I won't be responsible for my actions."

"He wouldn't dare wake up while I'm holding him," crooned the countess, nestling the baby at her shoulder. This was probably correct. If an annoyed Lady Irving awaited him when he woke up, Giles would keep his eyes shut tight indefinitely.

With a distracted smile, Lady Xavier settled herself at a writing desk and spread the papers before her. "Mr. Rutherford, will you open this box?" Richard darted over and slid the panels of the *ruiji* box, first locating the hidden key and then unlocking the box. Lord Xavier brought over an extra lamp to brighten the desk, and the young noblewoman began her study of the three sets of code.

The succeeding silence drew out thin and long as a wire. Richard cleared his throat. From his seat in a tapestry-covered armchair, Giles extended one restless leg, then the other.

"I'll require more than two minutes," said Lady Xavier without looking away from the papers. "Perhaps you would all like a drink while you wait?"

"God, yes," said Lady Irving.

Lord Xavier stood and moved to a sideboard topped by a cut-crystal decanter and glasses—along with a pile of books. "If you get drunk and drop the baby, I shall be very displeased."

"Aunt Estella hasn't dropped a baby in years, Alex." Lady Xavier again. "It will be all right."

Her husband declined to reply. Holding the decanter at arm's length, he squinted and poured a generous inch into four tumblers. "So, Rutherford. You are a jeweler?"

"I will be soon." With thanks, Richard accepted the brandy.

"And you, Mr. Giles Rutherford? How do you occupy your time?"

Giles took a glass from the earl. "I am an architect." The word sounded good in his mouth, and he echoed Richard's reply. "At least, I will be soon."

"Do you work with buildings that are getting all ragged and starting to fall down, or do you only draw up new ones?"

"I have been trained in both types of work."

"Ah, that's convenient." Lord Xavier held up a tumbler of brandy for Lady Irving, then with a warning look, set it beside her on a table. "Don't get drunk and drop the baby. *Please.*" Turning back to Giles, he added, "I ask because one of my stables in Surrey was partially destroyed in a storm, and I'm looking for a good man to rebuild it. It's not a large commission, but it's yours if you're interested."

His first commission, just like that. Good Lord. It was frightening and exhilarating at once, like stepping off a cliff and finding out that it was not a plummet, but a great smooth glide. "I thank you, my lord. Though I should note, I've done no practical design and building since leaving university. You might wish to consult someone with more recent experience."

"I'm not worried. I know you'll do well because Lady Irving is looking as though she will have you eaten by tigers if you do not. I cannot offer more incentive for success than that." Their host swirled his brandy, then tossed it back. "I know it's only just noon, but I've been awake for so long that it feels like evening. Our young rogue seems still to be nocturnal."

Giles took a sip of brandy, strong and sweet and smooth. The heat that spread through him was more than just that single sip, though: It was the sudden promise of a future. A future he could build one job, one building, one brick and stone at a time.

With a future in England, he might be able to stay. One job, one brick and stone at a time, he might be able to earn a place near Audrina. He could never be a part of her lofty society world, but he could be near her.

Near was good. Near was much better than being separated by the Atlantic.

While Giles tumbled into this fit of fantasy—a fantasy constructed as much of curling black hair and wicked hands as it was of building—the conversation had meandered on.

"Lady Irving is thinking about marrying me." Richard's feet jiggled. *An adventure!*

Lord Xavier fell into a chair. "Oh? And what are you thinking?"

"I've been asking him the same thing," said Giles.

"Out of curiosity, of course." The earl smiled. "Not disbelief."

"Er . . . right. That's what I meant, too."

"Hmph." Lady Irving sidled closer to her brandy. "That wasn't at all a bad idea about feeding you both to tigers, Xavier."

"Tut, tut." Xavier stretched out his legs with utter calm. "Not your nephew-in-law and your possible future stepson. What a family scandal that would cause."

Lady Xavier spoke up, squinting into the comparative dark away from the lamp. "Mr. Rutherford, is this the way all three puzzle boxes appeared? With the names, and then a quotation, and then these letters?"

Richard perked up. "Yes, exactly like that."

"I made as exact a copy as I could," Giles added.

"Good, thank you. It must be significant that there is a trio. If I try . . . no, then it would start with KYT." With a scratch of her quill on a sheet of foolscap, she went back to her notes. "JXS? IWR?"

"That last one at least sounds like English," Giles said.

"Yes," muttered Lady Xavier. "I . . . W . . . R . . . then would come another I . . . T . . . E. Oh, my Lord—I believe that's it. Yes!" When she looked up at them, her pale face beamed with animation. "It's a Caesar cipher."

"I don't know what that means," said Lady Irving. "As far as I'm concerned, Caesar is merely a stone head for Richard to plunk a wreath onto."

Richard managed to laugh and shush her at the same time. Quite a talent, that.

"I don't know what *that* means," Lord Xavier replied, and this time his wife waved him off with a grin.

"This message uses a substitution cipher," she explained. "It's called a Caesar cipher because Caesar is thought to have used it. It's not difficult to solve because it always uses the same letter in place of a coded letter. For example, if I wanted to say *genius*—just a word that comes to mind—then I would encode the message by shifting each letter back or forward some number. *G* would become *F* or *H*, and it would always be represented by that same letter. Caesar liked to shift three places—and so, it seems, did your late wife, Mr. Rutherford."

"Three places, three boxes." Richard's voice held awe.

"Shockingly simple, yes." The roll of Lady Irving's eyes was visible from across the room. "I feel a complete idiot for not thinking it out myself. No credit for you, Louisa my girl." Her tone was filled with pride.

"The clever thing Lady Beatrix did," added the young noblewoman, "was to encode the message across the three boxes, so it can't be solved without having all of them. Do you see? She put the first letter in the message of Box One, the second letter at the beginning of the message of Box Two, and so on. So on its own, each message is gibberish. But if you integrate them . . ."

The men sprang from their seats to surround the desk at which she scribbled a quick line of figures. Lady Irving, still holding the sleeping young lordling, glided over to join them after swallowing a quick gulp of brandy.

Giles read the familiar lines of nonsense:

Box 1

LLWVUKEGGBPBPKHSBLKBZOHBNHHWR
UDYLQDFHNZHRHQRHKKDKHYBDIJHLHS
RLDLRRRDGQUDRWQHUJIZGRIZGRDHXW
HHHFKRU

Box 2

ZWKIPXDDDILZDDPUHVDRLRGPHDZKXH
WHQJQRWQRDWUGYDRHVDOHRORLWVF
WQFUNZXYQYWHUUKWVDKRDLRRDWXG
QURWUDKHZ

Box 3

UHLRBVQQQDOHBYBDUWWXOQDDSFLB
UOLVHOGPRRQQKDOHFWULYRGXOUYK
GHLUKGQBOHDHXIPHDKWLWUUONUUR
UYWHJKVUWWH

Below these, Lady Xavier spaced a message with the letters integrated as she'd described.

LZULWHWKLVIRUPBKXVEDQGDQGDQBID
PLOBZHPDBKDYHPBSUDBHULVWKDWBRX
ZLOORQHGDBPDNHSHDFHZLWKBRXUUH
ODWLYHVLQHQJODQGFRPHWRNQRRZZRQ
HDQRWKHUDQGORYHHHDFKRWKHUDVLK
DYHORYHGBRXDOOIRUJLYHWKLVGHFFHS
WLRQULFKDUGLNQRRZBRXORYHDQDGYH
QWXUHIDUPRUHWKDQWKHVWUDLJKWWI
RUZDUGLORRNNIRUZDUGWRRXUDGYHQ
WXUHWRJHWKHUVHDUFKWKHWRZHU

"That's a beautiful message," Lady Irving said drily. "So poetic, I could cry. All those *Z*'s! They put me in mind of my childhood journey to Italy."

Amused, Giles shot her a sidelong glance. For a someday-stepmother, she might . . . not be terrible.

"You are a bottomless fount of entertainment, Lady Irving," said Lord Xavier.

"You rogue. You've no idea about the state of my bottom."

"If anyone is interested in the actual message, I can work that out." Lady Xavier wiped her quill. "If you'd all rather talk about Aunt Estella's bottomless fount instead, I shall need a brandy before this conversation goes any further."

"Vulgar." Lady Irving, of course.

Her niece murmured something that sounded like "I learned from the best" as she returned her attention to the paper.

Giles craned his neck to look over her shoulder as she wrote, but her shoulders—and the shoulders of the crowded-in Richard and Lady Irving—blocked the way. Several frustrating minutes followed; minutes in which the future seemed just out of reach, and the past seemed too far away. Thirty-five years ago, his mother had pieced out a message among three girls in northern England. A message Giles had not believed in, even with the evidence of Lady Beatrix's own final words.

Now that he knew it was real, it was like hearing her say hello again when he had almost forgotten her voice.

Another reason to be glad he had embarked upon this journey. And by now, there were reasons upon reasons, stacked like beautiful piers.

Lady Xavier slashed her pen between letters, dividing them into words; then she sat back. "I think that's done it. Does it make sense to any of you?"

I write this for my husband and any family we may have. My prayer is that you will one day make peace with your relatives in England. Come to know one another and love each other as I have loved you all. Forgive this deception, Richard. I know you love an adventure far more than the straightforward. I look forward to our adventure together. Search the tower.

"Canny Beatrix. Very canny," said Richard after reading the message. "She was so sorry that our marriage displeased her family. She must have guessed I would not return to England simply to make peace with them, but she knew I couldn't resist a treasure hunt."

"An adventure." Giles shook his head, an unwilling smile curving his lips. "*Two* adventures. As though saying it once wouldn't have been enough."

"Two adventures are far better than one," Richard replied.

Come to know one another and love each other, Lady Beatrix had asked. The Newcombes had given them houseroom as they plodded from one estate to another, but it was more a matter of duty than fondness. How could they be fond, though? They were nothing but strangers who happened to be bound by blood.

Put that way, duty wasn't a bad beginning.

Lord Xavier held out the paper and squinted at it. "So those quotations she added in there are meant to encourage love or forgiveness?"

"Forgiveness, bah. What I want to know is, where are all those diamonds she's supposed to have left behind?" When everyone looked at Lady Irving, she scoffed, "Don't act so missish. You were all thinking it.

That's why you Rutherfords came to England: to find diamonds. There must be something to that final bit, that 'search the tower.' She wouldn't say that if there was nothing to find."

"A tower that's part of her ancestral home, perhaps?" asked Lord Xavier.

Giles cast his mind back over the marquessate's family properties, all visited fruitlessly at some point in the past few months. The house in London was a neat stone slab in a row of identical town homes, just like Xavier House. It had no claim to a tower; the only structure to break the straight line of the roof was the chimney pot.

Richard's mind seemed to be working along the same lines. "Not the property in Devon . . . no, no tower that I recall in Shropshire. Derbyshire? Giles, was there—hmm. No. There is no tower there either. They're just . . . houses. Grand houses, but none of them possesses a tower. I can't imagine what it refers to."

"Not to worry." Giles pitched his voice low, mindful of the sleeping baby cradled on Lady Irving's—argh—bosom. "I'll start working on a list of every tower in England, and we'll search them all from south to north."

"Maybe just the ones in London," said Richard. "And Yorkshire, since that's where the puzzle boxes all ended up. Oh, no—Lincolnshire, too."

"A joke, Father. A joke." Giles skimmed the paper again. "There must be some other clue we're overlooking. The names of the girls?"

Lady Xavier fiddled with her quills. "Since they were real girls, their names might simply have been a way to link the puzzle boxes together. What about the

Bible verses, though? If I could look at the other two original boxes . . ." She held the small *ruiji* box beneath the bright circle of lamplight.

"She might have hidden the jewels in a church," Lady Irving suggested. "Bible verses, churches have towers, et cetera."

Giles stared at her. "That . . . makes sense. Huh. Her parents wouldn't have balked at letting her go to a church, no matter how angry they were with her."

"You needn't sound so surprised, young Rutherford. Remember, I'm the only one who recognized one of those canticles for what it was. The rest of you were shamefully ignorant."

"So." Richard rubbed his hands together. "We only have to search churches now. This is good!"

"There are about fifty million churches in England," grumbled Lady Irving. "I don't know why she couldn't just write, 'I hid my diamonds here. Go get them.'"

"*Thank* you," said Giles. "Yes."

"But that wouldn't have been an adventure," Lady Xavier replied.

"*Thank* you." Richard grinned.

Giles raised his eyes to the ceiling. "That, yes. But the code also kept anyone from finding the jewels."

"Only the perfect partnership could have done that." Richard smiled.

Lady Irving groaned. "Spare me the sentiment or I'll be sick in a bucket."

"Oh, nonsense. You love it," said Richard, and he stretched an arm about her shoulders. She went stiff—and then, after a tense second, she relaxed like a cat in the sun.

"I'll be sick in a bucket instead," said Giles.

"You love it, too," said Richard.

"No, I really don't."

"You don't have to love it, damn it, young man," said Lady Irving. "You just have to respect your father's decision."

Giles's mouth fell open.

When he managed to close it, it was smiling. And so was Richard's. "Well said, Estella. Thank you."

Lady Xavier, heedless of this tiny upheaval, was continuing to mull over the verses from the puzzle box. "These are an old translation, but I recognize the text. *Nunc dimittis, Benedictus, Magnificat.* They are the three Canticles from the Gospel of Luke."

"Hidden in a church with a tower," Giles mused. "Gospel of Luke. Is there a Saint Luke's in London? Or in Yorkshire?"

Lady Xavier blinked up at him. "Of course there's a Saint Luke's in London. That's where William Caslon's grave is."

Lady Irving sidled toward Lord Xavier. "Take this baby away, Xavier, so I can shrug properly. Louisa, my girl, I am certain I speak for everyone here when I say that I have no idea who William Caslon is."

Her niece granted her a sheepish grin. "He designed a rather lovely typeface. Why, most of these books are probably printed in Caslon's typeface." She shook her head, dismissing this topic with an apparent effort of will. "That's beside the point, though. Yes. There is a Saint Luke's in London. And it does have a tower; a rather famous one."

"Could the jewels be in London?" Giles questioned his father. "The puzzle boxes were all in the north of

England. I thought she gave the puzzle boxes away when she was at the marquessate's Yorkshire estate."

"We met in London and—ahem, decided to elope here. Maybe she posted the puzzle boxes to her young friends. I don't believe I ever asked Sophy if she received the puzzle box in person or through the post."

"So. London. Saint Luke's. The tower." Lady Irving looked from one of them to the next. "Well, shall we go right now?"

"Not yet." Giles's heart gave a stutter. "We can't go without Audrina. She's part of this . . ." He paused. "Adventure."

"Good boy." Lady Irving beamed at him. "We've got a stop to make at Alleyneham House, then."

In his father's arms, the future earl gave a tiny yawn, as though nothing at all of moment had occurred—when almost everything had, or was about to.

Chapter Twenty-Three

Wherein the Tower Is Identified, Along With Other Items of Significance

Based on his last meeting with the Earl of Alleyne-ham, Giles thought the blustering aristocrat might have locked up his daughter, Rapunzel-like, until his fortunes were safe. Giles was perfectly willing to spirit Audrina out a window, but in the end, no dramatics were required. Lady Irving simply marched ahead of the Rutherfords up the stone steps to Alleyneham House, rapped at the door, demanded Lady Audrina's presence, and glared at the servant when he goggled at her.

"That glare of yours is a formidable weapon, Estella," marveled Richard.

"Enough of your love talk," said Giles. "We'll celebrate if she actually comes to the door."

Two minutes later, she did, descending with as

much grace as if she were floating down the grand staircase at a ball. The sound of a baby's cry and a thundering shout chased her, but as soon as the door closed behind her, all sound was shut away.

Dimly, Giles heard her greeting them, and then saying something about her sister Petra having arrived, and Llewellyn having been silenced—and somehow, a baby was involved in the whole affair. It was all difficult to follow when every speck of his awareness was working on drinking in the sight of her, the scent of her, wanting to embrace her and swing her around in that great dark bell of a cloak, letting it wrap about them both.

"Giles? Giles?"

"Hmm?" He bounded down the steps to catch up with them.

"I was just saying"—Audrina's lips curved with mischief—"that I have got my garter back from Llewellyn. It turns out the Duke of Walpole was not interested in having his wedding canceled. Also, I appear to be an aunt."

"You've had an eventful morning."

"I have, rather." When she clambered into the carriage, she took the backward-facing seat next to Giles. "My sister Petra insisted on studying art in Italy, but it was actually a ruse to hide a—a pregnancy." She blushed at the word.

"Vulgar," said Lady Irving from her seat next to Richard as the carriage began to roll.

"That's what Papa said, too. Petra will not say who the father of baby Adam is, only that he wasn't suitable for marriage, which made Papa shout all over again. Then the baby cried, and Mama held him. Then she shouted at Papa to stop shouting at her only grandchild." A dazed expression crossed her features. "And Petra said it wasn't a lie after all about studying art because she began to paint while in Italy and wants to return there. She has fallen in love with an Italian artist."

"Art is vulgar," said Lady Irving.

"Now, Estella, you're just saying things to make a spectacle of yourself. If you want me to pay attention to you, all you've got to do is say so." Richard's tone was mild, and he took her hand in his.

"Don't be ridiculous. Pay attention to Audrina's vulgar story." Giles noticed that she did not remove her hand from Richard's.

His own prickled—not with pain, but with the feel of Audrina at his side. So near, yet for the moment, still untouchable.

"That is the end of my vulgarity, at least in relation to this particular subject," Audrina said. "It seems I am no longer the most scandalous daughter in the family."

"Does that matter to you?" Giles asked.

Her hand slipped free from the folds of her cloak; her knuckles brushed his. "No. I have always only ever been myself."

"You said the Duke of Walpole arranged Petra's visit, though, didn't you?" Lady Irving demanded. "If so, your parents will come around. Especially if she takes herself back to Italy and gets married. Not to speak ill of your parents, but they would eat their own heads if a duke told them to."

"I don't even know how that would work," said Giles.

"I don't either, but it is true." Audrina laughed. "It is not as if the duke loves having an illegitimate nephew-in-law, but . . . how did he put it? He will not revise anyone out of his future wife's story. Something like that."

"Hmph." Lady Irving shoved at her listing turban. "Walpole might not be a complete horse's ass after all."

"I have begun to think he is not a horse's ass at all," replied Audrina.

"Steady, now," said Giles. "You two are going to send us into a swoon with all your profanity and your talk of other men."

"Vulgar," Richard said solemnly—though a smile broke across his features after a shamefully short interval.

Audrina's hand had settled in next to Giles's now, and shielded by the folds of her cloak, her thumb stroked his skin. As Giles's toes began to curl within his boots, she asked with perfect calm, "Now you must tell me about your own eventful morning. I presume something fascinating has happened for you all to come retrieve me in such haste."

They passed the remainder of the carriage ride catching Audrina up on the letters, the clues, and the deductions that were leading them these several miles through the cluttered streets of London. Had Giles been less distracted by the sly sweetness of her touch, he would have contributed much more. But the tale rolled on, just like the carriage wheels, and by the time Richard and Lady Irving halted, Audrina glowed like Yorkshire moonlight.

"You solved it," she said. "You all solved it. That is amazing. We are going to find those diamonds if I have to crush rock into gemstones myself."

"If you can do that," said Richard, "I'd be glad to offer you a position in my shop."

Her smile turned puzzled. "If we find these jewels, Mr. Rutherford, will they rightfully belong to the marquessate?"

"No, these jewels were given to Bea personally and irrevocably. Which means, I guess"—Richard tilted his head—"that they're now mine."

Lady Irving snorted. "They won't suit you."

"Would they suit you?"

She pulled her beringed hand free from Richard's. "No, I'd rather choose my own. I'll clear a finger for you, though."

Giles and Audrina exchanged *does that mean what we think it means* glances.

"Why, Estella!" Richard beamed at the countess. "I believe you just accepted my proposal."

Nonchalantly, she patted her turban, which was crusted with bright paste gems. "I believe I did."

A few more minutes' drive brought them to the possible home of Lady Beatrix's jewels. Saint Luke's was a small church of pale stone, simple in form, with lightly ornamented arched stained-glass windows. The small, neatly trimmed lawn and cemetery, now winter-dry, were fenced in by wrought-iron pickets.

"There's a tower," observed Richard as they disembarked.

This was not a particularly insightful observation, for the tower was taller than the church was long. A strange tower it was, flanked by small domes, all dotted upward with round and arched windows, and topped with a reeded obelisk. As they walked up to the entrance, Giles noticed something yet more odd: The windows had an alarming cant, as though bits of the church were sinking. Peeling away from the others, Giles prowled along one side of the building, noting signs of subsidence in the foundation.

Though this was bad news for the church, it was good, *good*, to allow himself to notice such details. Like greeting old friends instead of hiding from them.

Not wanting to test the others' patience too much, Giles strode back to join them, and the four entered the small church together. A robed rector was moving about the pews, a service clearly just over. He welcomed them and asked how he could help.

"We wish to look at the tower," said Richard.

"We need to pay our respects to a relative," Giles said.

"We're here to visit Caslon's grave," barked Lady Irving.

The rector blinked at them.

"What we mean," Audrina said smoothly, "is that we wish to do all of those things." She lifted her chin, that look he'd once thought of as haughtiness. Now it looked like confidence. *I have a right to be here.* "We will, of course, leave a generous donation in the poor box before we depart."

Coins jingled in her reticule, and suddenly the rector was tucking something into his pocket. "Take all the time you require. I shall leave you in peace."

"Peace be with you," called Richard after him.

"Papist," muttered Lady Irving.

They were left alone, then, with the smell of damp stone and just-snuffed candles and no idea where to look next. Giles's gaze roved the white-painted lines of the church, the small round stained-glass windows, the wall of stained glass behind the altar.

"Quit making flirtatious eyes at the windows, young Rutherford, and come smash up the floor." Lady Irving jabbed Giles's side with an elbow, then pointed to the pattern of tiny black and white squares.

"I am *not* going to smash the floor of a church." He rubbed at his ribs. "Besides, Mother couldn't have hidden anything beneath the floor or she would have had to smash the tiles herself."

"Damn. She couldn't have made our hunt easier, could she?" Lady Irving mused.

"Oh, she could have," said Richard. "But what would be the fun in a life with someone who made everything easy?"

"You and I, Father, are very different."

"Indeed we are." Richard clapped Giles on the shoulder. "And what on earth is wrong with that?"

"Nothing in the slightest."

"While you all are arguing, or agreeing, or whatever it is you are doing"—Audrina's voice echoed off the stone walls—"I have begun looking around the base of the tower, and I've found a stone with a date on it."

"Let me see!" Lady Irving was the first to reach her. "Oh, phoo—it says 1729. That's got to be the year the church was built. That doesn't do us a bit of good."

"Not that stone." Crouched on the floor, Audrina pointed to the beveled stone molding that joined floor and wall. "That one."

To bring his eyes to the level of her finger, Giles had to lie flat on the floor. He cast up a silent prayer of apology, then slid his hand after Audrina's.

"I felt it," she explained. "The rest of the stone is so smooth, and then something is chiseled into it. Once you know it's there, you can make out the numbers."

1785.

It was real.

Lady Beatrix had left behind jewels and puzzle boxes thirty-five years before. Her message, her gift to a family she didn't know yet.

"I never knew my mother had such a fondness for chiseling things." He traced the numerals, so small and faint that he doubted their existence—but there they were, tiny imperfections in the stone. He smiled as he sat up again, though tears pricked at his eyes.

She seemed found again, the woman who had been lost to long illness. When she scratched these numbers into stone, she was hopeful and happy and full of mischief, a laughing woman with Giles's blunt-fingered hands and rangy build, his freckled face and fiery hair. "I wish you could have known her," he told Audrina.

"I do, too," she said. "Though I feel I'm getting to, a bit. She certainly enjoyed an adventure."

"So there's something behind the stone." Lady Irving straightened back up, one hand at the small of her back. "Hmph. None of us brought a single tool with us, did we?"

Audrina pawed through the folds of her cloak and put a hand into the pocket of her golden gown. "I have a penknife. I picked it up earlier after writing some notes, in case Llewellyn caused any trouble." She said this matter-of-factly as she unfolded the flat blade from its ivory handle and extended it to Giles.

He caught her hand instead of simply taking the knife. "I love you. Did you know that?"

He hadn't meant to say that. But when the words tumbled forth, they were exactly right.

She sat back on her heels, brows lifted. "I didn't, actually, but that's good. I love you, too."

Each folded into a ridiculous pile on the cold floor

of the church, a stone and a knife between them—
they smiled. No, smile was too mild a word for what
Giles's face was doing. It wasn't just his lips; it was his
heart and his mind and every sinew of his frame, all
wanting to leap and jump with swooping delight.
"You do?"

"Yes."

She blinked, then laughed, a low bubble that made
him forget the hard cold stone or anything that wasn't
her face and her laugh and her kindness and her
brilliance, because *good Lord, the woman has a penknife
with her.* Giles caught her up and planted a smacking
kiss on her lips. "You amaze me, princess. You. Are.
Amazing."

"No doubt this is all beautiful"—Lady Irving's voice
filtered down as though from a great height—"but if
one of you doesn't use that knife on the stone, I will
use it on you."

Giles rolled his eyes. "Do you feel as though we're
being chaperoned?" Not that he minded, really. He
wouldn't mind anything right now. He felt as though
his face must be permanently folded from all the
grinning.

Taking up the penknife, he caught its tip in the top
seam of the stone molding. "Here goes." He pressed
down onto the beveled joint with the thin blade.

Something crumbled.

His hands shook. "It's joined with mortar. It's not
solid stone."

"Lady Beatrix mortared the hiding place? Was she
in the habit of carrying mortar about?" Lady Irving
sounded skeptical.

"Surely she would have brought what she needed to

hide the jewels," Richard said. "Mortar, tools—anything to hide her treasure."

"Keep working at the joint, Giles!" Audrina urged.

Giles needed no urging, though. Drawing in a deep breath, he steadied his hands and followed the line of the stone. A grating sound issued as the knife blade split the thin seam of old mortar. With a satisfying pop, the last bit came free and a plate of stone molding the height and width of his hand tipped forward. Audrina worked it free and set it gently aside.

"What do you see?" asked Richard.

Giles leaned back so they could all look together: a crack, likely from the settling foundation, which had been chipped out and widened into a space the size of a fist. Stuffed into it was a wad of faded, discolored velvet.

He caught his breath. Held it. Tugged free the fragile old cloth, which proved to be a small drawstring bag. It was weighty, promisingly so. One of the strings snapped, rotten, as he pulled it.

"Father? Will you do us the honor?"

Richard held out a hand, and Giles upended the bag into it. A jumble of glassy fire and gold fell forth, so much that he had to swoop up his other hand to cradle it in his palms.

Lady Irving uttered an admiring blasphemy.

"Yes," said Richard. "Yes, exactly." The diamonds winked and beamed at them.

Richard sat on the floor and began laying out pieces. A crescent-shaped brooch, a jeweled hair comb, drop earrings, a ring, and a necklace. They were great stones, baguette and emerald cut. In the necklace, each was edged by tiny winking gems with a generous-sized edge of more diamonds. Between these, two delicate lyre shapes, almost like a tulip bud, lay on their sides and supported a giant teardrop diamond.

It was a fortune in stones. It was enough to build a business on—or a new life.

Giles swallowed. "My father and I talked about this, Audrina. If we found the stones, we agreed that you should choose any piece you liked."

"Why?" She turned from the diamonds to look at him, puzzled.

"Because you were part of this quest. Because I don't want you to feel trapped, ever. You should have the right and the freedom to decide your own worth, in whatever way you wish."

Richard cleared his throat. "Let's give them a bit of privacy, Estella."

"You must be joking. This is better than an evening at the theater."

Before Richard marched her away, he turned out his pockets into the poor box.

Audrina watched them walk up the church aisle. "If you want to know what I wish, Giles . . . I wish we would marry. I know you said you would not, but if the only thing keeping us apart is your hands—and my pride—and all the happenstances of birth, and distance—"

"Oh, is that all?" Somehow, over his heartbeat's thumping agreement, he managed a mock frown.

"Well, yes. I said nothing about feeling or worth, did you notice? I feel more . . ." She considered. "Myself. I feel more myself with you. And I love you." She laced her fingers into his. "If we need to, we can use my whole dowry to treat your hands, and we'll live in a hovel. As long as you design it. Only if you think any of this sounds like something you might like to do, tell me at once because I am beginning to feel nervous." Not that her features betrayed a flicker of it.

Until he said, "It all sounds like something I want to do," and she let out a sigh that seemed to fold her in half.

"Let me do the thing properly." Helping her to her feet, he then knelt before her right there on the cold flags of the church floor.

"I see what you're up to, young Rutherford," called Lady Irving. "There's a ring right next to you."

Giles ignored this in favor of the pair of warm green eyes that studied his. "I want to marry you, Audrina. I want to be with you; I want to deserve you. I want to watch you laugh or set your jaw or ruin bread. I want to notice when your eyes well up—yes, just like that—and have a handkerchief for you . . . Oh, for God's sake, I don't have a handkerchief. I'm sorry."

She laughed. "I don't need to wipe these tears away."

"Everything you suggested sounds delightful," he said, "except for living in a hovel and tossing away money on medical expenses. I do not think that will be necessary. You see, there's a more than fair chance that I am . . ." What was the word? "Fine." *Fine* was as good a word as any.

She gaped. "How—when—how can you—" She shook her head. "Explain," she finally choked out.

So he did, a quick sketch of his mother's symptoms and his own, and—not insignificantly—the relief from pain that had persisted for a blessed interval after she stretched and rubbed his hands. "But even if that weren't the case, I would propose marriage to you. I wanted to, you know that. Between the two of us, we did a fair job of chasing ourselves apart. But I never wanted to go."

"I wanted you to stay." Her voice caught. "I wanted to lie in your arms in bed, in a room painted the color of your eyes. I wanted you to say that you wanted to marry me because a future together was worth fighting for."

"*You* are worth it." He paused. "You make me want a future of bright and infinite possibility. You make me appreciate the present more: this now, and all the nows that come after. On either continent, on either shore, I want to be with you."

"Why not both? Your father has crossed the Atlantic several times. Surely we could, too." The set of her jaw, that vivid look in her eye, that flush on her cheek: She was having An Idea. "When you wish, I will travel with you to America on two conditions."

"What are those?"

"First, we must live in New York, or wherever it is a man of imagination and skill can design buildings. Second, our home must always be open to your siblings—or mine, should any of them venture across an ocean. Oh, and there's a third condition as well."

He realized he was still kneeling. Holding her hand, he eased to his feet. "The first two would be my honor. What else are you thinking of?"

"We must get a dog. Since we left Castle Parr, do you not miss having dogs about?"

Chapter Twenty-Four

Wherein the Adventure Ends, and Also Begins

Had the wedding of Lady Charissa Bradleigh to the Duke of Walpole taken place in a fairy tale, the first day of the year 1821 would have dawned with sunshine and birdsong.

Instead, the sunshine was distant and reluctant, and any birds trying to sing forth the day were silenced by a belligerent wind.

But Audrina had grown used to stern weather over the past few weeks. She had developed a certain fondness for freezing rain and drifts of snow. She did not even mind being mired in mud.

As long as one had the right company.

And this morning, as seemingly all of polite society flocked to Saint George's in Hanover Square, she had the best company imaginable. Not the duke her parents had wanted for her, and not the scandal she had once sought for herself. No, she held the arm of Giles Rutherford, whose heart was both noble and roguish. And who loved her, just as she was—which was one of the most seductive thoughts a woman could possibly entertain.

Well. She could probably think of others, too.

With the crowds of guests and sundry onlookers, they passed beneath the grand pedimented façade of the church. Saint George's could hardly be a greater contrast to the small, echoing puzzle box of Saint Luke's. All soaring spans and ornamentation, it was floored in black and white marble, with sparkling chandeliers casting down their winking warmth. Giles whispered all sorts of observations into Audrina's ear, admiring comments about *clerestory windows* and *barrel vaulting* and *triforium*.

"From your use of strange and wonderful architectural terms, I gather you are enjoying yourself," she murmured back.

She was, too. After returning from Saint Luke's the previous afternoon, she had laid out the tale of her absence for Charissa, who was first shocked, then relieved by the pleasant resolution, and finally delighted by her betrothed's heroics. Then Audrina had kissed her infant nephew's fuzzy-haired head and listened to Petra's plans for the future. She had embraced Romula and Theodosia when they arrived, scarred but smiling behind their veils.

There was more room for *different* in her family than any of them had ever known. Tongues might wag behind closed doors or fluttering fans, but the family would soldier through. Today was an important part of that, as the silk-wrapped members of high society stood shoulder to shoulder in this grand church, with light spilling jeweled through stained glass, over dark pews and bright faces, to celebrate. To witness as vows transformed a man and a woman into a husband and a wife.

That was the essence of it. That was the heart of this day. And with her hand on Giles's arm, she felt the significance, the promise of it, as never before.

As the final words of the ceremony were spoken, Charissa grinned, and even the Duke of Walpole's inscrutable features were softened by a smile. Audrina noted that her mother clutched a handkerchief and tried to cry, while her father visibly sagged with relief. At last, one of his daughters had caught a duke. Or rather, she and the duke had caught each other.

The resplendent new duchess walked back up the aisle on her husband's arm. Her dress was fit for a princess: silver lamé net over a silver-shot silk, flounced with three rows of lace. Their mother had dithered and agonized over whether a fourth ought to be added at the last moment, but the arrival of Petra and young Adam had shaken up the countess's plans and saved the fingers and eyesight of the *modiste*.

Besides the new duchess's glow of happiness, her jewelry caught the eye of many. As His Grace and Her Grace passed, Audrina overheard murmurs: "Where could she have got that necklace? So elegant! I thought I had seen everything Rundell and Bridge had to offer."

She turned and recognized the speaker as an acquaintance, so she allowed herself a reply. "It is a Rutherford piece. Do you know the name? He will soon have a shop in Ludgate Hill."

When the lady mustered a knowing expression— "Oh, Rutherford—of course!"—Audrina turned back to Giles and whispered, "There, we knew good would come of Charissa wearing your mother's necklace."

Something borrowed and something old at once. It seemed it would bring luck not only to the bride, but to Richard Rutherford.

The guests filed from the church, and a crowd formed on the front steps as carriages lined up to take them to the wedding breakfast. The formality of the ceremony dissolved into a clutter of embraces and how-d'you-dos, and Audrina sighted familiar faces. Lord and Lady Xavier were there, as expected; the earl had taken off his spectacles as usual and was squinting at Lady Irving as she recounted the end result of Lady Xavier's puzzle solving.

And that snake, David Llewellyn, really had attended the ceremony. When he became visible in the crowd, Giles growled. *Growled*, like a beast.

"Shh." Audrina laid a calming hand on his arm, though the growl was most gratifying. "We have to act as though we don't want to punch him in the face. This is all part of Walpole's plan for diverting scandal."

"Scandal, scandal. Who gives a damn? I *do* want to punch him in the face."

"You sound like the lady who is soon to be your stepmother."

Giles went pale. "You shouldn't say such things."

Laughing, Audrina edged closer to the lady in question, still in conversation with Lord and Lady Xavier. She wanted to thank Lady Xavier for so handily breaking the codes within the puzzle boxes. She had never known the young countess well, but had admired her wit ever since they'd both attended a scandalous house party at Lord Xavier's country estate two years before.

As the words of gratitude were leaving her lips, another couple joined them: a small blond slip of a woman with loosely pinned hair, followed by a sandy-haired man with an expression of wry good humor on his features.

"Ah, Julia," said Lady Irving. "Did you get to hug your newly-wed friend? Most vulgar, of course, to show that sort of enthusiasm."

The blond woman was introduced as Lady Irving's step-niece: Julia, Lady Matheson. Audrina, mentally paging through the peerage, recalled that this lady—who was also Lady Xavier's stepsister—had married a viscount several years before, since which time the pair had lived in the country.

"I did hug her," said Julia, "and I didn't mind that it was vulgar, and neither did she." To the others, she explained, "Lady Charissa was my first friend in London when I arrived here several years ago. James and I don't return to the city often, but we couldn't dream of missing Charissa's wedding."

"I dreamed of it," said the man at her side. "It was the only dream I've had in weeks, now that our youngest has decided to spend her nights growing teeth instead of sleeping."

Julia gave her husband a tight hug. "Because you came along, you got to sleep in the carriage!" To Lady Irving, she added, "We're returning to Kent tomorrow. The nurse says she'll give notice if we stay away longer. Something about how our two children talk more than any four she's ever cared for."

"I considered it a compliment, really," said Lord Matheson.

"I did, too." Julia craned her neck. "James, can you tell whether our carriage is here? There's a tin of biscuits hidden beneath the seat, and I want to eat them."

"We're about to attend a wedding breakfast," said Lady Irving.

James laughed. "Just wait and see. She will still be able to do justice to the food. My wife is a woman of strong appetites."

"Vulgar," Lady Irving said. Audrina noticed with some delight that Julia, Louisa, and Giles all mouthed the word as she said it.

"So, Aunt Estella," added Louisa. "Do I understand correctly that you are soon to embark upon a vulgar state yourself?"

"If you mean that I'm getting married, yes. Eventually. Soon. You'll all have to start calling me Mrs. Rutherford instead."

"I'm not certain my nerves can handle the shock," James mused. "Will Mrs. Rutherford still wear bright turbans and bark out orders?"

A tiny smile. "Very likely she will, yes."

"Then I am happy for her. And I wish Mr. Rutherford all the luck in the world. Where is the fortunate fellow, by the way?"

This was a good question; Rutherford had melted off after the ceremony. Lady Irving waved a hand. "Something to do with those diamonds we just found. The new duchess will be wearing the entire parure for the wedding breakfast. Sounds dratted uncomfortable if you ask me, but she seems to like shiny things."

"Fortunately for the jewelers of London, many people do." Giles paused. "Stepmama. Oh, no, I can't do it. I'll have to keep calling you Lady Irving."

"You young rogue."

The carriage for Lord and Lady Matheson and Lord and Lady Xavier drew up just then, followed by the crested equipage of the countess-for-a-bit-longer. Farewells ensued, then Lady Irving elbowed Audrina.

"Audrina, what's got you standing like a looby? Get in, girl."

Even through their gloves, Audrina relished the warmth of Giles's hand. "I shall ride with Giles."

"Oh, is *that* how it is?" She harrumphed. "I suppose it's all right since you're betrothed. Mind you don't forget to turn up for the wedding breakfast."

Audrina dutifully promised—though in truth, would anyone notice if she and Giles were absent? Such a happy chaos of family and friends, of well-meaning strangers and one defeated Llewellyn. In fact, the only people Audrina could not recall seeing were her dear friend Jane, Lady Kirkpatrick, and her husband. They had begged off the wedding in favor of spending the Christmas season with Lord Kirkpatrick's family in Cornwall. If Audrina was still in London when the Season began, she would see the return of the Kirkpatricks in company with his lordship's sister, making her society debut.

If that young lady seemed inclined to sneak away from ballrooms in the company of strange and sinister men, Audrina could give her a bit of advice. But really, there were so many ways to find happiness that she would probably do nothing except wish them all the best.

At last, the battered carriage rented by the Rutherfords several months ago drew up before the church steps. "Lady Irving will see to it that your father gets a stylish new carriage," Audrina said as they climbed in.

"I have no doubt that Lady Irving will see to everything my father could possibly imagine, and a great deal more besides."

With a gentle jolt, the carriage set off for the short drive to Grosvenor Square. They could have walked the distance more quickly, but this way, they had privacy for a few minutes.

A few minutes they used to great effect. In this few minutes, they learned precisely what could be touched without creating telltale creases in one's clothing; they kissed, deep and sweet and all the more enticing for having to be so, so careful not to displace a single hairpin in Audrina's hair.

"I can't touch you enough," Giles growled before trailing kisses up the line of her neck. This growling was a rather intriguing new habit, and one that Audrina intended to investigate fully in a situation with more time and fewer clothes.

All too soon, the ride was over. Not a hint betrayed their interlude save for flushed cheeks and quick breathing.

Well—one thing might betray them. "Give me a few minutes to settle." Giles drew in a deep breath. He rapped at the ceiling of the carriage and ordered the driver to make a circuit of the square.

"We shall talk of innocent things. Perfectly innocent, not at all lust-inducing subjects." Audrina racked her brain, finding it more difficult than expected to think of a non-lust-inducing topic when alone with Giles, her skin tingling from the memory of his last kiss and the promise of his next. "Um. After the wedding breakfast, we shall be off to Surrey? You mentioned that Lord Xavier had a small commission for you."

"Yes. But eager though I am to begin, there are a few things I'm even more eager to do. First we shall get a special license, if your father is willing to put in a good word with the Archbishop of Canterbury."

"If he will not, Walpole will," Audrina said. "My new

brother-in-law seems eager that his wife's family should be happy."

"What a bright fellow. Your sister has chosen well." Giles flexed his hands. "I also wish to consult a physician about the pain in my hands and wrists, as long as I can locate a medical man who doesn't think leeches and galvanic shocks are the cure for every malady."

"I am no medical man—"

"Thank goodness."

"*But* I think I have an answer that will help." She slid away from him on the squabs and took one of his hands in hers. Pressing at the center of his palm, she worked at the joints until he sucked in a sharp breath.

"Yes. Yes, you do. Now stop that or I'll ravish you in the carriage."

"Is that meant to make me want to continue, or to stop? Because it's having the former effect."

Giles shut his eyes. "I can't tell the driver to go around the square again. I cannot. Cannot. Cannot. Others will notice."

"All right. Goodness. I am beginning to suspect that you are not as improper as you pretend to be," she teased, releasing his hand. "What after Surrey, then? Shall we see the world?"

"We might be able to see more of England first, if that's all right with you. My aunt, Lady Fontaine, cannot navigate her own home because she uses a wheeled chair. A nephew with some knowledge of building might be able to figure out ways to amend the structure for the sake of her comfort."

"That sounds like an excellent notion. I should like to see you make peace with your mother's relatives."

"Yes, I'd like that, too."

"There must be other such families," Audrina said. "Like Lord and Lady Dudley, perhaps. Families who need a bit of change in order to be comfortable in their homes. A man of connections—with an earl's family on the distaff side and a marquess's on his own—could surely find those people."

"I'll give it my all, though whether in England or America, we won't be a wealthy pair," Giles warned. "I know you say you don't mind, but we've just seen your sister wearing a fortune in silver silk."

She waved a hand. "You forget about my dowry. It won't yield income enough for a life in London society, but it will keep us comfortable. Think of yourself as my courtesan."

He choked. She grinned.

"It would be my honor," he said, "to see to your pleasure. Oh, damn—we're going to have to send the carriage around again. I'm in no fit state to climb out."

Audrina laughed. "And to think, when we first met, you said you were the end of my adventure."

He pressed a kiss to her lips, one full of tenderness and desire. "And so I shall be. But I hope for now, and for many years to come, that we'll share a new one together."

AUTHOR'S NOTE

Japanese artifacts would have been rarities in Regency England, because until the 1850s, Japan was almost completely closed to Western trade. But through Dejima, an outpost in the port of Nagasaki, Dutch merchants—such as those in Lady Beatrix's background—were permitted to trade with the Japanese on a closely monitored basis.

In reality, the type of Japanese puzzle box that plays such a significant role in this story—the *himitsu-bako* ("secret box")—didn't develop as an art form until about a century after Lady Beatrix's puzzle box made its way westward. But certainly a gifted artisan could have made a puzzle box in an earlier year. Historical romance characters often benefit from the *possible*, which gives much more scope for storytelling than the *likely* or the *everyday*.

A few medical notes: The term *arthritis* has been in use for joint pain since the 1500s, though it's not likely a Regency physician would have been able to distinguish between different types. Lady Beatrix—and her sister, Lady Fontaine—suffered from rheumatoid arthritis, an autoimmune disease that can strike at any age. Giles fears he has inherited that tendency, but his own joint pain is due to something many computer users are familiar with: carpal tunnel syndrome. The symptoms can mimic those of arthritis, but unlike his mother, Giles would have been able to make a complete recovery with rest and care.

On a more festive note, Regency Christmases were simple compared to the elaborate celebrations of the Victorian era (not to mention today). The tradition of Christmas trees hadn't yet begun, but perennial favorites such as carols, puddings, evergreen garlands, and—of course!—mistletoe were all part of the holiday observances at the time. Other practices have gone by the wayside; for example, the huge Christmas pie of a half-dozen meats that Mrs. Booth proudly prepared. You can find a historic recipe for that pie, along with free stories and other short reads, on the Extras page of my website at theresaromain.com.

Books by Bestselling Author
Fern Michaels

___The Jury	0-8217-7878-1	$6.99US/$9.99CAN
___Sweet Revenge	0-8217-7879-X	$6.99US/$9.99CAN
___Lethal Justice	0-8217-7880-3	$6.99US/$9.99CAN
___Free Fall	0-8217-7881-1	$6.99US/$9.99CAN
___Fool Me Once	0-8217-8071-9	$7.99US/$10.99CAN
___Vegas Rich	0-8217-8112-X	$7.99US/$10.99CAN
___Hide and Seek	1-4201-0184-6	$6.99US/$9.99CAN
___Hokus Pokus	1-4201-0185-4	$6.99US/$9.99CAN
___Fast Track	1-4201-0186-2	$6.99US/$9.99CAN
___Collateral Damage	1-4201-0187-0	$6.99US/$9.99CAN
___Final Justice	1-4201-0188-9	$6.99US/$9.99CAN
___Up Close and Personal	0-8217-7956-7	$7.99US/$9.99CAN
___Under the Radar	1-4201-0683-X	$6.99US/$9.99CAN
___Razor Sharp	1-4201-0684-8	$7.99US/$10.99CAN
___Yesterday	1-4201-1494-8	$5.99US/$6.99CAN
___Vanishing Act	1-4201-0685-6	$7.99US/$10.99CAN
___Sara's Song	1-4201-1493-X	$5.99US/$6.99CAN
___Deadly Deals	1-4201-0686-4	$7.99US/$10.99CAN
___Game Over	1-4201-0687-2	$7.99US/$10.99CAN
___Sins of Omission	1-4201-1153-1	$7.99US/$10.99CAN
___Sins of the Flesh	1-4201-1154-X	$7.99US/$10.99CAN
___Cross Roads	1-4201-1192-2	$7.99US/$10.99CAN

Available Wherever Books Are Sold!
Check out our website at www.kensingtonbooks.com